Praise for

'Pieper's use of a dual nar[...]
[and he] handles the contrasting journeys in different
time periods with ease and style.'
AUSTRALIAN BOOK REVIEW

'*The Toymaker* is a compulsively readable collision between
the past and the present that results in a surprising future.
Secrets and survival, optimism and opportunism are the kindle
that fuels this funny, furious and unforgettable book.'
SYDNEY ARTS GUIDE

'Compelling . . . explores how our secrets can shape our lives.'
SUNDAY LIFE

'Pieper writes superbly. *The Toymaker* gives immediate
and absorbing pleasure, and has similarities to JM Coetzee's
Disgrace in terms of the main character's wretched search for
redemption, both for himself and for humanity.'
BOOKS+PUBLISHING

'Powerfully affecting . . . An important new testament
to the horrors and secrets of the Holocaust.'
AUSTRALIAN WOMEN'S WEEKLY

'Haunting, dark and enthralling,
Pieper's storytelling spans the gamut of situations
guaranteed to provoke extreme emotions'.
BENDIGO WEEKLY

PENGUIN BOOKS

THE TOY MAKER

Liam Pieper is a Melbourne-based author and journalist. His first book was a memoir, *The Feel-Good Hit of the Year*, shortlisted for the National Biography Award and the Ned Kelly Best True Crime award. His second was the Penguin Special *Mistakes Were Made*, a volume of humorous essays. He was co-recipient of the 2014 M Literary Award, winner of the 2015 Geoff Dean Short Story Prize and the inaugural creative resident of the UNESCO City of Literature of Prague. *The Toymaker* is his first novel.

ALSO BY LIAM PIEPER

The Feel-Good Hit of the Year

Mistakes Were Made

THE
TOY
MAKER

LIAM PIEPER

PENGUIN BOOKS

PENGUIN BOOKS

UK | USA | Canada | Ireland | Australia
India | New Zealand | South Africa | China

Penguin Books is part of the Penguin Random House group of companies
whose addresses can be found at global.penguinrandomhouse.com.

Penguin
Random House
Australia

First published by Penguin Random House Australia Pty Ltd, 2016
This edition published by Penguin Random House Australia Pty Ltd, 2017

Cover design by Alex Ross © Penguin Random House Australia Pty Ltd
Text design by Samantha Jayaweera © Penguin Random House Australia Pty Ltd
Cover photograph by V.K.K.V.
Typeset in Adobe Caslon Pro by Samantha Jayaweera, Penguin Random House Australia Pty Ltd
Colour separation by Splitting Image Colour Studio, Clayton, Victoria
Printed and bound in Australia by Griffin Press, an accredited ISO AS/NZS 14001
Environmental Management Systems printer.

National Library of Australia
Cataloguing-in-Publication data:

Pieper, Liam, author.
The toymaker / Liam Pieper.
9780143784623 (paperback)

Family secrets–Fiction.
Families–Fiction.

A823.4

penguin.com.au

For Mumma

ONE

'Let me tell you a story about my grandfather.' Adam leaned into the sentence, taking care with the syllables, throwing emphasis on the 'my', weight on the 'grandfather'. He loved saying it; he loved to boom it out like he was the invisible, omniscient voice at the start of a movie trailer.

'My grandfather came to this country with nothing, but now, because of his hard work and sacrifice, I have everything. Grandpa was proud of his work, of every little toy that he made. That's why he was so successful. There's nothing more important than hard work and sacrifice. To spend your life in service to others is the best thing a man can do with his time on Earth. When you work for a better world, when you are brave in the face of cruelty and stupidity, you earn self-respect, you earn dignity, which is the most important thing you can have in your life.' Adam paused, letting the import of this sink over the classroom. 'Because it lasts longer than your own lifetime. You get it from your parents, you pass it on to your own children. It's important you do that, more important than leaving them with money, although I don't think my own son would agree with that last part.' He paused for laughter, but none came, which annoyed him. He looked to the teacher at the back of the room, who gave him the wind-up.

Dickhead, Adam thought, but he smiled and obliged, skipped to the end of his talk. The kids looked bored anyway. Smack in the middle of their teens, they were too old to be excited by toys, and too young to understand just how exciting the sheer fact of his wealth was.

Standing at the head of this year ten class, he was grimly reminded that he wasn't a teenager any more, that he was starting to get old, that these schoolkids, surly and bored and secretly checking their phones under the table, weren't impressed by him. Then he remembered why he was there in the first place, that he'd been asked to address the students because he was rich and powerful, and a valuable member of the community. If they didn't know enough about life to be impressed by him, that wasn't his concern. They would learn what life was, soon enough.

He looked to the back of the classroom, where Clara was pretending to be absorbed by her phone. He'd known Clara since she was born, peripherally, through friends of the family, had maybe even been to her bat mitzvah, but hadn't given her much thought until he'd made her acquaintance again recently and found she'd grown from an awkward chubby dud into a voluptuous dark-haired milk-treat.

A fat little schoolboy sat next to her, casting her big-eyed mooning looks, in a way he must have thought was surreptitious. The kid was clearly in love with her, but Adam knew from long experience that until the kid grew a pair of balls she would friendzone him, at best. He wished he could warn the kid about that, considered walking up to him after class and giving him some wisdom: 'Listen, buddy, just make a move.' But no, everyone had to learn on their own. It would be character building for him to lose a few times – Adam couldn't stand entitled children. He wrapped up his talk, said goodbye to the teacher, and went to the car park to wait.

He felt like coming the second Clara took him in her mouth, so he forced his thoughts elsewhere. He looked away from his lap, where his fist was knotting her hair into a rough ponytail, and out the window, across the school oval to the swimming pool where kids were taking turns to dive off concrete platforms into the water. He clearly remembered the day that pool opened, as at the base of one of those diving blocks was a small plaque thanking Adam Kulakov for donating the funds for it.

He'd done that when his son, while on a school excursion to the Shrine of Remembrance, had used his pocketknife to carve his name into the side of a statue commemorating the dead of the Second World War. Kade had been suspended and threatened with expulsion from the elite P–12 college, until Adam and his lawyers worked out recompense. A few hundred thousand dollars later, on top of already extortionate tuition fees, and the school had a shiny new swimming facility. To try to deny little Kade his rightful place at the school, and the attendant place at a sandstone university it would culminate in, was an act of unwarranted aggression from the principal, a pathetic greying man who clearly resented Adam's status, but not nearly as much as Adam resented him for taking it out on his son.

As Adam thought about the way he'd handled that situation, the calm gravitas with which he'd talked down the furious school board, slammed the chequebook on the desk and signed the problem away with a flourish, he swelled with pride and came all of a sudden, surprising himself as well as Clara, who gagged briefly but then smoothly swallowed, not missing a beat.

The calm, practised way Clara had with sex was both appalling and irresistible to Adam. With her he felt a frisson he hadn't experienced since he had been a teenager. It wasn't just the way her freshly minted body pumped away atop him in the back seat of his BMW X5. Rather, it was the kind of singular beauty that bloomed at fourteen as the Ashkenazi time bomb of her genetics deployed her puppy fat strategically about the chest and hips, transforming her in the space of a year from big-boned hockey captain to rangy artwork, and rendering her, for the next decade or so at least, delectably fuckable – a beauty he wouldn't have been able to appreciate when he was fourteen, or even thirty, but at forty, his palate had expanded to fully savour it. Only with his own youth faded had Adam understood the aphorism: youth *is* wasted on the young.

He knew that part of it was the danger as well. Sitting in the car park across from the oval at lunchtime, waiting for her, he had found himself growing excited even before he saw her striding across the oval, swinging her schoolbag lazily over one shoulder, spitting out her gum as she got near the BMW. There was an extra little thrill in running his hand up under her skirt while they cruised down the main drag of his beachside suburb, past boutiques and cafes that threatened at any moment to disgorge some gossip-prone acquaintance or another. The possibility that he would be caught, busted, his life brought crashing down around him, was profoundly erotic. That's what drove him to take these risks – half the fun was pushing the envelope: buying her expensive dinners at his usual haunts, taking her out for cocktails in places he used to go drinking with his wife.

Clara righted herself, wiping her mouth and sweeping her hair back behind her head with one graceful gesture, and then leaned across his lap to where he kept a bottle of Coke in the beverage holder. She rinsed her mouth, gulped, and smiled.

'How do you feel?' she asked, lightly.

'Better,' he croaked, his mouth dry. 'Thank you.'

She leaned back in the seat and crossed her arms, pursed her lips. 'I wish you wouldn't thank me. It's not like I'm doing you a favour.'

'It seems that way to me,' he grinned.

'If I didn't like it I wouldn't do it.' It made him happy to hear her say that, although he didn't believe her in the slightest. He couldn't really understand the joy with which girls like Clara put themselves through what he considered to be a fairly grotesque chore. With his wife, Tess, oral sex had become something of a mirage; on the horizon but always out of reach, and one that had evaporated almost entirely a few years into the marriage.

Clara, on the other hand, really seemed to enjoy it, along with other acts he found sparing in his marital bed – complex, pretzeled positions – and had even hinted tantalisingly at a fondness for anal, all of which he attributed to a generational shift. Girls like Clara had grown up with unfettered internet access and had learned about sex from the coalface. They'd practised with boys who were raised to believe that sex started with a blowjob, shifted through a rigmarole of missionary, cowgirl and doggy style, and ended with a facial. What a time to be alive.

He'd met her on Tinder, where, using a pseudonym, a carefully blurred photo and a spirit of cavalier paranoia, he swiped right on any girl he thought could keep a secret. Clara had been one of the only ones to respond, and he had nearly died of shame and fear when they met in real life and he realised who she was. Once he'd calmed down and she'd convinced him that she wasn't bait in some elaborate predator trap, he'd set about seducing her.

Now as they rolled out of the car park, Clara put her legs, sun-tanned and hockey-toned, up on the dashboard, and Adam looked away, suddenly stricken with regret. Whenever he was with her, in the moments just after he had come, Adam felt disgusted by her, seized by a desire for her to slip out of the car and leave him alone.

The problem with infidelity, as he saw it, was the melancholy that filled him up seconds after he emptied out. Since he'd been a boy, an orgasm was always accompanied by a rush of endorphins that turned his mind into a vacuum, into which crept the terrible suspicion that he was ridiculous. It was always the same feeling, whether thirteen, surrounded by wadded tissues and listening in hushed panic for his mother's footsteps in the hall, or at forty, climbing off a teenage girl in the back of his car. His natural urge was the overwhelming desire to get as far away as he could, but over time he'd learned to ride out the unsavoury reality of post-coital company, long enough to endure conversation, cuddles, the drive home.

'Are you hungry?' he asked her.

She cocked her head and shrugged. 'What did you have in mind?'

He laughed. 'How about some junk food? I feel like being naughty.'

'Do you now?' she said, pouting. 'I could be up for that.' She leaned across and gave him a squeeze.

'Already?'

'Nearly your naptime, Granddad?'

He laughed again, but it was a little more forced this time. The BMW pulled into the KFC drive-through, where Adam barked an order into the microphone. At the cashier's booth, he found his wallet was devoid of cash and clicked his tongue, annoyed. He didn't understand where all his dollars went. No matter how much money he pulled out at the machine, his crisp handfuls of green and gold wilted and vanished by day's end. Adam frowned, and reached over to search the glove box for change, necessitating an awkward reach under Clara's calves perched on the dashboard.

'What's the matter, Adam?' she asked with mocking sweetness. 'Do you need to borrow money?'

Adam forced a smile, hoping the angry flush creeping up his cheeks wasn't visible. He fished out a company credit card that the girl at the counter swiped, before asking him to drive up to the next window. There, a pale brown kid with glasses and acne handed him a paper bag. He was short and slight, and had to lean right out of his station to pass a tray of drinks to Adam, which was how he caught sight of the schoolgirl in the passenger seat, her legs up on the dash so that her skirt bunched around her hips, and his eyes stuck stupid on her thighs, his sentence trailing away.

Clara, who had been absorbed in her phone, looked up and caught his eye, twisting her lips in annoyance. Her eyes burned with all the glacial beauty she could summon at a moment's notice, which was plenty, and froze him to the spot. 'See anything you like?'

The kid blanched, looked at Adam, then at Clara, then at Adam again. He paused, half out of the window, holding the tray of drinks aloft. 'Yes. I mean no. I mean . . .' the kid started to stutter and Adam felt sorry for him, and amused by his discomfort, and impressed by the scorn Clara could turn on like a spotlight. 'It's just, just, a very nice car,' the kid finished lamely, and dropped his eyes to the wood-panel interior of the vehicle.

'Yes,' Adam agreed curtly. 'It is.'

'Is it a Mercedes?'

'No, it's a BMW.'

'It's nice.' The poor boy's eyes flickered around the cabin in alarm, landing like a skittish bug on the steering wheel, the gearstick, the DVD player, the beverage holders, anywhere but Clara or Adam. He still held the tray out awkwardly towards the car, and only leaned back and dropped his gaze shamefacedly when Adam took the drinks and tapped the accelerator to end the excruciating moment.

Adam hated eating and driving at the same time, and parked in the deserted car park behind the restaurant, where they would be shielded from the passing traffic. He wolfed down a burger while they laughed about the drive-through clerk's discomfort.

'I think you've got a friend back there,' teased Adam. 'Do you want me to get his number for you?'

Clara's laugh was icy. 'Sure, why not? I love black guys.'

Adam's face fell. 'What?'

'Black guys. They have great skin.' She grinned. 'And big dicks.'

'Oh.' Adam frowned, suddenly jealous, inexplicably, because he was not racist, and besides, the kid wasn't even black, not properly, he was brown. Indian, or more likely Pakistani, and he wasn't about to feel jealous of a Pakistani.

Clara saw that she had ruffled Adam, and turned the same mocking smile on him she'd just turned on for the clerk. 'What's the matter, Mr Kulakov?' Her voice was earnest but her eyes were cruel. 'Are you jealous?'

'No, it's just . . . Should I be?'

'No, don't worry about a thing. You have a perfectly nice penis.'

Her smile widened, almost imperceptibly.

'Nice?' Adam winced to hear himself trip on the word, squawking when he meant to smirk.

'Yes, nice. Perfectly fine.' She smiled, carefully wrapped her half-uneaten burger, put it on the dashboard, then leaned over to unfasten his belt buckle. 'Don't you worry about a thing, Mr Kulakov.'

The bracelet he'd bought her tinkled as she worked, and the white-gold charms caught the sunshine and cast dancing sparkles of light around the cabin. Again, a sheer sense of wonder at Clara's ability came over him, and he tried not to think about how a girl this young could throw herself upon him with a skill that combined instinct and experience for such a result. When he'd asked she'd assured him that he was her first older man, so he guessed that it was simply luck that he'd stumbled upon her. Better him, after all, than some creep.

He was hard to bursting now, and climbed into the back seat, hit the release levers so the seats swung back into the boot, making one long cargo-bay of the cabin. Clara clambered across and positioned herself on all fours so that he could squeeze up behind her. As tall as the cabin of the SUV was, even with the seat laid down flat, Adam had to crouch with his head bowed and one leg stuck awkwardly out to the side to steer himself into her.

Clara let out a gasp and began moaning and bucking against him. After a few wild jabs he found his rhythm, and started to grunt and thrust. She switched rapidly between soft, barely breathed words of approval and excited, high-pitched yelps of joy as he accelerated, and she tossed her hair over her shoulders so it lay in a hazy dark fantail across her back. Glancing across to the other side of the cabin, he caught a glimpse of their reflected image in the tinted windows.

The sight of him thrusting into her made him at once ferociously excited and sad that he would have to end it, tonight probably, after they were done. He wished he didn't have to, but practicalities were piling up. The logistics of running an affair were difficult enough when both parties were adults with driver's licences and homes of their own, and besides, nothing could last forever. Still, she looked good, she really did.

Inspired, he reached out to where his iPhone sat cradled in the bluetooth bracket and snatched it up, then, with one hand on her back, he swiped his thumb across the screen to activate the camera. He took the first shot surreptitiously, which was abysmal, just a blur of skin and hair. Judging her too busy to clock what he was doing, he reached right out across the car to take a wide-angle snap. The photo was perfect, but he had to break rhythm to get it, and Clara groaned, 'Come on, fuck me,' and reached back to grab his arse and pull him deeper into her.

The convergence of the dirty talk, the sensation of sinking deep into her and the perfect image on his phone, which showed him ploughing away, his face gritted and manly, her head thrown to the side and her eyes closed in ecstasy, was too much, and he came, grunting mightily, then collapsed across her back, still inside her. He lay dazed for a second, her skin sticky and warm against his chest, then propped himself up on his elbow and looked out the window to find he was staring straight into the eyes of the clerk who'd just served them.

———

An alarm, a sweet ringing note like an angel breaking a wine-glass, startled Tess, and she realised she'd allowed herself to drift away, that for some time her eyes had been focused not on the spreadsheet but on her reflection, wan and sleep-deprived, in the computer monitor. She did not consider vanity one of her flaws, nor inefficiency, and so to find herself staring moon-struck into her own eyes on a workday was mortifying. She frowned, pinched herself mentally, and then when that did not seem to fix her pique, on the soft skin of her left wrist, between a lacquered thumb and forefinger.

She kept pinching, harder now, as she turned to the computer and opened the expense report. The chime was the most soothing sound Apple Computers offered, and she'd reserved it to ring out every time anything was charged to the company's expense account. The account had been set up as a slush fund to woo potential clients, but Adam, ever impulsive, was in the habit of handing out expense cards to their staff as a way of rewarding their loyalty. It was a nice idea, but impractical – and expensive – as each staffer grew bolder with discretionary purchases by the day. Adam, through his well-intentioned largess, had made a mess of things. He was a destructive power both insidious and spectacular, a great storm front of a man who would tear the roof off your life even as floodwaters rose to claim the rest of it.

It was his fault, for instance, that Tess had found herself, at thirty-four, running a toy company. She wasn't groomed for it, really wasn't qualified to clean its toilets; her only training was in the arts, specifically in making puppets.

She'd been raised in a sprawling Irish-Australian dynasty of artists and bohemians, and puppetry had seemed the only career unique and avant-garde enough to make her stand out from her siblings and cousins.

Her grandfather, Connor Coughlin, had been at the vanguard of Australian modernism at the precise time that it became briefly fashionable in international art markets, and a certain kind of antipodean swagger could lure pounds, francs, rubles and lira across the equator. In his half-century on Earth, Connor had managed to amass an unbelievable fortune, and nearly a dozen children, sired to Tess's long-suffering grandmother as well as a rotating stable of models, students, servants and patrons. When he died, this expansive and genetically diverse dynasty immediately began decades of litigation and bacchanal that eradicated the fortune, but not before it had fostered a generation of painters, novelists, poets and musicians who could not comprehend that the money would one day run out.

For a while Tess had tried to be a musician, then a writer, then, after being dragged to see a puppet show by an interminably dreary date, she stumbled upon her calling. She'd sat through it, Eric Bass's *Autumn Portraits*, and watched five puppets paint a portrait of an old man's waning life in ways that made her thoughtful, fascinated and, despite herself, joyful. By the end, when the bashful, mild-mannered puppeteer crept out from behind the curtain to bow, tears were streaming down her face, and she knew what she wanted to do with the rest of her life.

Encouraged by her theatre-critic mother and novelist father to pursue her dreams, she dipped into her trust fund and flew to New York to study with the Jim Henson Foundation. Three happy years there learning her craft and developing her show, then another making a name for herself touring Europe and North America, before flying home triumphant to find that her parents, having long ago hocked their last Connor Coughlin original, were broke. For the first time in generations, the Coughlins would have to make their own way in the world.

Too proud to take a job that didn't fully utilise her expensive, useless education, Tess worked as an entertainer for children's parties. At first, she put on revamped variations of her show for wealthy families, which she would perform behind a screen while the children sat cross-legged and bored, as their parents drank wine and smirked at the double entendres. She did quite well but gave it up after running into an old rival, now married to an achingly handsome man and towing an even more beautiful toddler, and whose happiness and security eviscerated her and plunged her into an existential crisis. Was that what happiness looked like? How a person was supposed to spend a life? Had she already wasted hers on an art that was, she was beginning to suspect, fundamentally silly? To validate its worth she vowed to take her puppetry out of the small-time and carve an empire from it.

She booked a spot at a children's entertainment expo, to try to sell her puppet designs to the champions of the toy industry who had come to purchase new intellectual property. She performed as long and hard as she could, throwing herself around behind a canvas screen until she was sticky and exhausted. The representatives from company after company watched for a while, then walked off expressionless. Taking a break for lunch, she sat dejected and nursed a takeaway coffee and a bucket of chips. Tess refused to give in to self-pity, but she had few other options. Across the aisle, a trampoline company was taking in much of the foot traffic, having hired a couple of sexy teenage dancers to bounce and frolic at regular intervals throughout the day. She was watching the teenagers, wondering where it had all gone wrong and what she was going to do, when a man walked over to her and stole a chip.

'Hey!' she protested, unnerved. 'What the fuck?'

'Sorry,' the man said. 'I needed an excuse to come and talk to you.' He smiled, and she smiled back, charmed by a move that years later he would admit that he'd read about in *The Game*, but which at that time seemed spontaneous and fun. It made her smile again at him when he asked, 'Why so serious?'

'Ugh,' she said. 'I'm trying to sell my idea to one of these fucking idiot toy companies but they wouldn't know a good thing if it grabbed them by the balls.'

'That's weird. I don't mean to boast, but I like to think I'm an excellent judge of character, especially when grabbed by the balls, and I happen to own one of these fucking idiot toy companies.' He handed her a card with a picture of two smiling dolls, one boy, one girl, with the colourful legend 'Mitty & Sarah' scrawled underneath. Flipping the card over, she read white text on a black background: 'Adam Kulakov – Owner'. Tess looked up from the card and gave Adam the once-over. He was wearing cargo shorts, runners and a zipped-up motorcycle jacket. It was such an incongruous look that she thought he must be either an imbecile or some fashion-forward genius.

'You don't say,' she said.

'I do. What's more, I'd like to know what you're selling,' Adam said. 'Why don't you let me buy you some more chips?'

Tess let him buy her some more chips, and later on dinner, where she drank too much and slept with him, and in true Coughlin tradition, fell pregnant almost immediately. When she realised she was with child, the first thing she did was get roaringly drunk with her friends. 'You need to get the abortion quick-smart,' they advised her. 'Wait too long and it'll start messing with your hormones and trick you into keeping it.'

It wasn't her first pregnancy. In Berlin a couple of years before she'd managed to pick one up, like a nasty infection, from the guy who tended the bar in the small theatre she played for a season, and she'd had it taken care of in brisk German fashion, at a walk-in clinic, without ever telling the man. But this was her first since she'd found herself broke. It rankled to have to ask Adam to help with it, but then again, it was half his mess to clean up. All she needed was a couple hundred dollars.

'I'm afraid,' she told him, conversationally, in the same tone with which she might send a meal back, 'that I'm a little bit pregnant.' Across the table, Adam gasped, but otherwise said nothing, just boggled at her, his big square jaw reaching for the floor. The next words out of her mouth were to be, 'I'll take care of it, don't worry,' when she realised *he* wasn't worried, not at all.

His happiness was so sudden, so delirious, so infectious, that she found herself unable to tell him that she wanted to terminate, and then, suddenly, realised that she didn't want to. He was kind, he came from good genes, all careless, clumsy muscle and easy smiles. He had – let's be honest – money, and while she was still sporting a bohemian carelessness, she sure did miss money.

When Adam proposed soon after, it gave her the unique sensation of feeling all her dreams of creative supremacy die at once, simultaneously replaced by a prefabricated, beige, quite wonderful and quite ordinary life. She could recall nights spent dozing, while the hormonal chicanery of the baby bombed her brain into contentment, concentrating on her breathing, one hand resting on her stomach as it rose and fell, like her, into a future that she'd never imagined.

For one thing, she'd never imagined her life could be so abstinent. After baby Kade came, her sex drive returned with a vengeance, even before her stitches were out, but Adam's had not. She remembered him sliding her sensible knickers down her thighs and pausing, the tiniest frown on his face as he surveyed her ravaged body.

It was a cliché, the husband whose home fires had gone out, but clichés often held true, such as the fact that, in the time between their first night together and the birth of their child, she had fallen in love with him. That was the worst realisation of all: that 'making love' was not a figure of speech; that the toxic industrial by-product of dirty sex was sweet, unadulterated, selfless love for the goof who, through the heady, sleepless first years of parenthood, she saw less of every day. For the first months he'd been faultless, a creature of inexhaustible paternal joy that kept her buoyant even as she forgot what sleep was. Then, Adam had gone back to work, and started staying longer and longer there, calling just after five o'clock with some excuse or another why he would not be home in the evening. At first she'd been sympathetic, then argumentative, but then, by the middle of Kade's terrible twos (another cliché, another truism), she would just hang up, put the child to bed, take a valium and order pizza. It was as though her epidural had sent her into a fugue state, from which she woke several years later to recognise nothing of the world, all her friends, and especially her husband, changed beyond recognition. She had found out, too late, like everyone, that the tragedy of marriage was not sociological, but geographical; she'd had no idea she could be so lonely.

When Kade was old enough to be put in childcare, she'd had a vision of what she'd become – a housewife, placated, bovine, schlepping from lunch to gym in her Lululemon widow's weeds – and had gently pitched the idea of joining the company in some capacity. Adam had been enthusiastic, and set her up in the office next to his, where he could ignore her just as easily as when she had been at home with the baby. No matter; nobody could have it all.

The quest for perfection was a mug's game; the secret to happiness was triage. Shortly after the birth of Kade, their squalling little bundle of joy, she had realised that there were no longer enough hours left in her lifetime to accomplish all she wanted to do. Sacrifices would have to be made, quickly, without thinking, and she'd jettisoned hobbies, dreams, friends like dead weight from a sinking airship. She loved her job, loved the company, loved the wealth it brought them, her husband of course, their son most of all, or at least, she was sure she did, and would be able to more fully if she could just get a minute to breathe.

By the time the baby could walk, she'd found that every pleasure she'd once enjoyed now came with a twinge of guilt because her time could be better spent with the child. She'd been told that becoming a mother would make everything else in her life seem unimportant; no one had warned her that it meant she would never be happy again.

To parent was to be perennially penitent, mired in micro-regrets, endlessly guilty and cranky. Things had been dire in the first years, but had improved rapidly when she'd made peace with her fallibility, and learned to parcel Kade away for bliss-ful stretches of time: crèche, kindergarten, school, babysitters, Adam's Grandpa Arkady, or, as a last resort, her own family. Little Kade did not need to be around his mother every min-ute of his life; apron strings are elastic things.

She herself had been thrown off the cliff like the Lion King and had learned to survive. Little Kade would be just fine. She loved her child so much that sometimes she thought her heart would burst Ahab-style through her chest. She loved him even more when he was not around.

She'd tried therapy once, and towards the end of the session the shrink had asked her to think about her ambiva-lence towards motherhood, which had made her bristle, and fire him. She was not ambivalent, she was exhausted. It was funny, how priorities changed over time; now she craved food less than sleep. Her hierarchy of needs was all scrambled, and the entirety of her life outside of work was sandwiched on Maslow's pyramid somewhere between shelter and wi-fi. What she needed, more than therapy, was the chance to take a break without worrying about steering the finances of the company away from the red they veered towards anytime she took her hand off the wheel.

Just now, for instance, she was, through her fug of exhaus-tion, searching for the errant expense the alarm had signalled. It took her a moment and when she found it, her heart leaped. The charge was small, under twenty dollars, and it was pro-cessed by a KFC in an area of town that nobody with a charge card had a reason to be. With mounting excitement, Tess checked back through the financial records and found another inexplicable transaction in the area, then another.

Several meals, a tab at a kitsch bar she'd once frequented but had grown out of long ago, a jeweller, a hotel; a couple of hundred dollars at a Sportsgirl. A fucking Sportsgirl! Tess could smell blood. If she had found an employee embezzling money she would be so angry, she thought happily. The company was bleeding money, and any excuse to terminate an employee was something to be treasured.

They could certainly use the spare pay cheque, as Adam was about to start a second meeting with a new assistant, which, now that she thought about it, was another thing she was late for. She would have to track down the rogue expenses later on; it would be something to look forward to.

Through the glass wall between their offices, she could see Adam preparing for the employee induction by rehearsing his speech, going over some passages with a forefinger, his lips moving slightly as he read. Tess slipped into the office to take her place at Adam's side, reaching over to give his leg a surreptitious squeeze. He smiled, a million beautiful, goofy teeth, and lightly smacked her thigh.

A knock at the door and the inductee came in and sat nervously while Adam shuffled papers at his desk. Then he stood, strode over to the window where – cast into silhouette by the light streaming in through the corner office – he would say, 'Let me tell you a story about my grandfather.'

I will not live much longer, Arkady said to himself, and the thought brought a smile to his lips.

He did not subscribe to the science, which had been so popular in occupied Prague when he'd lived there, that ascribed racial characteristics to individuals. However, he would admit to a certain Russian fatalism, and he had decided less than a day into the journey that he would not survive it, and if he did, for not much longer after that. Arkady knew he was dead long before the train arrived at his destination; he'd heard whispers of what was happening in Poland, had them confirmed by drunken soldiers on leave in beer gardens.

He was surrounded by people who, if apprehensive, did not know what was coming, although they had enough bits and pieces of lost nightmares to speculate. The collected hypotheticals almost drowned out the rumble of the engine, the scream of sleepers below the carriage, but did little to dampen the whimpering and the wailing from some sections of the cattle car.

The assault on his ears was not as bad as that on his nose. An animal smell: metallic blood, acidic vomit, excrement and fear. The smell ran in rivulets from the passengers; it poured in torrents, in rivers, so that everyone was soaked. It pooled on the floor and steamed through the superheated air of the carriage, the condensation on the ceiling forming thick droplets that shook and rained down on them whenever the train shunted or lurched.

The people, packed tight as herrings in a jar of brine, swayed and jolted as one, seethed against each other angrily, jostling for a little space, enough to fill tired lungs with air, or wriggle out of a coat.

Towards the end of the journey, most wore their shirtsleeves or less, cotton and wool waterlogged with perspiration, skin slick against skin. Arkady had been careful to position himself against a wall when the soldiers had forced them into the train, and he'd been grateful to have one surface to lean against that wasn't a human being.

Then the train stopped, shuddered and stilled. The people stopped with it, held their breath, waiting, waiting, a minute, an hour, and then the carriage doors slid open and the humanity poured out.

Arkady stumbled, shaky on legs used to swaying with the carriage, and he gasped icy air gratefully, but only for a moment before the wind threaded bitter fingers through his coat and caressed the soaking cloth underneath.

The passengers shuffled forward, slowly at first, then moving faster as soldiers set to them with truncheons and pistols on either side. They were marched down the platform until they reached a sorting station, where a *Schutzstaffel* soldier waited, neat and surly, with his SS death's-head logo shining from his black uniform. As waves of arrivals reached him he yelled out the same phrase, like a grocer hawking goods.

'Men to the left! Women to the right.'

Four bodies up in the line a young father struggled as they took away his wife, and an officer drew his pistol and fired, then waved the stunned widow on with the pistol, his expression bored and businesslike. All at once Arkady felt grateful that he was here alone, that he had nobody to care for, or to care for him, that everyone who would mourn him was a world away in Moscow, or, better yet, dead. He moved to the left.

'Form fives!' another soldier barked. 'Lines of fives!' Here, the line split into left and right again, the wave of people breaking when it reached a figure who stood eyeing the arrivals. He was striking, handsome in a severe kind of way, sharp in a black SS uniform, with a white doctor's coat over it. He held a baton, and as the prisoners approached he asked them questions and waved them left or right.

When he found himself in front of the German, Arkady stared at the ground, trying to look both non-threatening and useful, as the man looked Arkady up and down.

'Age?'

'Twenty-two.'

'Profession?'

'Farmer.' A lie, but why not? If they thought he was a worker, it might keep him alive a little longer, for whatever that was worth.

The baton waved to the left.

A long night followed, cold as hell, running from one humiliation to another. He was stripped, his clothes confiscated and discarded, his watch pocketed by a grizzled kapo – one of the prisoners bumped up to overseer who did the Nazi's dirty work for them – who spotted it shining on his wrist. He was allowed to keep his boots, which he was glad of, because then he was hustled through snow into a long, cold concrete room where he was shaved, head and body, and covered with acrid delousing powder, which crept into the thousand tiny cuts the blunt clippers had torn in his chest so that when a bucket of steaming hot water was thrown at him, it almost felt soothing.

He found himself running, now through a long warehouse corridor, now through the snow, naked and absurd, and then standing in another room, being handed a pair of striped slacks and shirt by another kapo. Even at arm's length, the funk of the garments, with months' worth of fear and labour soaked into the cloth, made his nose wrinkle, which did not escape the attention of the kapo.

'Is something wrong,' he asked Arkady, 'princess?'

'These are dirty,' he replied, in his ugly but functional German. 'Do you have clean clothes for me?'

The kapo grinned now and dashed the bundle from his hands. 'You are too good for our clothes? You are a fancy man! A lawyer? A doctor?'

Arkady shook his head. 'A farmer.'

The kapo reached out and ran Arkady's soft hands between his own, the calluses grating on his soft, pink skin. 'These hands have never touched dirt. You are some kind of professor, maybe? Someone important?' The kapo's finger pointed at his own shirt, where a green triangle pointed from his heart to the mud. 'Do you see this? This means I am a killer. It means I am in charge here. It means the world is upside down. Do you understand what I'm saying, professor? Do you need an interpreter? Here it is.' The man held up his fist for Arkady to admire, then sunk it into his solar plexus, dropping him. Although he hadn't eaten in days, he vomited a little, to the delight of the kapo, who walked off laughing. Another kapo, this one a little kinder in the face, helped him up and escorted him to a sorting room.

Two SS men prowled through the room, appraising the men, visually measuring their muscles, squeezing biceps, reaching into mouths to check the health of teeth and gums. One of the SS men noticed Arkady, came over to inspect. As the German poked and prodded him, Arkady realised that the muscles he had worked so hard to acquire, putting in endless hours with kettlebells and press-ups and sprints, were the reason he'd caught the attention of the SS. His friends back in Prague had always teased him, when he came back from a run breathless and ruddy, that his vanity was going to kill him one day. He almost smiled at the thought that they were right, but the kapo had already taught him how dangerous anything less than a blank facial expression was in this place.

'You are strong. Can you work?' the SS asked him. Arkady nodded. 'Good,' the SS said, then yelled over his shoulder in German, 'one more! One more for the Sonderkommando.'

He was taken to a new room and given a greatcoat to wear over his pyjamas. After checking their papers, he was held still by two kapos who tattooed a number into his left arm and attached a triangle to his shirt, just above his heart. Then they explained to him that he had been chosen for a special work detail – a Sonderkommando made up of the strongest men, where he would be rewarded for extra duties – and that he was very lucky. For a moment, flush with exhaustion and grateful for the coat after running through the snow all night, he almost believed it, until he was marched with the other prisoners into Auschwitz and he passed under the lie fashioned in wrought iron over the entrance, and marvelled at its cold practicality: how perfect the euphemism, how much sense it made when you learned the only freedom you could look forward to.

TWO

'Let me tell you a story about my grandfather. Arkady Kulakov was a hero, a survivor of the Holocaust who came to Australia to find a better life. He came to this country with nothing, nothing at all. He came with no money, with no English. He'd lost everything to the Nazis. In Russia the Communists took everything he had, so he went to Prague, trained to be a doctor, became a physician, and then had that taken from him by the Nazis. So do you know what he did?'

Adam turned to his new assistant and repeated the question. 'Do you know what he did?' She shook her head, nervous, which pleased him. He liked to make people nervous. 'He was a hero, my grandfather. When the other prisoners were sick, he healed them. When the other prisoners were hungry, he fed them with his own rations. When the other prisoners gave up, he kept them going. Do you know how?'

The assistant shook her head again, and Adam was, for a second, annoyed at the bovine way she blinked, but he smiled and went on. 'He made toys. He understood people, and understood that the only things keeping the adults going were their children, and if the children in the camps were to lose hope, all would be lost.

'So he worked out how to keep the children going. He stole bits and pieces from the Nazis, and taught himself how to make things to distract the little ones from the horror. Stuffed toys at first, then simple carvings, then, finally, things of great beauty you would not believe could come out of a place so dark.'

Adam warmed to the story, as he always did around this point, putting a little boom on the word 'hope', a little righteous scorn on the 'Nazis', and, as he came to the 'things of great beauty', he reached into the display case on the wall of the office and pulled out a doll, offering it to the assistant.

She took it, sat it in her lap, blinked at it. It wasn't beautiful, not at all. The doll resembled a little girl, but only in a rudimentary way. Rough-hewn articulated arms and legs hung limp off a torso that was just a sanded-down block of timber, wrapped in a dress fashioned from rough wool. Running a finger over one of the arms, she could feel where a blade had whittled the wood down. The doll's head, a rough wooden sphere, dangled from a crude ball-joint that attached it to the body. Its features, plump red lips and shining brown eyes, were painted unevenly over the face, but the hair was surprisingly lustrous and silky. The whole thing was covered in a patina of grime, and when she turned it over in her hand, she could see the edge of a yellow triangle peeking out of the fabric where it joined the seam of the dress.

'She's . . . beautiful,' said the assistant, uncertainly.

Adam grinned proudly. 'That is Sarah. She's the first real toy my grandfather ever made. She's named after a little girl he looked after in the camps, and when he emigrated to Australia he left behind his whole past except Sarah, and everything she represented. Strength, charity, hope.' Adam retrieved the doll and, opening the display case back up, carefully placed her on the shelf next to another doll, similar in design, but this one a boy. 'In some ways, the Mitty & Sarah dream was born in the camps, a spark in the darkness, but it was only in Australia that it truly came to life. He survived Auschwitz, the worst place the world has ever known, and chose to come to Australia, but they would not let him practise medicine in this country. After everything he had been through, however, Grandpa Arkady was not going to let that hold him back.

'Living out of his workshop in Melbourne, Grandpa carved these beautiful dolls by hand. The second he could afford to, he hired an assistant, Rachel, another survivor from Auschwitz. In time, they fell in love, and she became his wife, my grand-mother. Together, they grew the company from an idea to a concern that has employed hundreds of people, most of them new immigrants, survivors from the war who came to Australia to start again.

'This company is built on my grandfather's hard work and sacrifice. He built it from scratch and made not only his fortune, but a dream that gave all of Australia hope.'

Adam finished his speech and beamed at his new personal assistant, who sat bolt upright, having slumped further into the chair as the spiel ground on. 'That's what this company is all about. That's what we work towards every day.'

He moved to a chair and spun it around so that he could straddle it and cross his arms over the back of it, facing her with his muscles flexed to assert relaxed dominance. This was a trick he'd learned from pick-up manuals but it worked just as well in the corporate sphere. 'Do you have any questions?'

He'd finished the dramatic part of the induction, so Tess took over and talked the new girl through the rest of it: how over the decades the company had grown from a boutique toy manufacturer to a key player in the worldwide toy market with partners throughout Asia, America and Europe; their annual turnover, their annual growth rates; all the dry, boring stuff. As they walked out, Tess listing some of the various lines of toys they sold, Adam's eyes fell to the new girl's arse.

He had a good feeling about his new assistant. She was quiet, seemed competent enough, and was very plain. He made a point of hiring unattractive women because he wasn't the kind of businessman who relied on a beautiful assistant to make him feel important.

It was also designed to put Tess at ease. He wanted her to know that he could work late without the temptation of a wanton secretary, although he was sure that this one would be into it. With some girls you could just tell. He watched the new girl's hefty buttocks wiggling as she took the stairs down to the factory floor, and imagined weighing them in his hands.

It was important to him that Tess knew she was safe with him; that if he slept with other women from time to time, it wasn't that he didn't love her, quite the opposite. But not long into the marriage, in the months after the arrival of little Kade when he been unable to bring himself to touch his wife, he had been surprised and pleased to find that he didn't feel guilty for cheating on her. He was, after all, a man of the old school, with a man's desires, the need to let off steam, the pressure inside him like tectonic plates crashing and raising mountains. His straying didn't hurt anyone, and he never let anything drag on for too long.

In the murky past, in the hot, primordial months of their marriage, there had been situations where he had seen other women and let them get attached. He was smart enough now to concentrate on girls like Clara, young things sure of their beauty, vain enough to glory in seducing an older man, but too proud to boast about it to the wrong people. He'd found that perfect bravado of callow youth complemented his calculating predation.

He would miss Clara. After the encounter with the peeping tom in the KFC car park, she'd overreacted, and they'd bickered, and finally he'd dropped her off around the corner from her family home, after a bitter goodbye.

She thought he'd handled the situation badly, but what choice did he have but to take care of the little shit who'd pressed his face against the window during their congress. Perhaps she was right. But who would have expected the boy to bleed so much? Or Clara to freak out so much?

He'd been furious and jumpy after the fight, but as his adrenaline had cooled he'd started to fret about all the attention the incident had drawn. It was only when faced with the spectre of being caught cheating on Tess that he felt any remorse. He began to imagine Tess's tears and fury, the consequences and counterattack, the lawyers swooping and her taking his kid and his car and riding off into the sunset.

So, with the night already ruined, he'd broken it off with Clara. He'd expected her to cry, or at least to be upset, but she agreed that yes, they should break up, and accepted that yes, he was too old for her, and yes, lots of boys were probably dying to be with her. She took his dismissal with such good grace that he was filled with sudden jealousy at the thought that she had another boyfriend. If he was honest with himself, it was not so much her teenage body that turned him on as the fact that she had chosen him over some muscled jock in her class, that his second-hand physique could still make a young girl happy.

Slumping back into his office chair, he thought of Clara and thumbed idly at his budding erection, then, with the moral fortitude of a man who's just reaffirmed his marriage by discarding his mistress, he decided against onanism and dropped to the floor for a brace of push-ups.

While he was cranking out a quick hundred, he remembered the kid he'd caught spying on him. At first he felt a twinge of regret about the way he'd handled that, but as he rounded fifty and the hormones started to race through him, he found himself reminiscing about the satisfying crunch his knuckles had made on the boy's eye socket and wishing he'd hit him harder. For the last ten push-ups, he fuelled himself by replaying the fight in his mind, this time throwing in a few meaty stomps with the heel of his RM Williams boot.

He smiled to himself. There was work to be done, and the day was growing late. As he stood, he reached into his pocket for his phone, and realised that he had, at some point during the day, lost the fucking thing, and his mood crashed.

———

Adam came into her office without knocking, startling her, and asked her if she'd seen his phone. She hadn't but she called it, let it ring out, while Adam looked on, hopeful, then downcast.

'I've probably left it in the car.' He smiled then slipped out, and Tess returned to her accounts. She was trying to hunt down the person behind the abuse of the company charge card, or had been, but she'd become distracted by finding more and more fiscal misconduct. It wasn't a few indiscretions – someone was systematically ripping off the company.

She was having trouble tracking the extent of the problem. It might be achievable, even easy, if the company finances were more straightforward, but they were, like all else, a mess. Although she was ostensibly CFO, Adam insisted on approving every transaction – both their signatures were required to make money move. When she'd challenged him on the pointless bureaucracy, he'd confided that it was an exercise in 'projecting power'. 'I want every employee to know that I'm watching them all the time,' he'd said. 'The more afraid they are of me, the better productivity will be. I want them to know that if they step out of line they'll be gone, like that.' He'd clicked his fingers for emphasis, twice. Like. That.

The company's core function wasn't complicated – they imported toys produced in factories overseas, processed them in the warehouse that sprawled behind their offices and shipped them out to toy stores – but administering it was a labyrinthine task, managed by a workforce whose jobs Adam made almost impossible with his oversight. He had an erratic way of jumping excitedly into a particular project, derailing it with his inspirations, then leaving it a smoking ruin.

Tess had found herself running the company by default so gradually she didn't notice it happening, picking up a new job here or there, until she seemed to hold the entire hierarchy like a bar of soap in the bath. Every couple of months a new batch of business cards would arrive for her, along with new duties that put her in charge of the minutiae, or, as Adam framed it, gave her 'shared executive power'. The way he said it, he could have been tapping her on the shoulder with a sword, rather than bequeathing to her the endless chores that he was too busy buying magic beans to manage.

She looked over at Adam rummaging through his desk drawers, oblivious to the world and, specifically, her, and the old loneliness began to wrap itself around her. So she did what she always did when she felt low, which was to call Arkady, waiting through the ringing for his thick Eastern European 'Hchello'.

'Arkady, it's me.'

'Lubovka!' he boomed happily. His nickname for her, roughly 'Little Love Thing' – which, as he joked, was about as affectionate as Russians got. 'How are you, my dear?'

'Oh, can't complain. How are you?'

'Terribly shit!' he exclaimed, and laughed long. 'I'm a hundred years old. Of course I'm shit! Let's talk about something else, anything else.'

They talked for maybe an hour, this and that, the weather, the family. She spent, probably, more time talking to Arkady than anyone else in her life. She loved her child, adored her husband, but Arkady was her best, possibly only, friend. He was the one she turned to when she had a problem, and she relied on his unflappable old-school charm to cheer her up and steer her towards a solution. So, conversationally, almost breezily, she brought up the abuse of the company cards.

'I think we've got a thief in the company.'

'Excuse me, Lubovka, what do you mean?'

'Someone is stealing from us, the petty cash accounts . . . Some money has gone missing.' There was a long silence on the other end. 'Arkady?'

His voice was serious now, solemn. 'Do you know who it is?'

'Not yet.'

'Well then, relax!' Arkady said, his voice jolly again. 'It's probably a misunderstanding. I'll tell you what, put away your books and go outside and play. It's a beautiful day! And tomorrow I will come into the office and help you track down this scoundrel.' Arkady signed off, and Tess hung up.

Not long after she'd first joined the company, she'd found herself trying to process a complicated set of invoices at Adam's request, while he was away on a business trip in China. She'd been sitting at her desk trying to work it out, her child throwing a tantrum on the floor, she herself past the point of tears, when she'd looked up from blowing her nose and found Adam's grandfather standing at the door, staring at her.

Even though he'd passed the company he'd founded on to Adam, Arkady still dropped by occasionally, unexpectedly and unannounced, to go over the books. She stopped immediately, embarrassed and unnerved that the dapper old man, wearing a three-piece suit despite the sun beating down outside, his hat held politely in front of him, had caught her crying.

She'd met him only briefly, in the run-up to their shotgun wedding, and didn't even speak more than a few words to him on the day, although she'd felt his pale blue eyes following her, up the aisle, through the reception, across the dance floor and out to the limousine. It was a strange, searching look, not quite like the one she usually got from men; she couldn't shake the feeling that the old man was weighing her. At the time she feared he'd marked her as a gold digger, some silly rich girl fallen on hard times and trying to get her hands on his family's fortune. He'd given the same appraising look in the office as his eyes flicked from her tear-streaked face to the stack of orders before her.

'What is it?' he'd asked, his voice so soft that the purr of his

European consonants was barely audible. 'Why are you crying?' He walked in and stooped to address his screaming name-sake, then swiftly scooped him up and spun him around. The baby, suddenly airborne, was startled out of tears and started laughing. Little Kade had forgotten he was ever unhappy, and, suddenly, so had Tess.

They'd started talking, and she'd been surprised and pleased to discover that she was having fun. She'd heard his story from Adam, many times, about the war and his time in the camps, and had expected someone bitter and broken by life. Instead, she found him warm, kind and unexpectedly funny.

For perhaps the first time since little Kade was born, she found herself having an adult conversation, realised she'd had no idea how starved she'd been for it. She found herself complaining about the weird turn her life had taken, how in a matter of months her bohemian wonderland had shrunk to the space of a beautiful but claustrophobic house, one that some-how had grown even smaller since her son was born. That she had tried to fix her malaise by coming back to work, a development that only made everything worse because of the endless, stupid tasks that Adam gave her. 'He doesn't know what he's doing!' she wept. 'He's like a child, and he passes it off to me the second it gets hard.'

The old man stared at her, impassive. She realised that she'd blown it. 'Oh God, I'm sorry,' she snuffled, and the old man laughed.

'Do not apologise to God,' he smiled. 'He owes us no favours.'

'I mean, sorry, Mr Kulakov. I didn't mean to insult your family. I'm just very tired.'

'My name is Arkady, please call me that, if you like. And it is fine. You are right: my grandson does not know what he is doing. He is sometimes like a child. A nice child, but still a child. But that is why we must help him.' Arkady Kulakov came in and pulled up a chair next to her, resting his hat on the desk and pulling a ledger towards him. 'I will show you how.'

Sitting down next to her, Arkady opened a stack of invoices, and, taking a fountain pen from inside his jacket, started to show her his secrets. He was methodical, businesslike, his voice gentle and soothing as a lullaby as he took her through the alchemy behind the money. Soon she found that she not only understood but was enjoying herself.

After that he often visited her, helping her navigate the convoluted path that money took in and out of the business. At first she couldn't understand why the old man was paying so much attention to her. She suspected that he was, in the way of powerful men at the end of their life, indulging in a not-quite-decent flirtation – enjoying the proximity to her youth, and what was left of her beauty – but before long she realised she'd not given him enough credit. Bonded to her, unexpectedly, through blood, fate and chance, he'd decided that she could be trusted to look after his legacy: his family, and the company.

'The very first Sarah, she was made to cheer up a little girl during the war,' Arkady explained to Tess one day, fiddling with a doll's arm, bending it back and forth to make it wave. For a second he was subdued, lost in thought, then he went on, in a louder voice. 'After the war, in Melbourne, I used to carve them by hand, but it was very slow, even when I hired help, so I found a factory in Japan. Australia was starting to get rich, and Japan, well, we had just won the war, and they had workers desperate for purpose. In this factory, the workers make the same carvings, but do them fast and cheap. Then I import them and sell them – same old Sarah, but much more money.'

Then, going to the ancient filing cabinets that stood gathering dust, Arkady pulled out reams and reams of paper showing Tess how Sarah was now made: the raw parts for the dolls were lathed in India, then shipped to China for assembly and dressed in clothes sewn by hand in Bangladesh, all orchestrated from Melbourne, where the shipping containers full of Mitties and Sarahs would arrive pre-packaged to be driven across the country. 'You see, Tess, it is always more complicated than it looks. Everything, always so complex.'

The old man wasn't lying when he played up the complexity of the organisation. In recent years, the company had been trying to update its systems of commerce and tracking from paper to digital, but half a dozen failed attempts now meant the systems were strung across a makeshift platform of shining Macs, hulking IBM server towers and rows upon rows of old-fashioned filing cabinets, which, after all these years, only Arkady seemed to know his way around.

As time had passed, and Tess had started to grow closer to Arkady, she found a visceral thrill in the making of money, in the warp and weft of it, and began to marvel that she had ever wanted to be an artist, or any kind of entertainer. She'd been raised to believe that there was no higher pursuit than to reach somebody through art, but now she could see what a pointless exercise that was. It was a finer thing to sit on top of the world, steering the fate of a multinational that provided jobs, homes and self-esteem for thousands of people across the world, bringing joy into the lives of millions of children every day.

Tess, who worked alongside Arkady to learn the secrets of the company, knew that one smiling child was worth a million self-absorbed adults stroking their chins and applauding her artistic vision. Here was something she was good at, something that made the world better, that made her useful, something that nobody else could touch.

The money could be touched, however, and someone was stealing hers. First alerted by the spending spree on the company card, she'd gone back to check through expense accounts looking for further evidence, and found that not only were staff expenses out of control, but someone had, very clearly, very deliberately, been cooking the books, sneaking false expenses onto invoices, overhead reports, cost appraisals.

It was across all departments, on dozens of accounts, clearly an inside job, almost impossible to see if no one was looking for it, and who would look? She was inundated; Arkady was retired. Money was being spirited away. On a payment to a factory in Shenzhen, for example, twenty thousand yuan had disappeared in the transaction, whisked off to a side account via some fine print encoded in the order. She'd been investigating for only a few hours and had already found thousands of dollars missing. Who knew how far back it went? It could be years of grifting. It could be hundreds of thousands of dollars.

Someone was robbing the company, and therefore her family. She would track them down and bring Arkady their head on a pike, finally putting an end to the low-key imposter syndrome that still accompanied her to work every day.

'Do you see, Tess?' Arkady had asked her on the day she started to understand the business. His eyes sparkled bright from the wrinkles that framed them. 'We have a critical mass now. Money, when you have enough of it, becomes an abstract although, unlike most abstracts, it has gravity. It has mass. When you get enough of it, it draws itself in. Now we just maintain, slowly, slowly, gently, we live. The rest will look after itself.' He'd laid a warm, worn hand on her shoulder and squeezed it. 'The hard work is done. That is all in the past. All we have to do is protect it.'

———

At the end of the first month's work in the Sonderkommando, Arkady's opinion of his captors had been revised upwards, at least in comparison to his view of some of his workmates, those in the Sonderkommando who seemed to enjoy their jobs.

Each unit was divided into work details. Given a choice, he would have liked to be one of those who took receipt of the bodies and processed them for raw material: the barbers who shaved the hair off the dead for recycling into textiles, the kommandos with clever fingers who harvested the gold pulled teeth and earrings and sent them off to be melted down. His unit was tasked with leading the new arrivals down the stairs into the gas chambers, then waiting outside while pellets of hydrogen cyanide were dropped through hatches in the ceiling into four mesh pillars. While he waited for the screams to die down, Arkady would try not to imagine what was happening. He wondered if there were other doctors hiding in his unit who had the training to appreciate what the gas was doing to the people trapped in the chamber, the cyanide starving their cells of oxygen, the panic that set in at a biological level, even before the mind knew what was happening.

First they started to drool, and froth, as seizures struck them. The screaming would peak, as people fought each other, climbing over their friends and family to try to get away from the gas that rolled out along the floor before rising to the ceiling. The weakest – the old, the infirm, the children – died first, their bones broken by the panicked hordes, pushed down into the gas and the tangle of limbs and vomit, blood and excrement expelled by dying bodies.

Arkady had learned, after a tooth lost to the butt of a pistol and a night spent hanging from a hook with his arms wrenched behind his back, the full weight of his body sawing at the ligaments in his shoulders, to cooperate.

So now he worked the ovens, hosed down the gas chambers, helped with the murders to stave off his own death, even though it was killing him.

He was aware that he would already be dead if he was in the general barracks where the men who had been murderers

and rapists on the outside sat at the top of an awful hierarchy, elevated to overseer by the green triangles they wore. They
would beat you depending on the symbol on your shirt: for
being a Gypsy, for being a Jew, for being the wrong kind of Jew.
The colour of the triangle on his own shirt would be a death
sentence if the wrong kapo saw it.

In the Sonderkommando barracks, life was good, compar-
atively. Elsewhere in the camp people were dying of empty
stomachs, or eating bread made from sawdust and gruel and
still starving to death, bellies bloated from malnutrition. Out
there he watched people who were now barely more than skeletons walking to their work details and imagined that he could
hear the rumble, deeper even than the despair, of stomachs
wasting away.

In his barracks, he was warm, slept on a straw mattress; he
could bathe. There was a steady supply of food, cigarettes and
medicine brought into the camp by those destined for the gas
chambers. Best of all, there was alcohol, and most nights you
could drink yourself into a dreamless sleep.

Every day he reported for work in the crematorium, where
he'd had the luck to be assigned to a detail that cleaned up
the murders after the fact, rather than facilitating them; moving the bodies from the gas chambers to the ovens, loading
the ovens on a bad day; or, on a good day, collecting the outfits
hung neatly on numbered hooks in the entrance hall, waiting for owners who would not return. He told himself that he
would have refused, and been shot, if he'd found himself on the
team that lured the new arrivals to their deaths.

Dion Baro, the Hungarian who wore the red triangle of a political prisoner, was always the first to volunteer, even when he wasn't asked, insisting that he be among the kommandos who met the trainloads and truckloads of innocents. He coaxed them into the gas chambers where they would strip and be led into sealed rooms where, under the pretence of getting clean, beneath fake showerheads hung from the ceiling, they would be murdered.

When the prisoners piled out of their transports, Dion would be the first to greet them, trotting up and shaking hands warmly.

'Come! Come!' he would urge. 'You poor things, you look miserable. Come inside and have a nice hot shower, get clean, and into some nice warm clothes. This way! This way!' He would scurry along, collecting the stragglers, directing them to ignore the soldiers loitering in the crowd and hurry to the comfort of a hot shower. 'Hang your clothes on the hooks; be careful to keep them separate from your neighbours. The faster we get you showered and settled, the faster we can reunite your with your families.' When he encountered resistance, he would improvise. 'Faster, faster, now. The water is going to get cold, and if you miss out, you're going to blame me,' he would chirp, adding a rhetorical flourish, 'faster, faster, there's bread and soup waiting for you on the other side. Look at me!' he might chortle, lifting up his shirt and slapping his belly. 'I do not need all the food we have back there.'

After they were all inside, the jolly mask would slip from his face and he would stand, grimly smoking a cigarette pilfered from the clothes in the entry chamber, waiting for the screaming to stop. When some of the other prisoners confronted him at night in the barracks about the glee he took in the work, he was unapologetic. 'I'm going to survive this,' he said fiercely. 'I have a fiancée waiting for me back in Budapest, and her family is connected. I just have to wait it out.' Dion's gung-ho cooperation with the Nazis meant warmer clothes for him, better food, occasional cigarettes and cognac, even a visit to the brothel the Nazis had set up to reward collaborators. If asked, Arkady would admit that he, like most of the kommandos, did not have plans that extended beyond surviving another day. Part of him admired Dion's faith in his future.

Dion died one day when he finished his cigarette and took his place dragging the corpses out and over to the ovens. He was tugging at the leg of a woman to free it from the pyramid of black and blue bodies when he recognised his fiancée, not, after all, back home arranging his freedom, but a prisoner, like him, now dead. And he could not be consoled, raging and weeping until the SS had, exasperated, beaten his face to a puddle, his breath ragged and bubbling, the air forced through lungs pressed by cracked ribs.

Dion lay until the end of the shift as his own blood pooled and chilled around him, when the other men from his unit carried him back to the barracks and dumped him on the floor. He lay there undisturbed until his moaning got too loud and woke his bunkmates, who then kicked him silent.

By the time Arkady's own shift had finished, he could tell that the man didn't have long to live. Still, he was a doctor. He might never have taken an oath, but he knew what to do, and he did what he could. With a packet of cigarettes he'd been holding on to, he bribed one of the kapos to bring him a kettle of hot water, and tearing up his bed sheets into bandages, he cleaned the wounds on Dion's face and body as best he could. The nose was broken, and Arkady snapped the cartilage back into place with the heels of his hands. Dion whimpered but he didn't wake up. Scrunching up cotton into little balls, Arkady soaked them in boiling water and cleaned out the mouth where Dion had lost teeth, then pressed little balls of cotton into the gaps to staunch the bleeding. Deciding that was all he could do, he cleaned the blood from his hands with the last of the hot water and stood up, to find he was being watched.

A cigarette glowed in the darkness, and behind it, a voice, soft, in German. 'You are a doctor?'

Arkady shook his head. 'No. A farmer.'

'You understand it's a very bad idea to lie to me.'

Arkady shrugged. 'I studied to be a doctor, very nearly, five years, but then, the war, and your people closed our schools down.'

'What is your name?'

Arkady recited the number that was tattooed on his arm, as he'd learned quickly to do, when talking to an SS man.

'No,' the shadow said, 'I asked for your name.'

'Arkady Kulakov. Who are you?'

The shadow moved forward, offered him a hand. 'I am Dr Dieter Pfeiffer. How are you with a scalpel?'

Arkady laughed. 'Are you going to give me a scalpel?'

'Would you like one?'

'Would you trust me with one?'

'Trust is earned.' The doctor finished his cigarette, ground it out, lit another and offered it to Arkady. 'I need an assistant to help me with my research. Pathology, blood work, dissections.'

'Thank you, but, with respect, working with a Nazi doctor is not something I am interested in.'

The doctor clicked his tongue, frowned. 'That may be, but I am offering you an alternative to death, a pointless death that will certainly come soon.' Pfeiffer lowered his voice and leaned in, so that the other kommandos watching from their bunks would not overhear. 'This is not the first generation of Sonderkommandos. It will not be the last. In another month or two you will all be executed and replaced. If you live even that long.' The doctor suddenly reached out and grabbed Arkady's coat, which he wore over his camp-issue striped uniform, and pulled it back to reveal the pink triangle sewn over his heart. 'Do your friends know what you did to end up here?' The doctor spoke louder now, for the benefit of the kommandos who had fallen silent to eavesdrop from the shadows. 'Do you think they would approve? We had another man of your disposition who was discovered by his bunkmates, and let me assure you, his death was awful, even by the standards of his awful place.'

Arkady flushed, angry and humiliated and suddenly afraid.

'Come and work with me,' the doctor offered, returning to his soft, mild tone. 'Your friend here, whom you have commendably tried to save, is already dead; he is beyond what medicine can do. You will be too, soon, sooner than you think.

Unless you would like to work with me, and then you will live, and live well. We will take your pink triangle and exchange it with that of our friend here, and then you will become a political prisoner, and he the . . .' Pfeiffer paused, considered, 'degenerate.'

Arkady flinched at the word, and Pfeiffer knew he had found his mark.

'So,' he asked, 'what do you say?'

THREE

Adam loved to eat, but he scanned the menu he held with a growing sense of dismay. It went for pages, yet held nothing that appealed to him.

It seemed to him that the sinister creep of postmodernism had ruined every fancy restaurant in the city. It was all too weird, too self-conscious, too many chefs trying to prove how clever they could be, jamming together as many incongruous and incompatible flavours as possible. The waiters had just served a tiny ball of chicken, prawn, chilli and mint wrapped in a betel leaf. He sighed and poked it with a chopstick, making it wobble. He ate it and found it tasted faintly rotten.

Adam didn't understand this obsession that modern diners

had with trickery and subterfuge. Wasn't it enough to have plentiful and good food? Why go fucking it up like this? He'd read in *Men's Health* that you shouldn't eat anything that your grandparents wouldn't recognise as food, and he subscribed to that. What, he wondered, would his no-nonsense grandfather make of the great pretence, where nothing did what it was supposed to do?

'Isn't it wonderful?' asked Violet, his mother-in-law, more accurately his stepmother-in-law, leaning in to catch his attention over the clamour of the restaurant and nodding as the plates were cleared.

'It's something, all right.'

'I just love coming here,' his father-in-law, Trevor added. 'It's probably my favourite place to eat in the world – outside of San Francisco, of course.'

Adam shovelled more food into his mouth, a strategic move, because chewing would save him from being drawn into a conversation about the wonders of a slow-food diet. According to the menu, they were due another six interminable courses before the lemongrass panna cotta and aloe vera meringue signalled an end to the night. He gestured for the drinks waiter.

Adam had little time for Tess's family, particularly her father and his wife, the third Mrs Coughlin in a decade, but barely distinguishable to Adam's eyes from the second, or the first. She was a thin woman, wiry and yoga-fit, but turgid with old-money pretension and creaking socialist politics that were unbecoming on a woman of advancing years. The sort of politics that only people who had never really worked could hold. They liked this restaurant largely, Adam suspected, because the sheer amount of time you spent ploughing through a banquet made eating feel like an achievement.

Adam hated the place right down to his guts, with its cavernous dining room, which was not just dimly lit, but pitch-black outside of the pools of red light cast by the lamps over each dining table. When Adam looked out across the rest of the restaurant, each group of diners seemed like they were on a tiny island. He supposed it was designed to promote a feeling of seclusion and elitism, but it just made him feel stranded at the table with his mediocre family-in-law.

He wished he had his phone so that he could make a show of checking his emails to get out of talking to them, but it was still missing. When he called, it went straight to voicemail. It hadn't been in the car, or in his office, or the dozen other places he'd directed his new assistant to search.

Feeling naked without it, Adam cast about for a distraction, and was grateful when a waiter dressed all in black appeared out of the darkness with a tray of drinks, only to be barrelled into by little Kade and his cousins, who'd been careening about between tables. Even through the ambient house music and the delighted screaming of the kids, Adam could hear the tinkling of breaking glass and the pushed-down fury in the waiter's voice as he apologised to the table. After sending him back for more drinks, Adam called the children over and leaned down so he was at their eye level. The nephews had the excitable inbred quality that lurked inside all Irish, expressing itself like bad poetry across the features. While the genetic lottery had blessed Tess with the clean white skin, inky hair and eyes of the Black Irish, these two unfortunates had the snaggle-toothed, rough-finished pug look that suggested they'd been hacked out of parboiled potato. The effect was enhanced when they stood side by side in the gloom, all big ugly teeth and straggly red hair.

'Listen,' Adam said to them, 'why don't you guys sit down and talk to your grandma?'

'That's boring.'

'How do you think your grandma would feel if she heard you say that?'

'She wouldn't hear us!' yelled one.

'Because she can't hear us!

'Because she's deaf!'

'Because she's a big shithead!' they both chimed and dissolved into hysterical laughter. Adam winced, and for a second fantasised about dragging one of them to the ornamental fountain in the centre of the restaurant and holding the little ranga under the water while miming deafness at the other twin. *I can't hear you! What is it? What's the matter?* The image brought a smile to his face.

'Look, if you just go back to your seats and sit for one hour . . .' Adam checked his watch. 'I'll give you twenty dollars.'

'Fifty!' said one.

'Each!' said the other.

Adam glanced wistfully at the fountain and agreed. 'Don't tell your mother, okay? Our little secret.' The kids mimed zipping their mouths and dashed off to sit placidly at the table. Adam turned back to his father-in-law, who shook his head disapprovingly.

'You know, we did things differently. We never chastised or disciplined our children, because we trusted them to develop a sense of social responsibility. We never once yelled at Tess, because we trusted her to evolve to her full potential on her own.'

'Well, you certainly did something right with that one,' Adam said brightly, biting his tongue. Privately, he was amazed that Tess had turned out half as well as she had, given the kind of dipshit hippy nonsense she'd been raised on. He thought briefly about the string of sleazy men that Tess had let into her life in the years before she'd met him and wondered if her folks would have been so proud of her if they'd known.

Adam suspected that he was the best thing that had ever happened to Tess. When they'd met she'd been full of arty pretensions that had made conversing with her both exhausting and intimidating. Thankfully, they'd faded with time, and he'd only become fonder of her over the years. He was still blindsided by her mind, which grew sharper as the rest of her softened, and it was a rare week that he didn't stop to glory in his luck in marrying her; the sheer fact of her as she went about her day. He glanced over at her, hoping she would catch his eye and come to his rescue, but she was studiously playing with her food with a seriousness that implied she would rather avoid the conversation across the table.

He closed his eyes and listened to the burble of the room,

the low rumble of other powerful people doing important things, and for a second he could pretend that he was at a real business dinner, making real decisions, instead of being condescended to by these subhuman hippies. He reached for his phone and, finding the empty pocket in his jeans yet again, felt suddenly furious.

Excusing himself, he went out the front of the restaurant to find a payphone. The night was suddenly chilly, the way Melbourne got in the summer when it stopped being a city by the bay and remembered itself as a windswept hamlet under a mountain. A few diners were smoking cigarettes held carefully against the wind and swishing glasses of wine while they spoke. One finished a story and the rest of them burst into laughter.

Pushing coins into the payphone, Adam checked the answering service at the office and listened to a few work-related calls. He considered calling Clara and swinging by to see her, but remembered that they'd broken up, and he felt that it would be a moral weakness on his behalf to call upon her, like pulling into the McDonald's drive-through and stuffing his face on his way home from the gym. There was still credit in the payphone, so, on a whim, he punched his own mobile number in. It rang, and, after a few exhilarating trills, it was picked up.

There was silence on the other end. Adam listened, and thought he could hear, faintly, someone breathing.

'Hello? Hello?'

'Hello, there.'

'Hi.' Adam, caught on the back foot by hearing a strange voice answer his phone, struggled to think of what to say. 'Don't hang up.'

'Don't worry about that, matey,' said the voice on the other end. 'I'm not going anywhere.'

'So you found my phone?'

'Could be. What's it worth to you?' The voice was rough; cigarettes and suburbia.

'I'm happy to give you a reward . . .'

'A reward . . .' The voice on the other end rolled the syllables around thoughtfully. 'A re-ward, yes. I reckon a reward is just about right.'

'Where are you? Would a hundred bucks do?'

'It's a start, but what you're asking me to do here is be a good Samaritan, and good things happen to good people.'

Adam thought hard about whether he should meet the voice on the other end of the phone. The man sounded like a fairly scummy piece of shit, probably a bit of a drug addict, maybe a bit desperate, capable of violence. But then, Adam was a big boy – literally, he could bench a tenth of a tonne without breaking a sweat – and he could always run away if things got weird. And he needed that phone, bristling with apps and notes as it was. He also didn't fancy having to explain to Tess that he'd lost yet another phone. And besides, his instincts told him to meet the man, and his instincts were rarely wrong.

They were to meet in one of the forgotten car yards along

the Nepean Highway, the first place that had leaped to Adam's mind when he thought about privacy. It had gone into receivership a year or two earlier, and now was just a dark strip of asphalt where nothing moved but the fading dealership flags whipped by the sea breezes that blew in from the south. It was permanently deserted, except for the occasional carload of bored teenagers who parked there to smoke pot or have sex – he'd gone there with Clara more than once – choosing it because the big concrete shell of the showroom office blocked the view from the road.

When Adam pulled into the parking lot, the other car was waiting for him, a beat-up old Ford Falcon. He slowed, felt his tyres give slightly as they rolled over cracked bitumen and clumps of weed breaking through the concrete. He turned off the ignition, waited, suddenly frightened. What was he doing here, in the middle of nowhere, in the middle of the night? Why wasn't he still at dinner with his family? Or, better, home with Tess?

He wound down the window. Warm night, sea air blowing in from two suburbs over. The other car made no move. Eventually he flashed his lights and, after a moment, a man climbed out of the car and sauntered towards him.

'No need to be scared, mate,' the man, the same man he'd spoken to on the phone, yelled across the parking lot. White teeth flashed against brown skin. 'Come on out and say hi.'

Adam started to feel foolish, remembered who he was, remembered what he stood for, and climbed out of the car, strode out tall to meet the man, and gave him the once-over:

Adidas shoes, Puma tracksuit. The man offered his hand, and Adam ignored it.

'You've got my phone?'

The man's smile dipped, but quickly returned. 'I do, my friend, I do. And it's all yours, but I'm going to ask for a little finder's fee.

'A hundred dollars.'

The man grimaced, sucked air through his teeth. 'Oh, mate, I'm afraid I'm going to have to ask for a little bit more than that. You see . . . the boy who found the phone, the one you assaulted, he happens to be very dear to me.'

Adam started, a little jag of adrenaline, the quick rush of fear; he was about to be jumped. He took a step back and turned to look at the Falcon, saw four other people waiting in the car, faces shadowed under baseball caps.

The passenger-side door opened, and the boy from KFC, the one he'd caught watching him and Clara, leaned out, called in a weedy little voice, 'Oi. Tariq. Hurry it up, mate.'

At the sad adolescent squeak, Adam's fear left him as quickly as it had come. He remembered that desperate people, despite having less to lose, were frightened of people with power, people like him. They were like snakes; all he had to do was stamp his feet to scatter them.

'Okay, look, Tariq, is it? I'm sorry I lost my temper at your friend, but he was . . . spying on me.'

'Oh?' Tariq raised his eyebrows, 'Spying on what, exactly? What were you up to?'

'That's not your business.'

'Poor kid just wanted to have a look inside the car. He doesn't get a chance to check out fancy cars very often, where we're from. Didn't know what he'd find behind the tinted windows. What were you doing, anyway, made you so upset? His doctor bills! All those stitches.' Tariq frowned, whistled, raised his hands towards his face, elbows tight in a what-can-you-do gesture.

'So how much do you want?'

'A grand should do it.'

Adam almost barked with laughter, but supressed it, held out his hand. 'Okay. Fine. But give me a look first? How do I know it's my phone?'

Adam took the handset, booted it up and saw that yes, it was his. He nodded, then, reaching behind him as if going for his wallet, he dropped the phone to the concrete and raised his foot to stamp on it. He heard it shatter, felt the satisfying pop as the case shattered under his boot, and saw the equally satisfying shock on Tariq's face.

'You know what? You keep the phone, Tariq. Sell it. Buy yourself something pretty.'

Tariq looked down at the phone, up again at Adam, grinned. 'Oh, Adam. Adam Kulakov. What have you done, mate? That seems a little wasteful, doesn't it? Think of all the poor kids starving in the third world, mate.'

'Fuck you,' Adam bristled. 'You fucking scabby bogan cunt.'

Tariq moved forward, but Adam was already skipping back, climbing into his SUV, spinning the wheels. He roared past Tariq and his Falcon, flipping the boy in the passenger seat the bird on his way past. His instincts had proven right. The men were bad news, and he'd rather see his poor phone destroyed than pay them a dollar of his hard-earned. You never give in to bullies; you fight them on your own terms. That, more than anything, was what Grandpa Arkady had taught him about life.

———

Adam left before the end of the meal. Tess had seen him get up from the table and go outside earlier in the evening, and then he'd come back distressed. He ignored the food and fidgeted with his cutlery, and even in the dim light she could see his face and neck were splashed with the red splotches he got when he was working himself into a panic.

Then he stood up abruptly to go, cutting Trevor off in the middle of a story, lurching awkwardly to his feet and nudging the table. He said his farewells to Tess's step-mum, nodding anxiously to get away, then he was beside her chair, kissing her goodbye clumsily. 'I've just remembered something I need to take care of at work. It's urgent, but it'll be fine. I'll see you at the house.'

And he still wasn't in when she arrived home. She started to call his mobile, remembered that he'd lost it, so got little Kade showered and into bed and padded down to the kitchen. She poured herself a large whiskey, then fetched her pills.

The pills were a grown-up iteration of a habit she'd picked up in her youth. She'd learned early that she could manage her mood through drugs and alcohol, and she saw no reason to ever stop. If scientists and pharmacists of varying degrees of sophistication and legality had worked out how to tweak a hormone or synapse so her moods could be played like a synthesiser, then why on earth would she object?

Most nights, to still the endless stream of numbers that coursed through her mind at bedtime, she had a little valium, of which she kept a healthy stockpile, replenishing it once a month by visiting one of the overworked doctors in the bulk-billing clinics she rotated through. She selected a five-milligram pill, necked it with whiskey, then lay down on the couch to listen to the silence.

As a young woman, whenever she felt overwhelmed by life, she would lock herself away in her room and marinate in sad music until she felt better. Putting on a CD by Leonard Cohen or Patti Smith she would smoke a little pot and steep herself in misery for hours. At the end of it, she always felt much better, the bittersweet artisan angst like a colonic for her own, coursing through her and scouring out her own anxieties, leaving her clean and light. She'd tried to describe the sensation to her roommate once, who'd laughed and said, 'Yeah, we all do that. In this world you are either unhappy or an idiot. So what?'

These days, overwhelmed by familial and commercial emergencies, and frequently an unholy fusion of the two, the pockets of silence she found through the day had the same fortifying effect. It was rare that her child wasn't tearing through the house on a manic upswing about a new toy, or bawling about a skinned knee; it was even rarer that Adam wasn't doing the same. There was nothing more valuable to her than silence, and she sunk into the couch, trying to bury herself in the cushions, to sink completely into the fabric. She grabbed a throw rug and pulled it up over her face to make a little shrouded cubby and drown the world out. Soon she was snoring.

Tears startled her out of sleep. She sat bolt upright, embarrassed, woken from a dream where she was standing over a coffin, weeping, and the sound of her own wailing had woken her. For a while she sat there, teetering between sleep and wakefulness as the world reassembled itself and the dream retreated. She could still hear sobbing, and she realised that the whimpering she could hear through the house was not an echo from her dream.

Foggy, drugged and half asleep, she went upstairs to check on Kade. She took her time moving through the rooms, taking the stairs carefully, letting her eyes adjust to the soft, precise and expensive lighting in her home. Kade was still in bed, snoring gently, his nightlight, which Tess was fighting a losing campaign to have taken away, wrapping him in cosy shadow. She watched him sleep for a moment, and then checked Arkady's room.

Adam's grandfather had been living with them for the better part of a year. For a while after she'd first become involved in the company, Arkady had seemed content in retirement, happy to just pop by every couple of days to show Tess the secrets of the business. In time, though, as Tess grew more comfortable and he had less and less to do, he'd started to decline. It seemed to her that Arkady simply didn't know what to do without work. She'd read that a lot of men, especially quiet, powerful types like Arkady, just gave up on life when they were no longer useful. Still, she had been shocked by the change in the old man.

The accoutrements of wealth he'd accumulated went unappreciated. He owned a Mercedes sedan that he'd bought new in the seventies and kept in pristine condition his whole life. He'd loved that car like a child, but it had been an age since he'd taken it out of the garage. In fact, he never took himself out, spending all day moping in his sprawling house by the river. A lady from a service picked up his laundry once a fortnight and came back the next day with racks full of neatly pressed suits and shirts, and a sweaty, harried man from another service delivered him frozen meals he ate straight out of the tray, then left them to pile up around the house until the cleaning lady came. As far as Tess could tell, Arkady had no interests, no friends beyond his business associates, all of whom had promptly vanished when he stepped down as director, and no interest in taking up a hobby. He seemed to have nothing to look forward to except the times he dropped by the office to double-check the books.

The old man had worked fourteen-hour days, at least, every day for his whole life in Australia. According to Adam, he seemed to barely tolerate quality time with his family, even on the holidays his wife – a devout Jew, observant even though she had married an atheist, her faith unshaken, even after Auschwitz – insisted on celebrating, when he would fidget his way through her prayers, bolt down some gefilte fish, before heading off to the office again. Arkady had particularly despised Yom Kippur, the day of atonement when work was forbidden, and would sit in sullen silence in the lounge room until it was time to go to bed. When his wife passed away, he stopped observing the holidays altogether.

In the months after Tess had finally mastered the business, Arkady had stopped coming in to visit and had abruptly gone downhill. He'd even stopped listening to his records and then stopped eating. After some debate about what to do with him, he had moved into one of Adam and Tess's spare rooms. There were plenty of spare rooms – they'd bought a house with room for a much larger family than theirs but, without ever really discussing it, had decided that one child was enough for them. Arkady had moved in, his mood had improved, he'd become engaged with the world again, and, at her suggestion, started coming in to help her with the books again, although they both understood it was unnecessary.

Truthfully, Tess had missed Arkady's time in the office as much as he had. The most peaceful times she could remember that didn't involve a handful of tranquillisers were the endless afternoons spent working in silence alongside Arkady, tilling their abstract fortunes into neat, fertile rows. That was happiness: the toddler bouncing on his great-grandfather's knee, her husband in the next room making an elaborate sales pitch to some new clients, her mind slowly ticking over with steady, quiet accomplishment, and Arkady, friend and mentor, watching over the lot of them with a secretive half-smile on his face.

One afternoon, there was a knock at the door and Shubangi, their head of product, entered. She and Tess had a brief conversation about overheads on the new toy line, and then Shubangi left. As Tess returned to her work, Arkady started laughing at her.

'What?'

'You talk like a different person when you're doing business. Like a – what is the English? – a robot.'

She blinked. 'What do you mean?'

Arkady made circles of his fingers, raised them to his eyes in a parody of her reading glasses. 'Hello, Shubangi. Please come inside, and talk to me, Tess, about deliverables. Then we will discuss what learnings we have achieved from the outcomes. And then we will engage the stakeholder and also discuss the synergy.'

'Hey, old man!' She feigned outrage. 'That's not fair.'

'What is not fair,' Arkady said, dropping his impression, 'is what your generation of professionals has done to the poor English language. I speak five languages, and I have no idea what on earth you are saying.'

'Perhaps you're right. I'm sorry. It's a bad habit. I never thought it would happen to me, and it has. I wonder how else this job has impacted me as a person?' She put her hand to her mouth, gasped in mock horror. 'Oh, God. I used impact as a verb. How can I go on?'

'There there, Lubovka.' Arkady reached over and patted her hand. 'You'd be amazed what you can live with.'

•

Arkady wasn't in his bedroom, but he had been. His room, which, since he'd moved in and re-engaged with the world, he'd kept in a state of medical-grade cleanliness. Now, it was ruined. The bed, normally carefully made with hospital corners seconds after the old man woke up, was upended, the sheets scattered and torn, the mattress flipped onto the floor. The wardrobe door swung open on its hinge and the suits inside spilled half out and across the floor. It looked for all the world like the house had been knocked over while she slept. She felt a stab of fear, that someone had broken in, had left with her valuables, or, worse, was possibly still in the house.

'Arkady?' she called softly from the doorway. Feeling foolish about her wimpy little croak, she did it again with more confidence and stepped into the room: 'Arkady?' His turntable was spinning; the record had finished and the harsh scratch scratch scratch of the needle crept up her spine. She moved over to it and lifted the stylus, then, almost reflexively, slipped the record back into its sleeve and returned it to its spot on the shelf, where Arkady's records rested next to his late wife's, all jazz, all gathering dust. Arkady hated jazz, resolutely refused to listen to it: bebop, big-band, anything with a horn provoked his ire. If they were eating in a restaurant that played easy-listening, Arkady would slip away from the table and ask them to turn it off.

In the silence that filled up the room, she could hear the weeping that had jolted her out of sleep again, and she realised it was coming from outside.

Arkady'd had a magnificent garden at his old home, and, although it had been tended by a contractor, he'd seemed to enjoy it. When he'd moved in with them, Tess gently suggested that gardening might help him fill the days, and he had agreed. Now, rows of tomato and string-bean plants climbed stakes, basking in the watery sunlight that bounced off the swimming pool, and on nice days she would see Arkady out there, sweating in his shirt and waistcoat, picking caterpillars off leaves and muttering under his breath.

That's where she found him, crouched on his hands and knees, scrabbling in the dirt. It was raining, a soft, dismal fall that hid the tears running down the old man's face, if not the sound.

Arkady's crying was clearly not meant to be heard by anyone; here were tears that had been stored somewhere deep for the longest time until they broke out again, geysered up under pressure to become a loud, animal wail which finally broke down to a whimper.

Tess stood shocked for a minute, watching this man, who to her epitomised restraint and dignity, weeping face down in the mud. She stood, vacillating between wanting to put her arms around him and to slink off pretending she'd never seen this, while the rain picked up and the rising hiss of it hitting the pool drowned out the sobbing. She watched as he uncurled from a fetal ball and his hands plunged into the loose soil around the roots of the plants. Unsure what to do, she approached him slowly.

'Arkady?' she asked softly, then again, louder, 'Arkady?'

Arkady's head snapped around, his eyes wild. They stared right through her.

'*Verzeih mir,*' he choked out. '*Wir wussten nicht.*'

Tess approached slowly with her palms stretched out, making cooing noises. *This is ridiculous*, she thought, *he's not a dog.* Still, it seemed to work, and he let her approach, then collapsed quivering into her as she put her arms around him. As he got close she realised, much to her surprise, that he stank of booze. Arkady, for the first time since she'd known him, was drunk, falling-down drunk.

She got him inside, and, worried, wanted to call Adam. Where was he? What was she supposed to do?

After thinking hard for a moment, she decided to do for Arkady what she would want should someone find her face-down in the garden, inconsolable. She gave him a valium with a glass of water, and he took it without questioning. She then led him to his room, where she used a hand-towel to clean his face and hands before she made his bed and helped him get undressed. It felt indecent to be undressing the old man, who stood docile while she unbuttoned his vest and shirt, even raising his arms like a child to help her take off his sodden singlet. Underneath, stark against the sagging white skin, a mess of crosshatched scars covered his shoulders, down his back, stretching from his shoulder blade to his rib cage. A jagged surgical scar traced up his chest from navel to throat. She bit her lip to stop the swear words that crowded there, and the questions.

Arkady had told her that he'd been hurt in the war, spent

time in Auschwitz, but this was much worse than she had imagined. She helped him into a fresh flannel pyjama shirt, and as he threaded his arms into the sleeves she caught a glimpse of the crude, faded number tattooed into his forearm. She thought about whether she should remove his trousers, but they seemed dry enough and she decided against it, instead gently moving his legs to lever him into bed. She pulled the covers over him, and stroked his hair back from his face, making soothing noises like she did for her son after he'd had a bad dream. Soon, the old man's face relaxed, and he slept.

She craved a cigarette and fetched one from the pack she kept hidden behind the shelf of classics that Adam liked to talk about at parties, but, she suspected, had never read. Adam would be disgusted to know she still enjoyed the occasional sneaky cigarette, but *fuck it*, she thought, *if he's going to vanish on me at a time like this, then he doesn't get a say in the matter*. Walking outside, she inhaled furiously, and started pacing by the pool, wondering what she was supposed to do. Words jumped out at her in the darkness, serious words, words with consequence: stroke; aneurism; dementia. Where the fuck was Adam? She found her mobile and tried her husband, then finally, giving in to a nagging fear in the back of her mind, decided to call an ambulance to come take Arkady to the hospital.

Her smoke had burned down to the filter, and she walked over the vegetable patch and threw it into the dirt. It landed in the mud and extinguished with a small hiss. Using the toe of her shoe, she pushed the butt into the mud to better hide it, and her foot nudged something hard. Squatting down, she reached into the mud and felt around, pulled up a parcel, something hard swaddled in a towel. When she unwrapped it she found she was holding a doll, the original design from Arkady's empire, the hardwood, floppy-limbed Sarah doll.

———

Dr Dieter Pfeiffer liked Arkady, found his assistance invaluable. There were gaps missing from his education, of course, cut short as it had been by the war, which Arkady had tried to fill with his own study. The results were mixed; some things you just couldn't learn from books. Dieter would need to give him extensive training before he trusted him to perform surgery, for example, but autopsies, vivisections, pathology, removing blood and bone specimens from bodies – everything that the lab needed help with – he had a natural talent for.

Arkady was a big man and when he sat at his station his hulking back hunched uncomfortably over to dwarf the desk, but if Dieter peeked over the man's shoulder he would see him using his fingers, each a gnarled Slavic club, as gently as if he were rescuing a butterfly that had fallen in a pond. The way he prepared a blood slide was a thing of beauty, a perfect circle in the middle of the glass square, the platelets and the plasma dancing for the microscope. It was a rare day that went by that Dieter wasn't thankful for discovering the Russian languishing in the Sonderkommando. He was above that grunt work; a good doctor, in the middle of a Europe where good men, let alone doctors, were in short supply. For Dieter, who was buckling under the workload as Mengele's demands grew more erratic and outlandish, Arkady was a godsend. He needed all the help he could get.

The Russian was a quick study, but better than that, he was kind. He had a bedside manner that soothed the children, made them more relaxed and easier to work with, could even coax a laugh out of a little girl, even after her siblings had gone to the research rooms and not returned.

The start of their working relationship had been shaky. When Dieter had explained the scope and purpose of their research, Arkady had been outraged and refused to work, especially after he saw Mengele's zoo, the special barracks housing the twins that the doctor was collecting for his comparative studies. Dieter had explained Dr Mengele's scientific theories, and his method of using twins, one for the experimental factor you were testing, one for control. 'This way,' Dieter explained, 'you have the perfect measure of the effectiveness of a treatment or a pathogen. With identical twins, the biological data is identical, the sociological data virtually identical. You have one factor influencing the result, the factor you introduce into the equation.'

Arkady had been horrified. 'They are children!'

'They are subjects.'

'They are human beings.'

'Subhuman.'

'I'm not going to be part of this.' Arkady was quiet, but adamant, and Dieter frowned. He considered threatening Arkady, or summoning a guard to have him beaten, but he found all that distasteful. Besides, he suspected it would be ineffective. If he was to recruit Arkady he was going to need to appeal to him as a man of science, or as a humanitarian. And he knew a way to do both.

The selections happened every time a new trainload of civilians arrived at Birkenau, where SS men with attack dogs would greet the arrivals and divide them into groups. The strongest were selected for labour and sent three kilometres down the road to Auschwitz where they were assigned to work details in the factories. Everyone else – the elderly, children, pregnant women – was sent to the gas chambers. Arkady had already seen a selection, of course, when he arrived at the Auschwitz-Birkenau complex himself, and he'd seen its aftermath. But this was the first time he'd seen one from the outside, all the faces streaming forward, blank, hopeless, frightened. He'd thought he would feel more for them, he knew exactly what they were going through, but he found it impossible to think of them as individuals. There were just too many. One poor person on the way to the gas chamber was a tragedy. A million was a statistic.

A Nazi with perfect posture, a long white coat over his black uniform, strolled up and down the lines, a baton swinging at his side, whistling. Every once in a while he would stop, tap an arrival on the shoulder with his baton, gesture for them to get out of line.

'That's Mengele,' Dieter told Arkady from where they

watched on the sidelines. 'He comes down here to pick specimens for his experiments: twins, dwarves, giants, anyone with an interesting mutation. He is a genius of genetics. Very famous in his field.'

'Why does he come down here? Why doesn't he just send soldiers?'

'Because he is terrified of losing specimens to the gas chambers if he's not here to catch them. One time they brought in a family of seven dwarves; seven! And sent them to the gas chambers! Luckily, we were able to catch them in time and save them for the zoo.'

Together they watched Mengele make his selections from the children: a pair of twins; a little girl with heterochromia, one eye shining green, the other blue. The rest of the children not old enough to work were dragged away from their parents and marched towards the gas chambers.

'You see,' Dieter had said sombrely, as Arkady watched the young being escorted away, those too small to walk on their own being carried down the ramp by the older children, 'there is no place for children in Auschwitz. They cannot work, so we have no use for them. It makes sense.' The Nazi shrugged. 'Some children will survive, perhaps, but not without your help. If you work with me, I can help you to save these people. At least the children, at least some of them.'

Arkady weighed it up and made his decision. The war could not last forever, one way or another, and in the time he'd spent in occupied Prague he'd seen enough to know that it would not go well for the Germans. They were spread too thin; there was too little oversight of their worst excesses. The Third Reich was not the next age of mankind; it was a bunch of chicken farmers and thugs with delusions of grandeur, running out the clock. He would wait, and he would survive, and he would save as many of the children as he could from this mad scientist.

So he went to work, performing measurements and chest drains and bloodlettings on the children because he knew he would be gentler than anyone else.

And in return for his compliance, Dieter made sure that Arkady was kept away from the worst of it. When a subject had a limb amputated for no reason but to test immune response, he sent Arkady to another ward to distract the children with games. On the days that Dieter injected chemicals into the eyes of living subjects to try to change their colour, he made sure that Arkady was sent out to run errands.

Dieter had also started to think of Arkady as a friend, which he knew was stupid, knowing that the Russian would soon be dead and by his own orders. Still, Dieter liked him, he really did. The Russian was taciturn and gruff, but urbane. He had a dark, dry sense of humour and an encyclopedic knowledge, not only of medicine but also of art and music and culture and literature. To pass the time while they waited for a slide to develop or a bacterial culture to bloom, they would have long arguments about books they'd loved and hated. Arkady would rhapsodise at great length about Chekhov – 'a consolation prize for the rest of Russia' – and in the next breath contemptuously dismiss Tolstoy, whom he despised, especially the holy *Anna Karenina*: 'A 800-page pamphlet on agricultural reform and an argument about caviar by the most boring people to ever learn French.' Talking to him, Dieter realised how much he enjoyed the company, and that until now he'd been frightfully lonely. He found that at night, after Arkady had finished his work and returned to the Sonderkommando barracks, his laboratory and the adjoining quarters seemed empty without him.

He sometimes wondered at fate, at the mathematical improbability of life, of all the micro-decisions that had been made for Arkady to end up in this place, at this time, that they had found each other and become friends, of sorts. Physically, Arkady could have been his brother, with their shared blue eyes and jet-black hair. Intellectually, he could have been his peer, were he not deranged by his unfortunate illness.

Dieter had applied for a placement fresh out of medical school because he'd heard rumours of the brilliant research happening in Nazi facilities, and believed it would be an ideal way to fast-track his career. He had realised too late that the Nazis were brutes and bores: cruel and cunning at best, but for the most part dull-witted, chaotic and mean. There wasn't a day that passed when he didn't regret coming here. The only upside that he could see was that as long as the camp stayed busy he would be kept away from the Russian Front. Dieter did not want to spend his life treating frostbite and self-inflicted gun-shot wounds and risk being captured by the Soviets, whom he considered subhuman. He was surprised, then, to find he had such affection for a Russian. One day, he voiced his astonish-ment at the fact.

'Believe me,' said Arkady, 'I am just as shocked to find a Nazi who knows what to do with a book.'

Arkady appreciated the company too. He'd been lonely since Prague, hadn't realised how much, even as bleakness coloured everything around him, he'd missed having someone to talk to. He'd made no friends in the Sonderkommando. The ones who didn't go mad in the first ten minutes or take their lives after the first week were often a special type of man, the kind who could shrug off their humanity and wield cruelty and violence as adroitly as the tools for snipping hair, stripping cloth, pulling teeth. So in the evening, when the men would gather in the bunkroom, with their food and liquor and cigarettes, he would sit apart, and close his eyes and wait for the dawn alone.

Some nights, though, after work, before Arkady returned to his barracks, he and Dieter shared a beer or a glass of cognac and talked. One evening, as a reward after a grim day performing autopsies on young men who'd died of gangrene, they got tipsy and Dieter found himself confessing his doubts about the war, about the Reich, how much he missed civilisation, how much he missed his family in Hamburg.

'Do you have a large family?' Arkady asked him.

'Not very. One sister, my mother, and my father, for whom I am named.'

'Dieter Pfeiffer? Your father had a name that unfortunate and still inflicted it on you?'

It was a test, Dieter knew; the Russian was pushing the boundaries, trying to find out where he stopped being a prisoner and became a companion. He smiled, let it slide, and they went back to drinking.

Later, Dieter stepped outside to piss, and when he came back inside, Arkady was bent over the table, packing up the surgical instruments.

'Oh, don't worry about that,' Dieter said expansively, waving a drunken hand. 'You go on to bed, I'll clean up.'

It was only when he was stowing his tools away in their leather case that he noticed a missing scalpel. He paused, swayed drunkenly, blinked several times to try and sober up. He checked under the benches, in the basket of medical waste. No, the scalpel was gone.

Dieter felt rage, and, absurdly, stinging dismay, and found himself blinking back tears. He had thought that they were friends, truly, and he had not only trusted Arkady with his work, but with his life, turning his back on him while deadly medical instruments lay all about. He had been stupid. It was the height of foolishness to trust a prisoner, much less an *untermensch*, a degenerate.

Dieter conducted a careful inventory of the lab. Half a dozen blades of one shape or another were missing, along with several wooden splints, which could, combined, make handy weapons. Dieter sat, brooding, trying to think clearly. Arkady was now a liability, a security risk, one that would have to be resolved.

The doctor stewed for a moment, his thoughts now cold and clear if not sober, and made up his mind. He summoned a soldier who marched in, saluted, his heels tapping together and knocking snow over Dieter's floor. He waited for orders. 'Go to the Sonderkommando barracks,' Dieter told the soldier, 'and find prisoner Arkady Kulakov. His serial number is in my files. Take him to the Luftwaffe lab, and tell them he has volunteered for endurance testing.'

FOUR

Her phone was long dead. In the scramble to get out the door and follow the ambulance she'd forgotten to pack her charger. She'd nearly forgotten her son, too, had been backing out of the garage before she remembered, swore, and had to call around for a babysitter. She finally found one in her father, Trevor, who seemed overjoyed to head over in the middle of the night, a joy she wished she could ascribe to love for his grandson, rather than bald-faced salivation at Tess inheriting Arkady's estate.

She regretted running the phone battery down trying to reach Adam as she sat in the waiting room, forgetting time and again that it wouldn't work, getting angry at herself for thinking irrationally, then realising it was fine to be mad, because her husband was off chasing fireflies or whatever he did, at one of the few times she needed him around.

It wasn't unusual for Adam to vanish for hours right when his presence was needed, but it had never been quite this impossible to reach him. Every time the call rang out then went through to his drawling voicemail message: 'Hi, you've reached Kulakov. I'm busy, or just ignoring you, so leave me a message and I'll hit you back.' She'd been trying to get him to change it to something more professional for ages, and now, sitting and waiting for her father-in-law in the holding tank of this hospital, she felt a hot flare of rage as she listened to it yet again.

She was checking her email for the hundredth time when her phone went dark, the little wheel spinning out into the black, and she only realised when it was completely dead that she couldn't remember a single phone number off by heart.

'Shit!' she said, then, remembering where she was, tried to compose herself. Searching through her purse for distraction, she ate a whole box of Tic Tacs, crunching them before they could soften in her mouth, and when they ran out, a couple of valium.

By the time the doctor came in, Tess was halfway hypnotised by the glare off the glossy pages of the waiting-room magazines and the soft hum of the fluorescent lights overhead, all the roiling stress submerged under a chemical mellow. When the doctor took her into an office to deliver her diagnosis, Tess reacted as she might if a waiter came back to the table to tell her they were all out of the salmon that day.

'He's had a stroke,' the doctor said. 'At this point it's too early to know how bad it is, but it doesn't look good.'

'A stroke,' Tess repeated, softly. 'Yes, I thought it probably was.'

The doctor was professional but sympathetic, and, thought Tess, unreasonably pretty for someone working the night shift in the emergency ward, even in a mood-lit private hospital like this. She looked like a sassy medico from a soap opera. When did doctors start becoming younger than her?

Tess tucked her legs up under her in the chair across from the doctor's desk and swivelled back and forth while the doctor talked, using long, worrying words that meant very little to Tess: *cerebrovascular trauma*, *dilated cardiomyopathy*, *concerning imaging results*. Her bedside manner was soft and firm, and her voice raked Tess's scalp with pleasure, like being massaged by a hairdresser, even as she delivered the terrible news.

'He's had an embolism, most likely from a small blood clot breaking off from the heart and settling in the brain. It's led to a lack of blood in the area, causing an ischemic cerebrovascular accident, or stroke.' The doctor swung her computer around so that Tess could see, and called up a series of images. It struck Tess how much the inside of a person – the veins, the hydraulics, the surging thought and electricity – resembled the blueprints to any other machine. It could have been a schematic for a new product ready to be emailed to their factories in China.

'And I'm afraid that while this cerebral incident was serious, probably triggered by some kind of extreme stressor, it isn't Mr

Kulakov's first.' The doctor pointed at some dark blotches on the glowing web of Arkady's brain scan. 'This is necrotic brain tissue, and it seems to indicate that Mr Kulakov has suffered a whole series of micro strokes over the past few months.'

'That seems . . . I mean, why wouldn't he say anything? Wouldn't we have noticed?'

'Maybe, but probably not. They may well have happened at night, and this is the first Mr Kulakov will have known about it. In fact, he probably won't know about them. I'll be frank: the prognosis is not great here. As he ages, these incidents are likely to occur again, and the accompanying confusion and incidents like you experienced tonight are going to increase. It's not just this stroke – with the smaller incidents, you're looking at the onset of vascular dementia. His mental condition is likely to deteriorate rapidly.'

'So what does that mean? His brain is broken?'

'Not his brain, not exactly.' The doctor called up an image of Arkady's heart, and pointed at a shadowy mess in the middle. 'Mr Kulakov's heart shows considerable stress, and we see evidence of significant scarring on the wall of the heart. Some is new, natural wear and tear that we'd expect in an older man, but some is decades old. The scarring and arterial constriction is consistent with someone who's lived with hypertension and abnormal levels of stress for a long time. Basically, his heart's walls have weakened, meaning it doesn't pump as well as it should. This has allowed a thrombus – a clot – to form, and when bits break off, they have the potential to block smaller vessels. The brain doesn't get enough blood, the blood enough oxygen, and eventually the body will just wear out.'

'So how long does he have?'

The doctor shrugged. It seemed to Tess that doctors shouldn't be allowed to shrug, at least not during consultations. 'The speed at which vascular dementia progresses varies from person to person. We can't reverse the brain damage, but it might be possible to slow the progression of the disease. Medication, diet, exercise, all might help; but then, they might not.'

Tess took this in, tried to parse what it meant, failed. It was all too new, too big, too sudden. 'Can I see him?'

Arkady was dwarfed by the size of the bed, which was itself dwarfed by the size of the room. It was much, much larger than she'd expected; larger, in fact, than her old apartment in New York. It was vast, a sprawling vista populated here and there with feature lamps and pot plants. A heart monitor beeped among the bank of life-support equipment that buttressed the bed.

She'd seen a photo of Arkady in his youth, standing unsmiling in black-and-white at St Kilda Pier after being badgered into a family portrait – he was always strangely reluctant to be photographed – with his wife and son, and been struck by the bulging muscles fighting their way out of his sleeves, the unexpected pelt peeking out the top of his shirt. Now, his chest, bare and covered in monitor electrodes, was crumpled, the best part of it lost in the past, a balloon floating about long after the party had died. The doctor was tactfully silent for a moment, then cleared her throat and spoke quietly so as not to wake him.

'The human body isn't designed to hold up to the kind of stress that Mr Kulakov seems to have been under for some time. He's strong, but the wear and tear on his organs suggest that he's suffered from intense physical and emotional trauma for long stretches.'

There was a moment's silence in which Tess took Arkady's hand, running a thumb across the topographical map life had carved into his flesh, where the callused ridges on his hands turned into papery dry skin. 'He was in the camps, you know,' she said at last. 'In the war, over in Poland.'

'Jesus,' said the doctor. 'Well, that would explain some of the trauma on his internal organs. It could also explain his unusual behaviour. You see it a lot in older survivors of extremely traumatic life experiences; soldiers, medics, civilians caught in war zones may start to regress to previous traumas that they have repressed. In cases such as Mr Kulakov's, where the onset of dementia has occurred, there's the possibility of him becoming confused and returning to old behaviours. I've seen a lot of Holocaust survivors with dementia start to live in constant terror that they'll be returned to the camps, becoming fearful, starting to shoplift from stores because in their mind they're back in the forties, just trying to survive. That would all be consistent with the behaviour you describe: his wandering at night, his confusion, his hiding precious objects in the ground. I'm sorry to say, but these symptoms are likely to get worse.'

'So there's nothing we can do?'

The doctor smiled sadly, and together they watched Arkady's chest sink and rise with his breath. 'I know this is a lot to take in, Tess,' said the doctor. 'If you feel comfortable we have a psychologist on staff who's very good at helping to process the feelings that rise at times like this. We also work with a rabbi, who . . .'

'Oh no,' Tess said. 'No, I'm not Jewish.'

'Oh, I'm sorry, I just assumed that . . . Our files show Mrs Kulakov was in hospice care with us some years ago and she and the rabbi were very close.'

'Yes. Arkady's wife, Rachel . . . We never met.' Tess had heard a great deal about Adam's grandmother but she'd passed away long before Tess had come into the play. 'She was very religious. Arkady, not so much. He was a gentile, in the camps for political reasons, and he never converted after he married Rachel. She was upset, but what could she do?'

For reasons she had never fully understood, Arkady had very little to do with the Jewish community, although he had married Rachel, a fussy, fiery Polish girl who'd been in Auschwitz around the same time as him. In Melbourne, when they met, they had marvelled at the coincidence, courted and fallen in love, then conceived John, their only child, Adam's father, and who had himself married a shiksa, which Rachel declared had broken her heart and would drive her into an early grave.

Rachel had, in fact, died young, just a few years after her grandson was born. She'd been used as a medical test subject by the Nazis and one of the experimenters had injected her with something that had stunted her liver. It had never grown properly and childbirth had put too great a strain on it. When it became clear how serious Rachel's illness was, Arkady had raged against the Nazis, against the doctors who couldn't save her, against the God he didn't believe in, except in moments of blinding fury when he needed a punching bag big enough to take his anger. But nothing worked, and she passed away. After she was gone, Arkady, who had never been very social at the best of times, drifted away from the community, and now had almost nothing to do with them.

As Tess spoke about Adam's family to the doctor, she realised that her husband still didn't know his grandfather was in the hospital.

She was still awake when he got in late that night, after the requisite hours in the slow, digital alarm clock–lit purgatory of their bedroom, in which sleep refused to come to her no matter how many breathing exercises she dredged up from a distant yoga class, or how viciously she brutalised her pillow searching for a cooler side. He tiptoed in, undressed quietly, and slipped into bed beside her. She went to speak, and found her voice tight with rage.

'Where have you been, Adam?'

'Out. Out with friends.'

She considered herself a realist, and while she'd never managed to make a relationship last very long before Adam, growing up around her chaotic, fabulist parents had inadvertently educated her in exactly what a marriage was, which was a contract to be renegotiated time and again as the currencies brought to the table – sex, loyalty, companionship, family – waxed and waned. Yes, her husband could be one-dimensional, even simple-minded at times, evasive and daft at others, but he was, she thought, a kind man underneath it all. Disappointing at times, but reliably so, and a good father to Kade, whom he adored with a force that occasionally broadsided her, even after all these years. As petty and as bullying as he could be with his staff, he had never lost his temper with his son, or his wife. So, in return, she was as magnanimous as she could be about his frequent flakiness and not-brilliant evasions. Tonight, though, after his vanishing act when Arkady could have been dying, she'd had enough.

'What friends?'

'Just some guys . . . from school.'

'And what was so important that you couldn't stay at dinner?'

'There's a problem with our Chinese suppliers. I had to put out a bunch of fires.'

'What kind of fires?'

'There was a problem with a blueprint. It was urgent. Couldn't wait until morning. What's your problem?'

Tess sighed heavily, and turned back over. Adam sat up. 'What's the matter, Tess? Don't you believe me?'

'I do not.'

'Oh?' Adam sat up in a huff, summoning as much easy outrage as he could at a pinch, which was plenty, and demanded, 'So where do you think I was?'

Tess rolled over and curled into a little ball. 'I honestly don't care any more. Just do what you need to.' This sent Adam off on a long, angry screed about workdays and supply lines and duty, which she listened to until he paused to draw breath, when she calmly said, 'I just wish you had told me where you were going, because your grandfather is in hospital,' then paused, and, despite herself, smiled in the dark, enjoying the moral high-ground as she heard Adam derail mid righteous monologue, take a deep breath, and freak out.

———

After Tess had filled Adam in on Arkady's episode, he tried calling the hospital and lost his temper at the night nurse who kept asking him to call back in the morning. Adam lay next to his wife for ages, his mind ticking over, pinging like an overheated engine. Once he was certain Tess was asleep, her breath deep and regular, he slipped out of bed and padded, naked, down the stairs to the lounge room, through to the kitchen.

He hit the lights, and the halogen bleached crawling afterimages into his eyes that he blinked several times to clear, before retrieving a bottle of vodka from the freezer. He took a belt straight from the bottle, and another over ice in a tumbler that sloshed through his stomach without dislodging the hard, fluttering knot inside it.

He filled the glass and walked to his grandfather's room, surveying the disarray Tess had seen earlier. Since he'd moved in, Arkady's mind had run on rails, his habits on clockwork. In the mornings he would be at the table early, drinking a heavily sugared black coffee and frowning over the newspaper, having bathed and shaved long before anyone else had risen.

This mess seemed a far more damning diagnosis that something was profoundly wrong than anything a doctor could tell him. That word, dementia, was just a concept, an idea. This, the confusion that had led to the desecration of his grandfather's discipline – this was something to worry about.

Adam had been robbed once, back when he was at university. He'd gone out drinking and come home to find the back door smashed in, the whole house tossed. The thieves had wrecked the place, pulling out every drawer and dumping them upside down looking for valuables. He'd lost his computer and all his CDs, but the mess was what really bothered him. He could buy a new computer, but the sanctity of the place was ruined. The state of Arkady's room reminded him of that feeling, a physical revulsion, a crawling revolt under the skin. His grandfather would be appalled by the mess when he came back from the hospital, Adam knew, and he decided to clean the room for him.

Adam squatted down and started to gather up the spilled items when something caught his eye. A dull metallic gleam shone from the back of the wardrobe, invisible from eye level behind the hems of Arkady's old-school European greatcoats. Adam shuffled forward on his haunches and pushed the coats aside to reveal a stash of food. He reached into the back and started pulling out tins of canned carrots, pickles, beans, a large jar of vinegar stuffed tight with rolls of pickled herring – all the gross, fresh-off-the-boat food that Arkady insisted on keeping in the pantry.

He'd read about Holocaust survivors doing this, regressing to the camps and hiding under their beds at night, or hoarding food in the present while their ruined minds wandered the bombed-out ruins of Europe. 'Jesus Christ,' he muttered. 'Poor Grandpa.'

One by one he retrieved the cans and stacked them on the floor. To get right to the back he pushed aside a pile of junk that he'd hastily shoved into the wardrobe when the old man was moving in and his hand connected with his old jewellery box. Although he had long since forgotten its existence, the second he touched it, fingertips tripping over the fine engravings in hardwood, he knew what it was.

The jewellery box had been a gift from his mother on his sixteenth birthday, antique, probably priceless, utterly inappropriate for a teenage boy. It was characteristic of her in that it was expensive, tasteful and in no conceivable way something he would be interested in. She tended to buy things she liked on impulse, then, when bored of them, pass them on as gifts.

As a teen, Adam, who had never shown an interest in collecting either jewellery or antiques, had been crushed when he unwrapped the box, hoping against hope for the keys to a brand-new dirt-bike, or a Nintendo, or even a roll of cash for him to decide for himself, rather than this bullshit. He'd taken it to his room and cried, the tears hot and silent and muffled by his pillow, as he would be horrified if his parents knew he was weeping, even though he wanted them to understand how bitterly they had disappointed him.

He'd thrown the box against the wall in a fit of rage, wanting it to shatter, but the ancient hardwood bounced off with an unsatisfying bonk and fell open on the carpet, displaying the velvet interior with all its little compartments for rings and chains. When he picked it up he found the spring-loaded false bottom, and, delighted, immediately started hiding his drugs in there, congratulating himself on getting one up on his aloof, indifferent mother. Some nights, listening to CDs and blowing smoke out the window of his bedroom, he wondered whether his mum had known about the false bottom of the box and how much mileage he was getting out of the stash-spot, and, if so, whether that actually made the gift surprisingly thoughtful.

Lost in thought, Adam sat on the floor of the games room cradling the box, then on a whim, popped the false bottom to find a long-forgotten joint he had rolled on some late-night video-game binge and never smoked. Gingerly, he poked the dry, flaky paper to test its stability, and, satisfied, slipped out to the backyard to smoke it.

After a couple of puffs, Adam found himself calming down, the vodka in his belly now warm and soothing, the pot straightening out his tumultuous thoughts. He looked out over the backyard, where the pool lights made the water shimmer and throw twisting glowing ribbons across his property. His gaze came to rest on Arkady's little vegetable garden, some of it uprooted by the confused old man, the rest already looking untended, unloved, doomed.

Adam thought of the company. When he'd inherited it, it had been in similar shape to the garden, everything carefully planted and latticed, but growing out of control. His own father, John Kulakov, Arkady's only son and heir, had never shown any interest in running the family company, instead pursuing a career in the law. Adam's dad had met his mum, Sandy, at university, finished his articles while his mum carried him to term, and made partner by Adam's third birthday. By Adam's tenth birthday, John had worked himself into a paragon of achievement and a textbook example of obesity-related hypertension, and before Adam's twelfth birthday John Kulakov's heart had exploded, leaving Sandy unable to cope. She did the best she could, despite her grief and the stress of having to raise Adam alone, which she'd treated with a regime of benzodiazepines and booze. It was a diet she kept secret until one night when it made her fall asleep at the wheel on the lonely road back from the family beach-house, a little under a decade later.

He rarely thought about his parents, except sometimes in dismal insomniac hours like these. Adam knew that people thought his devotion to his grandfather was strange, but they didn't know what Arkady meant to him. His parents' marriage had been an unhappy one; they both drank too much, and would have loud, melodramatic fights during which either would use Adam as a weapon to batter their belligerent spouse with. His happiest memories from his childhood were of playing alone in his room, or better yet, with Arkady, who would regularly stop by, shame John and Sandy into acting like adults, and whisk little Adam away to the park, or the zoo, or, best of all, Europe.

Every year of Adam's childhood, Arkady had embarked on an annual buying trip to Europe, where he would visit the factories and workshops of storied old-world toy and game companies to scout for new products to bring to the Australian market. When Adam was old enough, Arkady started to plan these trips to coincide with school holidays, and together, while Australia baked and sweated, Adam and Arkady would tour Europe, which seemed to Adam to be one endless winter playground. His happiest memories were of long trips cruising winding European roads to factories in far-flung parts of Yugoslavia, Czechoslovakia, ever further east as the Iron Curtain rusted, warm and sleepy in a German limousine, listening to his grandfather mutter and crinkle the newspaper, while snow tapped against the windows.

As an only child, with few friends, these trips were a reprieve from the loneliness that hung heavy over his whole early life and, years later, in an effort to thank him, Adam had bought Arkady a Rolex to replace the scuffed vintage model he wore on his wrist. Arkady had taken the gift, read the accompanying card and burst into hysterical laughter until, finally, regaining his composure and dabbing at his eyes with a handkerchief, he'd explained: he had taken Adam to Europe as a guinea pig.

To better understand what would appeal to children, Arkady had taken Adam to all those foreign showrooms as a tester. He would just hang back and watch little Adam run out to play. Whatever he got fixated on, that's what Arkady would buy. Adam was Arkady's bellwether; he just had to go in the direction the boy took him.

When Adam had told Tess about this discovery, she'd laughed, and commented that, while that was kind of brilliant, it was also borderline psychopathic, wounding Adam. She did not understand Arkady like he did. Nobody did. He had been, and remained, the single greatest guiding force in Adam's development.

As a grown man, Adam sometimes felt a twinge of regret that he'd never really had an adult relationship with his mother, who'd already become a slightly floaty, ethereal presence by the time he emerged from adolescence, yet he had nothing but a smouldering resentment for his father.

Adam had barely known John Kulakov at all, and looking at photos from his childhood he could summon no memories of the man that didn't paint him as a short-tempered, burned-out workaholic. He remembered one incident when he'd burst into John's study seeking someone to play with, and his dad had looked up from his phone call and yelled at him that he had no time for games and to go play with his fucking toys. Later, John had gone to find Adam in his room, snuffling into his pillow, and apologised, or gave as much of an apology as he could.

'You know not to disturb me while I'm working.'

'You don't have to be so mean to me,' moaned Adam. 'Grandpa works too, and he's nice.' John had sighed then, and frowned, and finally moved into the room and sat heavily on the end of Adam's bed. He said nothing for a long moment. Adam kept his face buried in the pillow, but heard the bedsprings creak under his dad's bulk, could hear the unhealthy wheeze of his breath, could smell the afternoon bourbon on it. Finally, he said, 'Adam, I know you think the sun shines out of Grandpa's arse, and maybe he's good to you, but let me tell you, he was a shit father. A really shit father. And what's more, he's done some terrible things. Unforgivable things. You're too young to understand, but one day you will.' John had died not long after that, and although they must have spoken again, that was the last thing Adam could remember him saying. It had shocked him to the core, and even now, decades later, he had never forgotten it. How was it, he thought, that his grandfather could be such a selfless and noble man, and his father so rotten? Since the day his dad died, he had tried to be more like Arkady and less like John, whom he still blamed for shirking his duty to Mitty & Sarah.

John Kulakov had rejected the family business, considered himself to be above toy-making. Adam, for his part, thought there could be no greater responsibility than to take charge of the company when the time came, to protect and build on everything Arkady had created. He had a destiny, a fact that had weighed heavily on him over the years. Sometimes he would think about what his life would have been like if he'd chosen another path, but he was consoled by the thought that what he did gave so many people reasons to get up in the morning, which, when you thought about it, was a better use of a lifetime than any other.

Now, tonight, with his grandfather ailing and maybe not long for the world, Adam wondered if it was more than family commitment that had driven him to take the role. He didn't believe in God, necessarily, but there had been certain times in life when he could feel some invisible force at his back, guiding him this way and that. He'd felt it the first time he'd called a company meeting to outline his vision. The feeling had been there the night he'd met Tess, as well as the night they'd married, and the day Kade was born, and a half a dozen other perfect moments through his life.

The first time he'd known for sure that something was watching over him was at nineteen, when he'd been driving his first car, a boxy, unwieldy Saab convertible, down Toorak Road late on a stormy night, not exactly drunk, but too tipsy to be driving on P plates, or to notice the tram tracks which caught the edge of his rear tyre and spun the car out. It had rotated completely around, and then halfway round again before the rear end smashed sideways into a Corolla parked on the side of the road. He'd sat shocked for a minute, deafened by the rain on the roof of the cab and blinded by the deluge outside, as a thousand horror stories of young drink-drivers going to prison ran through his head. He'd scrambled out to find that, while the other car had been totalled, his Saab was unscathed, the chassis intact, the paintwork unscratched. He'd driven off without leaving a note, filled with a great surge of relief and faith that this was definitive proof that the world had a greater purpose for him.

Tonight he felt it again. He would have never admitted to his staff, to his wife, even to himself, that he was uncertain about his stewardship of the company, but deep down, the doubt had gnawed at him. Tonight, as the hours ran out and his glass emptied, his mind was changing.

Tonight, he could feel it, almost hear it – great invisible gears turning behind the scenes, tectonic plates shifting beneath him, daring him to lose his balance. He would not, though; he knew that very clearly. The universe was testing him; his grandfather's illness was as clear a sign as any that it was time for him, at long last, to man up.

It was a tragedy, sure, but so was the war that had forged his grandfather into the man he had been. Now, as the company struggled in a tanking economy, he would stand firm and rise to the challenge. He would rebuild the company from the ground up. He would be faithful and true to his wife. He would set a role model for his son worthy of Arkady's legacy. Just earlier tonight, he had stood up to the bully Tariq in the car park, handled it like a man, shrugged it off. There was no greater bully than fate, and Adam would meet his head-on.

The joint was finished now so he took a last draw and flicked the butt out into the night, where it arced lazily until it landed, hissing, in the pool. Adam thought about retrieving it before Tess could find it, but that would involve grabbing the pool net from the shed, and the cleaners were coming in the morning anyway, so he left it.

Dawn had nearly broken and, too excited to sleep, Adam got dressed and drove to the office, taking the road by the beach for as long as he could to watch the water change colour with the rising sun.

He gunned the SUV down the motorway and swerved to take the ramp that led to his office. When the speed bumps in the road signalled the gate into the car park he tapped the accelerator and hit them at speed, so he could enjoy the gasp and recoil of the state-of-the-art shock absorbers in the guts of his German-engineered machine. After he parked, he took a moment to savour the stillness of the new day before going in, luxuriating in the sight of the chrome and glass office, the gargantuan warehouse next to it. Yes, things were changing; this would be a new era, a new start. In his euphoria, he failed to notice his was not the only car in the car park, that the beat-up Ford Falcon that had been following him around all night had pulled in quietly after him and stopped, turned off its engine, going quite still, as if taking a moment to think.

———

Dieter watched the experiments through the one-way mirrored windows installed so that doctors could observe their subjects in privacy. He didn't want Arkady to know that he'd ordered his death. It was one thing to die; it was another to die without any friends. Better that Arkady perish thinking that Dieter was not responsible for what happened to him. There was no oversight of how the prisoners were used by the SS, and they were subject to random executions and punishments, a fact that Arkady knew very well. He should go to his death with the hope that Dieter would come to his rescue.

They froze him first, in tubs designed to test thermal endurance. He was stripped naked and directed at gunpoint to climb into a basin of iced water, where a prisoner, a huge red-headed Soviet soldier captured on the Front, was already freezing. Dieter had overseen this experiment before, and knew the water would be just above freezing point, and Arkady would stay submerged while it sapped the body temperature. As the subject became hypothermic, they would stop shivering as their homeostatic thermoregulation shut down, then they would stop responding to stimulus. At 32 degrees they would lose consciousness. Death would occur at 25.

Dr Pfeiffer waited, and waited. The 32-degree point usually occurred in less than an hour. Now, hour after hour, the two men sat, hunched into balls in the water, still shivering. Dieter left to have his dinner, and when he returned the men were still conscious.

The other man, long past stoicism, was growing furious. He swore loudly in Russian, turned to Arkady. 'Do you speak German?' he asked in Russian. 'Ask them to kill us. Please ask them to kill us.'

'They will kill us,' Arkady said grimly. 'But not soon. Don't expect mercy. These are bitch-whores, these Germans.'

'And stupid.' The other man laughed, unexpectedly. 'What kind of fucking idiot tries to freeze a Russian to death?'

Arkady snorted, and the two men laughed until they wheezed. 'Goodbye, comrade,' the Soviet said to Arkady. They shook hands.

Watching from the other room, Dieter ended the experiment. 'Take them out. Take their temperatures, and shoot the one with the red hair. Warm the other one up, and if he lives move him to the altitude program.'

Then Dieter watched through the double-thick glass of the pressurised chamber where they tested the effect of high altitude on the brain and heart. This was, like the freezing baths, a research initiative from the Luftwaffe, as they wanted data on how long a human being would survive if a pilot ditched in sub-zero temperatures, or what ejecting from a plane at high altitude would do to the body.

Once locked in the chamber, Arkady was given a free-flowing oxygen mask, and Dieter's colleagues lowered the pressure until it matched that of an altitude of a cruising warplane. Then, to simulate a pilot ejecting without a mask, the oxygen was turned off and the altitude dropped. Dieter went to the observation port and saw that Arkady was already twitching with convulsions. As the dial plunged, his legs and his arms stretched forward at a right angle from his body like a rabid dog. At 20000 feet of pressure he was whimpering, and at 10000 screaming. At zero feet, the chamber was depressurised and Dieter went in to inspect.

Arkady's eyes were rolling back in his head and he was gibbering, strange bits of words that tripped through gritted teeth. He had bitten his tongue and the blood oozed down his jaw. Dr Pfeiffer checked his reflexes by shining a torch in his eye, found no response.

'Open the chest cavity,' he ordered. 'Check the cardiac condition.' The aids retrieved Arkady's rag-doll body from the room and put him on an autopsy table. Strictly speaking, Dr Pfeiffer didn't need to dissect Arkady – his team had already performed hundreds of live autopsies – but he wanted to make sure the man didn't wake up, and, after seeing him survive the ice bath, he didn't trust Arkady to die on his own.

What were these Russians made of that they refused to die? They were savage, certainly, but they were also adamantine. He thought of the hopeless war being lost on the Eastern Front, and lamented that Hitler had lost the second he marched on Stalingrad. Once Dieter had examined an SS guard stationed at an Auschwitz satellite camp who had been wounded on the Eastern Front. As Dieter had checked on his slowly healing scars, the man had spoken about the horror of holding off a Russian advance, the hordes of soldiers who ran screaming across the battlefield, some without weapons, some without shoes, to overrun their position. He'd been the heavy-calibre machine-gunner on a panzer, and the Soviets just kept coming, no matter how many he gunned down, a sea swarming over the ice, until his machine-gun had overheated and warped. When the soldier finished his story, he paused for a second, and started it again. It was all he would ever talk about, the Russians who weren't afraid to die, had less feeling than steel, who had crawled over his crippled tank like insects.

This was an empire that had carved itself out of snow and sadness, a nation of people where each had been given both a life not worth living and an iron will to survive. There was no way that Germany could beat Russia, no possible scenario in which they came out on top. The Russians would still be there after the bombs stopped, after the thousand-year Reich was dust, after the Soviet Empire fell, when all else was rubble and snow. They would inherit the earth, the Russians, and the roaches.

Dieter knew what he would find inside Arkady. The pericardium – the layer protecting the heart – would be filled with fluid that would squirt out when pierced and the membrane would deflate. Then a piercing in the left ventricle would empty the still-beating heart out over a period of fifteen minutes, as the muscle slowed and stopped.

The assistant made the first incision, a quick deliberate scalpel swipe to open the epidermis, slicing Arkady open from the hollow of his neck to his navel. The blade returned to the initial incision point for the second cut, a deeper, firmer stroke through fat and muscles to get at the joins of the rib cage covering the heart.

'Stop!' Dieter said, startling the assistant, surprising himself. 'Close him up. We don't need this data, and I want to go home for the day. Close him up and take him to the convalescent wing. If he lives, put him back in the Sonderkommando.' Dieter walked back to his quarters, still unsure why he'd given the order. Arkady would still die, just more slowly now, from his injuries. But there was something snagged in the back of Dieter's mind, something about Arkady he could not quite let go of.

A little under a week had passed since they'd performed the depressurisation experiment on Arkady, and Dr Pfeiffer was trying to put it all behind him. He'd ordered a search of Arkady's barracks and when his missing surgical tools had failed to reappear, he had been annoyed but out of options. If he reported the theft it would only lead to bureaucratic snooping and awkward questions. Better to let them go, order replacements, move on.

On a whim one evening he stopped at the building where they housed Mengele's children and let himself in. He moved quietly, unlocking the door and swinging it open so as not to alarm the subjects. It was late and most of them were asleep, exhausted or drugged. Those who were conscious started in fear and pulled their legs up to their bodies, scuttling away from him to press their backs against the wall. One or two of them whimpered as he walked past their bunks. He didn't blame them: nothing good ever came from men in lab coats. The fear it sparked made handling them difficult. More than the company, Dieter would miss Arkady's way with the children. Even when things were really grim he was able to calm them down, relieve their suffering a little, make them pliable. Dieter's research would be much harder to accomplish without Arkady's help.

He reached the end of the barracks, sighed, turned to walk back, when his eyes caught something amiss. A little girl, maybe eight or nine, he thought, although once a child got to a certain level of emaciation it got hard to tell, was hiding something behind her back.

'Hello,' he said, not unpleasantly, squatting down so he was at eye level with her. 'What's your name?'

'Sarah.'

'What have you got there?'

The girl shook her head furiously. 'Nothing.'

'Nothing, hey? Isn't that a coincidence!' Dieter reached into his pocket and produced one of the bars of chocolate he and the other doctors carried to bribe reticent children. 'I have a nothing too! Perhaps you could have a bite of my nothing if you show me yours.'

The gears turned in Sarah's head, she made a careful calculation, and relented, retrieved a doll from behind her back, handing it to Dieter and falling upon the chocolate, while all the other children watched in dismayed jealousy, eyes shining in the dark.

Dieter turned the doll over in his hands. It was rough but serviceable, a little boy hacked from raw wood with a tiny sharp blade – scalpel strokes; just a plump wooden torso with a head and arms wobbling from it. It was dressed in crude white pyjamas, which, even in the dark of the barracks, he could identify by touch as medical gauze. The limbs and the head moved as he manipulated them, and looking closely he could see simple hinges made from refashioned surgical sutures.

'Where did you get this?'

'I can't tell you. It's a secret.'

'Did the nice doctor give you this?'

Sarah stared glumly at her feet. Dieter gave the doll back to her. 'Does he have a name, your little friend?'

'Michael.'

'That's a nice name,' said Dieter. 'Why did you call him that?'

'I didn't!' protested Sarah. 'The nice doctor gave him to me and said he could be my new Michael until real Michael came back. So I wouldn't be lonely.'

'I see . . . And where is real Michael?'

'He went away with one of the other doctors.' Sarah looked around, then whispered, 'One of the mean ones. That was days ago.'

Dieter nodded. 'And Michael is your brother?

She nodded.

He studied the girl's features, her hair, her eye colour, her cheekbones. They were familiar; she must have been the sister of a boy he'd finalised, just that morning.

Well, that's that, thought Dieter, but he said, 'Then is there a little Sarah doll? For Michael to have when he comes back?'

'Yes! But he isn't finished yet,' Sarah said, then bit her lip. 'And I'm not allowed to show anyone.'

'But you see, the nice doctor and me, we are friends. He sent me here to have a look at little Michael, and the Sarah doll, and to give you this!' He produced another chocolate bar, and then Sarah was leading him by the hand, out of the barracks, into the snow, to a patch of dirt under an awning. Using her hands, she dug in the mud and retrieved a bundle of rags. They'd once been a prisoner's uniform but mud had turned the stripes to a single grimy shade. Setting it down in the snow, he unwrapped it carefully and found a block of wood, half carved into a likeness of little Sarah. As he unwrapped the parcel, his missing scalpel fell out, along with a half-dozen surgical instruments, and odds and ends from the lab, now blunt and dull from woodcarving. Dieter picked them up and realised the mistake he'd made, the conclusion he'd jumped to.

Arkady had been making toys. He had stolen blades not to slit Dieter's throat but to cheer up Mengele's children. Dieter had been, he realised now, too emotional in his reaction to the missing tools, a little hasty in ordering Arkady's murder.

•

Dieter found Arkady on the floor, unconscious, barely breathing, in the middle of the barracks, a couple of prisoners tugging at his boots and so busy arguing over who would get to keep them they didn't notice him come in. Without stopping to think, he drew his pistol and fired it, point-blank, into the back of one of their heads. In the silence that followed, Dieter heard himself sniff and, pulling himself back together, he aimed the pistol at the remaining assailant.

'You, pick this man up and carry him to my offices. He needs medical attention, and he still has work to do.'

FIVE

Arkady hears boots thudding up the stairwell to the apartment and he smiles. Jan, fundamentally lethargic in his manners, work ethic and attitudes, is still prone to sudden bursts of energy in certain situations, like the childlike way he runs up every flight of stairs he encounters; no matter the time of day, his state of inebriation, the level of his fatigue, he will mount the first step like a toddler chasing a puppy.

As the boots round the curve of the staircase and barrel up towards the top floor where their apartment rests, Arkady puts down his pencil but doesn't turn around to face the door, pretends to be still absorbed by the anatomy book open on the desk. He is trying to set a good example for Jan, who, when the

Nazi state annexed Prague and closed the universities, immediately quit his studies and went on vacation. Jan has little hope that the schools will open again. The distant castle Hradčany that looms over the town now flies swastikas and a black flag embossed with two runic Ss. Its walls bristle with artillery which is aimed not outwards to ward off liberating armies, but down towards the Old Town, ready to eliminate the civilian populace at a moment's notice. It is, Jan argues, a poor sign for the resumption of intellectual life in Prague, and he won't waste the time he has left on schoolbooks.

Arkady, on the other hand, has kept going, as best he can. He is stubborn, and proud of how far he's come in life through sheer will. His stubbornness keeps him at his books in preparation for the day Russian tanks will roll in, the schools will open again and he will be rewarded, with his medical degree as official validation of his pig-headed optimism.

His friends, those of them left, make fun of him, but he has a sense of mission. The war will end, and when it does, the insanity that has submerged the world will recede, and it will need civilised men to help rebuild: architects, lawyers, doctors.

Jan teases him mercilessly for his naivety and Arkady is defenceless against his mockery. He teases Arkady's speech, his autodidact's way of reaching for words he cannot quite master. Arkady's German is a mongrel thing; a stubborn dog that will not heel. It was learned in the eye-widening, brain-searing tumult of experience his life has been since leaving Russia, and is tainted with stray bits of Czech, French, English and the ponderous Latin picked up from his textbooks. If he tries to speak German – something romantic, for example – no matter how carefully he constructs the sentence in his brain, it will invariably trip out mangled with some errant Latin conjugate that has forced its way in from his medical classes.

Jan, who has grown up in Krakow sandwiched between the Weimar Republic and the Soviets, speaks Russian nearly as well as he does German, and in the time they have been living together, Jan has worked hard to improve Arkady's language skills. It's a thankless task, though, both figuratively and literally, and so most of the time they speak in the strange bastard tongue that they have built between them, out of scraps of Russian and Polish. A messy jerry-rigged Slavic that only they will ever understand; a language built for two. Over time, a word will shrink into slang, reduced to the bare essentials. '*Spokojnie*' was something Jan said to Arkady every time he got excited, or angry, or scared, and over time it became '*spokoja*', and finally just '*spoko*'.

Spoko. Relax. Everything will be fine.

Arkady thinks Jan is too relaxed. Most days, while Arkady busies himself with his textbooks, Jan will walk down the riverbank to Most Legií, where he will cross the bridge halfway to the island in the middle of the river, then clamber down to the sandy banks to watch the clouds and drink wine. No matter how dire things seem in Prague, no matter what shortage is gripping the city, Jan is always able to find wine, so by the time he comes home he will be half cut. In truth, and in secret,

Arkady has started drinking earlier in the day too, staring up past his textbooks, out the window that overlooks the tranquil river and the medieval bridge and the wooded hills beyond it.

Nearly every morning they float the idea of going walking through those hills, and it quickly becomes an argument. The year is growing late and the leaves are starting to turn and fall. Jan often indulges his native Silesian urge to hike up every pretty hill he sees and conquer it with a picnic blanket, but has never been able to persuade Arkady to join him. 'We live in the most beautiful city in the world, and we would never know it. Let's go walk up a mountain! Look back down at the town! Glory in the majesty of creation!'

Arkady refuses, often because he knows refusing will start a fight, and he loves a fight; the fury, the tender resolution. They fight over the forest like they fight over everything, half seriously, for something to do, as a prelude. Jan likes the forest best in the autumn, as leaves fall soft and restive as you stroll. Arkady can stand the forest only in the summer, when the heat tears at his lungs as he huffs up a hill.

For him, the woods in winter are a utilitarian thing at best, full of shadows and superstition and memories from a childhood spent gathering wood to stay warm. Even the smell of autumn in the woods reminds him of the grim soviet workshops he worked in with his toymaker father. His hands are adorned with scars from the tools of those workshops, and when he finds himself staring absent-mindedly out the window, he will run his fingertips over those phantom cuts to remind himself of his mission. He can be single-minded, but he cannot help that, and no, he will not go hiking with Jan when there is work to be done.

He will, however, go to lunch. A man has to eat, and when Jan comes bumbling in, no doubt humming Beethoven's 16th, just the allegro, just one bar of it again and again, it will drive Arkady to distraction and off to fetch his coat. Then they will hurry to make the daily special at the Café Louvre, just like yesterday where, between the entree and the main, slowly, deliberately, Jan took his napkin from his lap, folded it to place alongside his plate and, with the slightest smile to Arkady as he sat across the table, rose to visit the restroom. He left a cigarette burning in the ashtray. It was a signal: to the waiter that he would be back to finish his meal; to Arkady to follow and find him in the WC.

Arkady waited as long as he could, the span of half the cigarette, before he slipped out of the booth and wove through the smoky bustle of waiters and into the cool silence of the toilet block. He found Jan at the basin washing his hands and stood next to him, glanced down. He towered over the smaller man. There was no one else in the room, but, just to be sure, Arkady threw a furtive glance over his shoulder before he reached across and ran a hand down Jan's back to cup the muscled curve of his buttock.

The men in the sharp, handsome uniforms who filled the dining hall would kill them if they saw what happened next. Arkady knew this, but only cerebrally, and clear thinking has nothing to do with the reality he shares with Jan.

Jan turned and embraced Arkady, reached up for a kiss,

which he cannot make, even standing on tiptoe, so planted his lips on the soft, bristled skin of his throat, sending a shock down the Russian's skin and spine, which came to rest pleasantly in his belly. Arkady bent slightly, tilted his head to meet the smaller man's mouth, lost himself there, found himself again a moment later pushed up against the marbled wall of the restroom, a pit stop on the way to the privacy of a cubicle, his breath frantic and his hands clumsy as they fumbled at buttons, belts, flies, and then, in another flash, they moved apart as the door swung open.

An SS officer stood in the doorway. He was a baby, no more than twenty-three, his uniform crisp and black. 'Excuse me,' he said, after an uncertain moment.

'Please,' Jan replied without missing a beat, in his perfect German, 'excuse us. My friend here never could handle his alcohol.' He smiled his winning smile at the Nazi, who seemed unsure of what he had walked in on.

Arkady, for his part, was terrified. Jan is Jewish, but lapsed in every way except for his swarthy Ashkenazi *je ne sais quoi*, with his tousled curls and jutting chin. He hadn't so much renounced God as slipped out of His house and on to a life of science and reason and breathless teenaged bacchanal in Berlin with men who'd given up their own gods in the trenches of the Western Front. His German accent is Berliner, but with a dangerous *Institut für Sexualwissenschaft* lilt to it, and that could have caught the SS's attention.

Jan's effeminate side is something he slips in and out of like an outfit, of which he has a closetful. He is a different man in the streets of Prague from the one he was around his large, wealthy family back in Poland, and another one altogether from the one who, in 1937, showed the newly emigrated Arkady around Krakow at the request of a professor who was hoping to entice him to enrol at the medical school there.

At first he was dismayed at the chore, but as the day wore on, Jan decided he quite liked the Russian, gruff and laconic as he was. They started with a breakfast of dumplings and beer, and then showed him around the old town, the castle, the market square, the church tower where once a day a trumpeter sounded a warning call.

'Why?' Arkady demanded.

'Well, the legend goes that in the thirteenth century an old watchman saw a Mongol horde advancing on the city, and blew his trumpet again and again and again until the city rallied and the archers repelled the Mongols, and Krakow was saved. But when they went up the tower to thank the watchman, they found him dead. Shot right here.' He reached up and touched Arkady on the throat, where the thick carotid pulsed up to the brain. The Russian smiled. 'Took a Tartar arrow to the neck and died still holding his bugle. So every day, to honour him, a trumpeter plays to remember the man who saved us from the Mongols.'

'It seems strange to hate the Tartars after, what, half a millennium? They haven't bothered you for some time, you know.'

'It's a tradition. They don't have to make sense. In fact, it's better if they don't. Don't you have traditions that don't make sense?'

'I'm from Russia. We don't have traditions so much as superstitions, but we have all of those.' He started to list them:

never say goodbye on a bridge; never look at a newborn baby, never compliment a newborn baby; never give someone a knife; never give someone a kitten.

'What happens if you give someone a kitten?'

'It invites the devil in and you will die.'

'Oy God.' Jan sighed. 'No wonder your country is fucked.'

'You've no idea,' replied Arkady. 'If only we'd had a trumpeter when the Soviets came.'

Jan smiled. 'Fine. I would like to show you one of my favourite traditions. I will take you to my favourite place in Krakow. But you must cover your head, or we will insult God. Here.' He took off his hat and placed it on Arkady's bare head, then removed his scarf and wrapped it around his own head, then wrapped it around his face. 'There.' He grinned at Arkady. 'Do I make a beautiful babushka?'

They turned and walked into the Jewish cemetery on Miodowa Street. Something in the grand cobbled walls, the oaks that grew scattered between the gravestones, gave tranquillity to the place. The Krakow air, usually a miasma of coal smoke and merchants yelling at each other, was clean and quiet here. Graves, old and grand, so ancient the inscriptions had rubbed off, were sinking into the ground, tipped over by creeping roots from the trees, listing through the years. The dead are tossed and tumbled by time, just like the living. No one stays the person they were buried, not for long.

A soft grey rain fell as they walked slowly down the pathways threading through the headstones, taking turns to read the names in Hebrew, Russian, Yiddish, German, with a rash of

German casualties from 1914 to 1918 filling up the gravestones.

'This seems a strange place to show me. You know I am not a Jew.'

'No, but I thought you would like it. It is peaceful.'

'I do.'

They walked a little more, footsteps crunching on gravel over centuries of bones.

'Why do you come here?'

'To be alone, to find some privacy.' Jan indicated with a tilt of the head that they should head down a path between the graves, where they found themselves sheltered between a small mausoleum and the cobbled wall, a spot shielded from sight elsewhere in the cemetery.

'Why do you need all the privacy?'

'Everyone is worried about the Gestapo. That they are coming for us, that they watch everything we do. They don't have anything on my mother and her friends, though.'

'So why don't you leave?'

'Ah, but I will. This is my final year in Krakow. I have studied previously in Berlin, and next year I am transferring to Charles University in Prague. I feel things will be better for my kind there.'

'For Jews?'

'Yes. And also . . . I am . . .' Jan turned suddenly, and, leaning forward, kissed Arkady on the lips, then stood back, waited to see how his gambit would land, his eyes as sharp as a cat's and as hopeful and trusting as a dog's. He was right. His instinct rarely failed. The scarf fluttered to the ground, and after a moment, Jan kneeled to retrieve it.

'Don't be scared. Nothing bad will happen to you, my friend,' he murmured, then took the Russian's hand and rested it on top of his head, where his hair was already starting to thin into a pale tonsure through the black. 'Just remember to keep your hand here. You do not want to anger God.'

The SS man stepped out of their way with a polite '*bitte*', and by the time they returned to their table their plates had been cleared. A waiter approached, asked if they would like dessert. Jan asked for the drinks menu to be returned. Once the waiter had vanished, Arkady glowered across the table.

'That was fun,' Jan said to Arkady.

'That was stupid,' fumed Arkady. 'If we'd been caught they would have killed us. He could have beaten our brains out right here without consequence.'

'*Spoko*. That's crazy talk. There are always consequences. For one, he would have gotten brains all over his nice new uniform. And besides,' Jan lowered his voice and smiled winningly as the SS soldier passed their table on his way back to his lunch, 'that boy isn't old enough to beat his own meat.'

Arkady snorted angrily, but couldn't hide his amusement. 'Grow up.'

'I actually think he's quite handsome,' Jan said, warming to the theme, casting a mock-smouldering glance over to where the SS was eating with a uniformed colleague, their voices low, their hands holding silverware in the efficient German fashion.

'Should we ask him to join us? The uniform is so dashing.'

'You shouldn't joke about these things,' Arkady scolded him.

'Who says I am joking? I would be joking if I asked us to take home one of those.' He wrinkled his nose and nodded at another soldier, one of the Czech *Vládní vojsko*, the troops the Nazis had deputised with rounded helmets and obsolete rifles and ordered to stand forlornly on street corners and train stations. 'These *vojsko*, they are as ridiculous as they look, flaccid little dildo men. But the SS! They would know how to fuck a man right.'

'Keep your fucking voice down, Jan,' Arkady growled. He was angry at Jan for his recklessness, his risk-taking in restrooms, and in the crowded corridors of trains and in bars down narrow alleyways in the old town, but he did not blame him. The secrecy was erotic, the danger an irresistible aphrodisiac, one quite removed from the reality of the situation. Since that first kiss in the Krakow cemetery, reality had been completely rewritten.

Outside, flurries of snow tapped against the window, but by the time the flakes reached the concrete expanse of the Národní Boulevard they had started to melt. The town was not ready for them, for the first snow of the season – the leaves had just started to fall, and the frost had not set in.

Jan was chatting with their waiter, taking his time to decide what he wanted to drink next, ordering then calling the waiter back. He was being a brat, deliberately testing the waiter's patience, but he knew the waiter would tolerate being toyed with for the tip he and Arkady would inevitably leave, carelessly strewn across the table, as though money is no big deal, even in wartime.

Arkady was not done sulking, and to keep his hands busy, he reached for his napkin and folded it in half, then cross-wise, then into a series of elaborate triangles. The very first toys he'd ever learned to make from his father, as a boy, before he'd learned the toy-making trade, before he'd given it up, running up loans and running away from Russia to become a doctor, were simple playthings from scraps of paper – a bird, a hat, a little boat seaworthy enough to race down the gutters of Moscow in the spring thaw. There was something meditative in it; he felt his mood lifting with every fold. By the time Jan had finally decided on two cups of hot wine and sent the waiter away, Arkady had turned his napkin into a tiny peaked cap, a cartoon version of the SS cap.

'There.' He reached across the table and fitted the cap onto Jan's head at a rakish angle. 'Now you can play dress-ups with your friends.'

Jan grinned, mugged in the hat for a moment, throwing clownish *sieg heils* out for the world, which, as far as he cared, consisted of just him and Arkady. Neither man saw the pair of SS on the other side of the cafe fall silent and start watching them, although Arkady did sometimes wonder what strangers saw when they looked at them. What do people see?

They looked, perhaps, like old friends catching up over lunch, although they aren't that, not exactly, or, in their expensive but ageing suits, like medical students taking a break from study, but they aren't that either, not since October 1939, when all the universities were shut down, their professors arrested. That prompted a thousand of their fellow students to protest in the streets, giving the Reich-Protector the excuse he needed to round them up, and all the intelligentsia, to be shipped off to a concentration camp.

When the wine arrived it was hot and bitter. Arkady dropped two sugar cubes into the liquid and stirred them. They refused to give, so he reversed the spoon and used the fat handle to crush the crystals against the bottom of the mug. Flecks of red wine splattered the tablecloth.

'You eat like a Mongol,' complained Jan. 'What part of Russia are you from again?'

'I just want you to feel comfortable with me, since you think like a mule.'

'You mean I fuck like a horse.'

'Your ignorance is showing, city boy. If you'd ever smelled a horse you would not want to fuck it.'

'I'm not sure. There have been times of the day when I feel I could fuck anything that walks. Four legs, or two. What? *Spoko!*'

'Even the swine?' Arkady nodded at the table of Nazis.

'Even the swine.'

Arkady sighs heavily. 'If you must. But not in our apartment, please.'

They have an agreement not to mind if one of them takes another lover now and again, but the apartment they share is inviolable, and both men love it, for different reasons. In Arkady's eyes it is a relic of *La Belle Époque*. In Jan's it is homely and humble, with its entry hall's worn stone steps and bronzed handrail buffed shiny with use, only the edges decaying into greenish grime.

They rented it shortly after they both enrolled in the Charles University, to have a place to make love away from the prying eyes in the student dorms. They paid in cash, gave false names, and, after the crackdown on students, they simply never went back to college. One night they went to bed as trainee doctors; in the morning they were nobodies, and slipped into their fake identities. A strange thing, to go to bed as one person, and wake up another, but then, when one thought about it, people did that every day. The Arkady who sailed paper boats down Moscow streets was a different one entirely from the one who walked into Krakow cemetery, and it was a different Arkady again who walked out.

As time passed, and the occupation intensified, Jan hustled some false papers for them. Truthfully, neither of them came to Prague for the education. They are there for each other, and they will stay together until the war ends and the world rights. To run would be foolish, and their best chance is just to wait it out, hide in plain sight, the Jew and his Degenerate. Nobody in their block of flats asks questions, now that everybody has secrets to keep. With the world turned the way it has, only the really bad men have nothing to hide.

After lunch they made their way home, only realising after they stood up that they had drunk far too much, and they stumbled out, giggling, nearly tripping into the table of soldiers, and, ignoring the dirty looks, down the marble staircase into the street.

On the way home they saw the crowd gathering to watch the astronomical clock strike the hour. The clock had stood in the town square for more than five hundred years, with the mechanical astrolabe keeping track of the heavens, four moving rings tracing the path of the sun, the moon, the zodiac.

When the hour struck, two windows opened above the tower and little wooden automatons of the Twelve Apostles filed out in procession. Beneath them, four figures flanked the clock tower, each representing the most despised human afflictions. On the right, Death, a skeleton ringing his bell, stood next to a Muslim soldier depicting Lust. Across the clock face, Vanity, a man admiring his own image in a mirror, stood next to a hook-nosed Jew clutching a bag of gold. Greed.

Below, on the cobblestones, jostled by the crowd, Jan looked up at the procession, smiled wryly, pointed at Vanity and Greed. 'I think they've captured us rather well, don't you?'

'Which one are you? Vanity? Or Greed?'

'Oh, don't make me choose, Arkady. Not so late in the day.'

As the clock chimed, Death's bell rang out, and with each knell the other figures shook their head.

It is a sight Arkady never tires of. Apart from Jan, the *orloj* is his favourite part of Prague. He marvels at the gears that have ground on through the centuries, both modern and ancient beyond reason. There is a legend that says that, after creating the masterpiece on the order of the city, the fifteenth-century clock master was blinded so that he could never build another. In return, the blind clock master sabotaged the clock so badly it could not be repaired for a hundred years. Arkady loves this story. It fits perfectly with his understanding of the world – of consequence, of cruelty. As a device, timepiece and narrative, the clock appeals to his very nature.

Arkady, who for so long had no one to share his thoughts with, is a terminally introspective man, but this has its advantages in self-awareness. He knows, for instance, that he is built from a sticky combination of Soviet pragmatism and repressed white Russian sentimentality. He is equal parts science and superstition, and often broods about human nature.

Love, for example, when examined from a purely physiological point of view, looks a lot like heart disease – a racing pulse, confusion, panic, wandering thoughts. When the figurative heart pumps with its fullest glory, the literal heart, the gruesome hollow chamber that keeps the engines of life ticking over, suffers. Descartes, so impressed with his own theory of duality, hadn't bothered to write that one down, that uplift of the soul meant derangement of the mind – Arkady had not been able to think straight since that day in Krakow cemetery.

Every day, when he can, he stops here. It has become a superstition – he feels uneasy if he misses the clock. He has no faith but science, but he adores astrology because it takes away our agency. The idea that who we are is determined by the month in which we are born is very soothing. He wished he could explain some of this to Jan, in front of the clock, but they dared not speak their Slavic in public, and he knew his boyfriend would tease him if he started tripping over his German grammar.

If he could have said so, he would have liked to tell Jan: 'Doesn't the idea of fate make it all a little easier? That we have no choices? That you and I are not degenerates and failed doctors. We are just two men, who were always meant to meet, always meant to be here. If we kissed right here —' then he would dart across to kiss him '— that was always in our stars.

'Everything we are and all we ever will be was decided by a gear forged long before we were, Jan. The horrible and wonderful thing is that we will never know that.' He would've liked to say all this, and then to point to where the skeleton would be ringing his bell, the greedy man and the vain man shaking their heads in argument. 'No more than they ever will.'

He wished he could explain some of this to Jan, but their improvised language failed to extend to the metaphysical, and besides, to pontificate on life all the time is boring, so instead Arkady slipped a hand into his boyfriend's, and gave it a quick squeeze. *Spoko.*

Perhaps it was that squeeze, or the SS man interrupting them in the cafe toilets, or a million other indiscretions, or something not even their fault at all – an informant in their building who traded money or freedom to sell them out. Whatever it was, he will never know; that knowledge will be shared only by the Gestapo, and the skeleton on the clock tower.

The boots are at the door now and Arkady thinks to turn, ready to greet Jan, but the next sound is not Jan's key scraping clumsily at the lock. It is an angry hammering on the door, and he realises, too late, that he has heard not one set of boots outside but many.

Escape is not an option. The window does not open, only affords a view away from town: the medieval bridge across the sparkling river, the motorcycle division rolling past the statues of the martyrs, and beyond them the patchwork orange, green and black of the forested hills, which every autumn morning have been a little rustier, and he knows now that he will never hike them after all.

Soon the leaves will all be gone, turned to be mush underfoot, where they will rot for a few days before snow will fall and cover everything in crisp, clean white. By then he will be travelling to Poland, crowded into a train with hundreds of other prisoners at Bubny, the quiet, suburban station where commuters looked on silent and indifferent as Arkady was jammed into a cattle car. Before all that, though, as the door splinters and falls open, and then blows the rain down, and he is dragged bleeding from his home – he will find himself somehow in two places at once: on the cool, marble staircase of his Prague home, and the polished concrete floor of a barracks in Auschwitz, as boots ring out over stone and hands grab and tear at him, and he will realise that of course Jan was right, always had been, that the leaves are at their most beautiful as they fall.

SIX

Adam couldn't hold still. He'd only just sat down at his desk, but after a few seconds of staring at the computer screen without taking anything in, he was on his feet again. He'd been like this since the night spent soul-searching in the wake of his grandfather's diagnosis – constantly excited, and beyond invincible. It was as though everything that had come before had been the first part of the story and a new phase had begun, a period of toil and altruism, which ended only when he came to work one day and found that his life was over.

He'd started his renaissance of the company by firing half the staff. You built up by cutting down; be the blood and bone on the roses, the volcano that spat lava across the land from which the verdant fields of Hawaii grew. There were several staff members who had been on the books for decades whom Adam simply couldn't see the point of. For example: they had a tea lady, who'd been hired in the seventies and had clung to the company while she raised her children and ground through two marriages. A fucking tea lady! Out the door with you!

He was, admittedly, a little weary. It was only in the past weeks, with Tess spending all her time at the hospital with Arkady, that he'd realised just how much work she did to keep the company running, far beyond the financial responsibilities – from organising events, getting media hits and maintaining the website, down to ghostwriting the Mitty & Sarah children's books that went out every Christmas.

And the endless, pointless paperwork! He'd finally got around to auditing the overheads of the organisation, starting with overstocked merchandise. Sitting back down at his desk to attempt it again, he found he simply didn't have the headspace to concentrate on the rows and columns of numbers, so, closing the document, he went down to the warehouse and climbed into the Kindergarten.

The 'Kindergarten' was the nickname for the storage area where they kept everything that would never sell again. Overstock, factory seconds, product damaged by flood or fire; it was all stacked up in three storeys of pallets, with the newest stock piled loosely in half-open crates on the top. The first time little Kade had seen it, with toys strewn everywhere and packing paper blowing about, he'd pointed out that it looked like his kindy, only much, much better, and the name stuck. These days, when Tess wasn't around and Adam was looking after their son, Adam would send him over to the Kindergarten and let him play with the toys.

Adam climbed up into the Kindergarten and strolled through the maze of product. Staring at the rows and rows of dusty, imperfect and outdated Mitty & Sarah merchandise, Adam realised that he'd walked past them nearly every day for five years and never wondered at their provenance. He climbed up to the lowest crate, peeled open a cardboard box and retrieved a vintage Mitty & Sarah model town – it was an item popular in the early nineties. Once a bestseller, these days it barely moved and thousands of units languished in the warehouse.

He sighed, sifting through his feelings, a complex mix of pride at what he'd built, annoyance at a world that was growing indifferent to the toys they sold, rage at the incompetence of his team that had let business stagnate, and the nagging feeling that he'd fucked it up somehow.

He couldn't tell how much overstock was here just by looking at it, and no great inspiration was coming to him, so he gritted his teeth and headed back towards his office. With no great desire to rush back to the tyranny of maths, he dawdled, made a cup of coffee, shot the shit with some of the factory hands, and trudged into his office, where he was dismayed to see someone waiting for him. A man was sprawled on his couch, his feet up on the coffee table, his hands flipping through Adam's latest *GQ*, which he hadn't even cracked the spine on yet. His temper rose, the bile flaring up at the intrusion, and the impertinence of someone barging in on him without an appointment, which quickly turned into fury towards his assistant for showing the man into the office. He rounded on her, moulded his face into an expression he hoped showed her she'd fucked up and that her job was forfeit, and asked with controlled rage, 'Who is that man in my office?'

'He said he was a friend of yours. T something? Tariq?'

'Oh.'

As he entered, the man made no move to stand, but swung his legs off the coffee table so that he was sitting hunched over, relaxed, his hands draped loosely over his knees. It was, Adam saw with mounting alarm, the man from the parking lot. In the daylight he was mid thirties, maybe, but a rough thirties: balding, with a worn, sunken face that had weathered too much too soon.

'Hello, gangster,' the man said. His accent was Australian, the double-thick accent of a young immigrant, adopting broad vowels to mask other cultural deficiencies, more Aussie than the real thing. 'You have a lovely office here. Very posh.'

'You aren't really supposed to be in here, Mr . . . Tariq, was it?'

'Lot of people aren't meant to be in a lot of places, Adam. Even when a fella's got permission, there's someplace a man shouldn't go. Call it a grey area.'

'What are you doing here?'

'Oh, well, see the thing is, you left your phone behind after our last date. Remember that night? Warm night, sea breeze. Charming conversation. So I followed you around for a little while, looking for a chance to give it back to you. Thing is, I followed you here, and I realised, that, actually, you maybe have a little bit of money.'

'Okay then.' Adam spoke through gritted teeth. 'What do you want?'

'I want to make you an offer, Mr Kulakov. One I think you'd do well to consider.' Tariq reached into his jacket pocket and laid a shattered iPhone on the desk. Adam, in full righteous flight, did not respond straightaway, so Tariq continued unfazed. 'Beautiful things, these phones, Adam,' he said. 'These new ones, they automatically back up everything onto a remote server, so, say you drop your phone, say the screen gets shattered, it's just so easy to get in there and download what's on it. Especially if you don't bother locking the thing. So nothing is ever really lost. Every note, every email. Every photo.' The man's eyes, big and black, twinkled, and a mocking smile crept up his face. 'And all that just sitting there, waiting. A man can just reach out and . . .' Tariq mimed reaching up and plucking a piece of fruit '. . . grab it. That's the best thing about living in the future, Adam Kulakov. No more secrets.'

Adam thought back to that almost forgotten night weeks ago and regretted the smugness with which he had smashed the phone and driven off. Now he sat down opposite the man, picked up the phone, examined it. The screen was shattered, but when he turned the power on, it booted up. 'Fine, tell me what you want. What did we agree on? One hundred dollars?'

'That would have been nice! But that was before I had a look on your phone.' Tariq shrugged. 'And before I started going through your happy snaps. Forgive me, but I found one I liked so much I just had to print it out.' He reached into his pocket again, and pulled out a photo that Adam had forgotten he'd ever taken, the one of him leering into the camera over Clara's back, his face clearly visible, her skirt with its school logo on it bunched up around her hips, and his world fell apart. He stroked the photo to see if it was real, and the cheap ink came off on his fingers.

'Of course,' continued Tariq, 'I can't say I blame you. I'd hit that too, if I was a younger man. The arse on it! I was always a sucker for a school uniform. And this photo, Adam, it really brings out your eyes.'

Adam breathed in, out, fought the rising panic. 'How much do you want?'

'How much do you reckon it's worth, Adam, for you to not be outed as a fiddler? That's what you are, Adam, a kiddie fiddler. This photo, well, it puts you square on the roof, doesn't it?'

'Tell me a fucking figure.'

'I thought we could come up with a figure together, can't we, Mr Kulakov? I thought you people were supposed to be good with money?'

'And what if I say no?'

Tariq smiled, shook his head sympathetically, then slowly, lazily, reached out and struck Adam across the face with the back on his hand. The blow caught him across side of the head, and he sat, shocked, as his assailant leaned in, smiling, and placed a collegiate hand on Adam's shoulder, which made him shrink away. 'Adam, look,' Tariq said. 'You need to understand something. I'm a piece of shit, a man with a record, one with nothing to lose. I'm everything your newspapers warn you about and I can beat the shit out of you and ruin your life, because I've got nothing to lose. Do you understand? Do we understand each other? But all I want from you is a little bit of money, and I'll go away, and you can go back to your charmed life making toys and raping girls and whatnot.' He stood, tugged on his hoodie to straighten it, and retrieved a slip of paper from its front pocket. 'Here's me bank account. I'll give you a week to pop fifty K in there, nice and easy. Otherwise, I burn your life down. Have a lovely day, now, pumpkin.'

Tariq laid the photo on the table beside the broken phone and took his leave. He stepped neatly around Adam and smiled cheerfully at the assistant on the way out.

Once he was safely alone in the office, Adam let himself panic. He picked up the photo and stared at it for a long moment, this cursed, profane, sacred object, the unearthly doom of Clara's beauty, the milky expanse of her flank, his own stupid, gormless face, teeth gritted in pleasure and concentration as he reached out with the phone to capture the angle; ruin. Stricken, he scrunched up the photo and tucked it safely away inside his leather jacket, in the secret pocket over the heart.

He paced back and forth, breathing hard, playing out the incident in his head, trying to think of what to do next. Abruptly, he realised he was making a weird keening noise in his throat and knew where he'd heard it before.

His son had a habit of curling into a ball when he was scared or nervous, and rocking back and forth making a high-pitched groaning noise, and the only thing that would calm him was if Adam scooped him up and stroked the boy's head, his fingertips shushing him gently until he relaxed. As little Kade had got older and wasn't growing out of the habit, Tess had started to worry, but Adam knew that children grow at different speeds. If the boy wanted his father, that was fine. Now, freaking out in his office, Adam wished someone would soothe him the same way, and with the realisation that there was no one to help him his wailing got louder.

He looked through the glass partition of his office at his assistant, who stared back at him wide-eyed. Mortification. Had she seen him cry? Had she seen him being slapped? He needed privacy, so he barged through the door, past the girl, all thoughts of firing her forgotten, and ran for the car park and the safety of his car.

He spun the wheels on the BMW, clipping the fence with the rear bumper as he skidded out of the lot. Frantic, he turned the wrong way through the estate and found himself looking for a way out. Rows and rows of identical factory offices stretched out, distinguishable from each other only by giant, colourful plastic signs perched on the front gate and the logos on the container trucks that rumbled up the drive. None of these factories had been around a few years ago; they had all sprung up not long after his, built cheap on cheap land. As he drove past the buildings he caught flashes of rolling green hills that were once eucalyptus forests, then grazing meadows, and in the next few months would become truck depots and canneries.

When the industrial estate ended, the residential area began, huge culs-de-sac reached with a sharp turn off the highway, all built around artificial lakes lying empty due to drought. The buildings here, too, were identical, homes bought off the rack and built cheap, squat and nasty, each little neighbourhood a landscaped gulag.

He'd calmed down a little by the time he reached his destination, a tight collection of chain stores clustered around a food court. The mall had been built in a rush, to serve the suburbs which had been built to service industry, and little thought had been put into the planning, with one roundabout leading in and out of the complex, which was thronged with a deciduous traffic jam. He inched through it, tooting impatiently, until he found a park outside his bank, where he ran to the ATM and started pulling out wads of cash. The machine wouldn't give him the money he needed, so he entered the bank and pushed his way to the front of the queue, where the cashier explained that she couldn't give out that kind of cash without notice.

Adam took this news badly, started yelling, and only stopped when he realised that cash would be no use to him anyway, that he was in a panic, wasn't thinking straight. He walked slowly out to the car, and as he climbed back behind the wheel he recalled that Tess had limited the amount of cash he could draw from any of their accounts to curb his impulse buying. Foolishly, he had let her, although at the time he'd argued, only half seriously, 'What about emergencies?' at which she'd patted him on the hand and said, sotto voce, 'If you need more than that, come tell Mummy and I'll take care of it.' He'd laughed then, but now Tess could account for almost every dollar in their accounts, and she had lately been asking uncomfortable questions about staff credit card purchases. There was no way he could get the money he needed without alerting her that something was terribly wrong.

As he digested this, a series of horrifying realisations unfurled inside him and the manic wave he'd been sailing on all month crashed. The sobs burst up from his gut, and, appalled, he tried to choke them off, which only squeezed them into strangled wails. Before long he was bawling, eyes squeezed shut, head pressed against the steering wheel, knees drawn up to meet it. He sat like that for a moment, knees smarting, the oak steering wheel pressing into his thighs.

With the stereo in his car turned way up, he screamed in frustration, at his unexpected nemesis, and at his wife, her claws encircling his money, at the injustice of this life. He felt a sudden urge to confess everything – to his wife, to the police, to his grandfather. That's who he could turn to: Arkady would know what to do. Whenever Adam had messed up as a child, he'd always gone to his grandfather to solve his problems, with his calm, old-world composure, unflappable in the face of any adversity.

Adam was on the verge of reaching for the phone when he recalled his grandfather's condition, lying broken and fading in a hospital bed, and his fear turned into shame once again.

What would his grandfather do in this situation? Adam reasoned that it was a silly question. Arkady wouldn't have let himself be manoeuvred into this mess, would have avoided it, would have kept his dick in his perfectly creased trousers.

Adam drove aimlessly for a while, and then pulled off the road to cry again. He stared blankly ahead, deep in thought, snuffling. He cast about for a tissue to blow his nose with, reached into his jacket, where his fingers touched the scrunched-up photo of him and Clara, and withdrew his hand with a whimper. Digging into his other pockets, he retrieved a couple of receipts, and then found his pocketknife. He had carried a penknife since he was a little boy, when it had been his favourite toy. His grandfather had bought him an authentic Swiss Army model in Europe and he still treasured it. Once, at the height of hostilities between his parents, Adam had run away from home. He'd packed his backpack with sandwiches, clothes, a blanket, the knife tucked safely in the centre of his bag, and had trekked tearfully into the park, where he'd sat by the pond, lonely, feeding his dinner to the ducks until long after dark. He sustained himself with the hope that some vagrant would appear and murder him; imagined his funeral, the tears, the recrimination, his mum and dad's shame over driving him from home, until finally, cold and hungry, he slid back into the house to find that no one had noticed him missing. That had stung, and he remembered folding out the main blade and looking at his warped reflection, as slowly his self-pity settled and reshaped itself into the realisation that his parents' apathy was a blessing; he could do anything, could get away with anything.

He stared at the knife now, blankly, until his eyes sharpened as an idea started to form. Inspiration struck, and Adam stopped mid sob. This situation was like any other, an opportunity. This goon with his clumsy attempt at blackmail had given him lemons, so Adam would make lemonade. He would make his own luck. All the money he would ever need was in the company, going to waste.

First he tried Marketing, told them he was working on a new project and asked them to work out exactly how much they could cut from the charitable spend of the organisation. The answer was distressingly low; all of it was intricately tied up with their tax return, and nothing could be spared. He would find no help there.

His next stop was the production department and Shubangi, the head of product. She was by far his favourite employee. She had a knack for taking his ideas, making them workable and then presenting them back to him as his own. Better, she seemed to genuinely like him. If anyone could help him out of this mess, it was Shubangi.

'Oh, hey,' she chirped as he walked in. 'What brings you to visit us long-suffering elves in design?'

'Can you keep a secret?'

'Possibly. This secret of yours, is it expensive?'

'Very.'

He explained that he needed to find fifty thousand dollars in savings for a new project he was working on, that he couldn't talk about it, and asked what could be cut from production. Shubangi thought about it for a moment, brows knitted in concentration, then sucked air in through her teeth unhappily.

'There's not really much I can do, imports-wise,' she said. As it was, the vast majority of the products they sold these days were not Mitty & Sarah designs at all. Instead, once a year, Shubangi handed Adam a catalogue of inexpensive toys from generic Chinese manufacturers that were predicted to trend in the coming season, he selected a bunch, and Shubangi sent away for them to be branded in Mitty & Sarah colours.

The idea was the same as when Arkady had made the switch from hand-carving the toys he sold to buying them from factories. The maths was simple: make a toy for fifty cents, sell it for a dollar; or better: buy it for ten cents from a factory in the developing world, and sell it in the first world for ten times that.

It was a business model that had worked for half a century, and had survived wars, outlasted the Soviets, outlasted even Communist China, the powerhouse that had quietly packed away its revolution and emerged the most savage capitalist state the world had ever known. In the end, there was no army, siege engine, weapon of war or ideology that conquered the world as effectively as the conglomerate. McDonald's beat Machiavelli, every time.

Unfortunately for Adam, the system was eating its young. As the money the West had pumped into China started to reproduce and send back its seeds to buy up huge swathes of Western industry, production costs in China were on the rise.

Now there was nowhere you could buy the toy you needed for the price you wanted. China was no longer desperate for wealth, and there was no fat left to cut.

Because of this, there were, Shubangi assured him, no expenses left to cannibalise. 'Our only really unnecessary overhead is the original flagship Sarah doll, which is a huge production cost. We've been running at a loss on that one for years. We could cut that line and save the money easily, although your grandfather might have a few things to say about that.'

Adam thought hard for a minute. 'Is there some way we could bring down production costs on the dolls themselves? I mean, where are they produced now? Is there someplace we could move them to where they could do them cheaper?'

'Well, yes, there are options.' Shubangi swivelled around in her chair and pulled up some files on her Mac. 'How do you feel about Jakarta?'

———

Tess, drawn away from Arkady's hospital bed and into the office by the nagging fear that the company was collapsing in her absence, didn't notice Adam slipping into her office until he'd slumped heavily into the chair opposite, startling her. She'd been googling vascular dementia, and had wandered for God knew how long between websites that spelled out in calm detail exactly how Arkady was breaking: his body, then his mind. She drifted from Wikipedia to dry government sites to earnest support groups to online forums and found herself lost in an endless round of people asking questions about symptoms that worried them, and responses, helpful at first, then meaningless, then mean-spirited, then nuts. She wondered what it meant about the species that the internet was the pinnacle of human achievement and democracy, and it had become a giant scream of loneliness and insanity.

'You look like shit,' Adam said. 'When was the last time you slept?

'Thank you.'

'You're welcome. Seriously, though, you look a little tired. How'd you sleep?'

'What's sleep?'

'Touché.'

In truth, she hadn't really slept since the first night in the hospital. She'd spent every minute she could by Arkady's bedside as he convalesced. His doctors assured her that he was making a strong recovery, but she couldn't see it. He was asleep most of the time, and when he wasn't he was sullen and uncommunicative. The idea that the old man was at death's door had retreated, but the fact that he might not be the person he was before the stroke was just as bad, perhaps worse. The thought that Arkady was lost to her was never far from her mind, especially in the nights when sleep would not come, and her pills just made the world around her dull, her thoughts thick and grainy, but didn't kill the anxiety, or bring oblivion. In the end, sleep would creep up on her unnoticed, and when her alarm went off at six she would crawl out of bed, unrested and barely able to rouse her son and get him ready for school.

In spare moments, she worked remotely, tried to wade through everything she hadn't finished the day before, and every night she found herself further away from the bottom of her inbox, a thousand little tasks lying scattered and forgotten somewhere on the desk. She hadn't been so overwhelmed by her job since the day Arkady had first taken her under his wing. Until his illness, she hadn't realised just how much she'd relied on being able to call him for advice when things got tough. All these years she thought she'd been doing the old man a favour by indulging his desire to keep on top of the business, but without his help, the work drifted in on her like snow, banked up and immovable.

It was made worse by the zeal with which Adam had embraced his stewardship of the company since the night of Arkady's stroke. He had been a blur of activity. In the past weeks he'd pored over catalogues of toys from suppliers in foreign markets and ordered dozens of new lines to be produced with Mitty & Sarah branding, items he seemed to have chosen more or less at random: pencil cases, water guns, teddy bears. Seconds earlier she'd been staring at an order form for ten thousand Mitty & Sarah yoyos and had a mild existential crisis executing it. She knew already that none of them were going to sell. People just didn't buy those sorts of toys any more. Every harried parent had a device in their pocket that could summon one of a million entertainment options, and children were expected to play with a fucking yoyo? She put the order through anyway, too tired to argue. What she really needed was some time off.

'I think you should take some time off,' said Adam, leaning over the desk to take her hand.

Tess burst out laughing, then caught herself. 'Really? Do you have any idea how busy we are?'

'Of course, but I'll cover your desk. You've got more important work to do right now.'

She was pleased to find, even after all these years of marriage, that Adam could still surprise her.

Their relationship was built on surprises, starting with the happy accident that had turned out to be little Kade. Even now, years later, the very idea that she was married struck her as unlikely. In her childhood, as she watched her parents go through increasingly calamitous marriages, the whole thing had seemed like a terrible idea. Then, as a teen, she had discovered feminism, not the watered-down white-bread socialist varietal of her parents, but something a little less messianic, a little more applicable: Greer, de Beauvoir, Wolf, Madonna. By her late teens she figured marriage to be a cynical contract that exchanged currency for procreation. None of that for her.

Marriage, or even monogamy, had always seemed impractical. Once upon a time she'd been callow and horny to the point of derangement. Back then, sex was pure pleasure, politically as much as physically, and through her under-graduate years she'd chosen her partners based on a complex algorithm of privilege, opportunity and guilt. An ex-con, a trans-woman, a black guy for whom she had learned to quote

James Baldwin and to apologise profusely for refusing anything he wanted in bed.

Back then, she had entertained a right-on perspicacity and she was particular about the words she used for sex. She remembered once shouting down a classmate in a college tutorial who had referred to a lover's penis in her poem. 'A lover doesn't have a penis,' she announced primly. 'A lover has a cock.'

Of course, nothing cures a bad case of arts degree faster than a decade of struggle, something she discovered as her youth, and her trust fund, waned. One does not want to headbutt against the world forever, no matter how idealistic.

And then, just in time, Adam. Halfway through their business meeting in which he was supposed to be acquiring the rights to her puppet designs, Adam leaned across the table and kissed her, and it dawned on her that he was not actually interested in her puppetry, but in getting into her pants; hence, of course, the expensive dinner.

As Adam broke off the kiss and settled back into his chair, she brought her hand up to her mouth to cover her shock, and then suddenly burst out laughing.

Adam wasn't laughing. He looked so crumpled and forlorn that she could see his hope that he would sleep with her that night leave him, so in that moment she decided to do it anyway. And then he had proven to be so much better in bed than she'd imagined, a surprising blend of instinct and utter selfishness.

What a relief to meet a man who just wanted to be her friend, to rampage over her body like a toddler in a ballroom and then take her to the movies. He was unromantic in the best sense; a world away from all the boys who were determined to see her as a mysterious, irrational cipher, or, worse, those who claimed her as an intellectual peer and then immediately started to batter down her self-esteem for fear of losing her. Finally, after a lifetime of reparational sexual conquest, it was nice to just have something uncomplicated.

For the first time in as long as she could remember, sex had stopped being a performance, and became fun. Adam had a guilelessness and playfulness in the sack that she'd sorely missed. He undressed her the way she'd once unwrapped Christmas presents, clumsy with eagerness, eyes alive with sheer gratitude as they feasted. A nice surprise, then a lull, a nap, and, when she opened her eyes later, everything in and around her had changed.

So nearly a decade later another surprise, this one also kind of pleasant, and probably exactly what she needed. Adam sat in the chair across from her and, in a hangdog kind of way, apologised for his recent behaviour, his weird mania, all the extra work he'd caused her, and just generally under-appreciating her.

'I'm sorry, basically. I haven't really known how to deal with the situation with Grandpa, I've been trying to ignore it through work, and I haven't acknowledged the toll that's been taking on you. So I thought it might be good if you take some time off.'

'Well . . . I mean . . . It's impossible, all this . . .' She waved her hand to indicate the invoices, the accounts, the world. 'It's too much to leave for someone else.'

'I can handle it. If I need any help I'll bring in some con-tractors.' Until now, Adam had never taken Tess up on the many times she'd hinted, strongly hinted, near-begged Adam to bring in outside help to audit their finances.

'Adam, I'm your wife, so don't bullshit me now. What are you up to?'

Adam looked down, bit his lip, used his leg to swivel back and forth on his chair. For a moment, he looked exactly like their son, and she felt a wave of affection for the ridiculous man sweep over her.

'Okay, look, in all honesty, this company probably needs you more right now than it ever has before, but Grandpa needs you more. I know you two have a special relationship, and I would be by his side right now if I could be, but things . . .' He gestured with his arms, a sweeping movement that could mean anything. 'I can't walk away from things right now. So I want you to take some time off. For yourself, and for Arkady.'

She smiled, and Adam smiled back, and a lovely moment passed between them, the sort that had been common in the early days of their partnership, but were made all the sweeter now by their rarity. 'Fine, okay. Good. I'll do it, thank you. When would this happen, theoretically?'

'Tomorrow.'

'Tomorrow? Oh, Adam, that's not possible.'

'Sure it is! Listen.' Her husband outlined how her job would be covered. Further, that she would need the time off to take Kade to school as Adam had to fly to China for an emergency meeting at their suppliers. 'Oh, that reminds me.' Adam produced a manila folder and handed her a sheaf of pages. 'You'll have to sign this before you go on leave.'

She glanced down at it, squinted, reached for her reading glasses. Adam leaned forward and put a hand on hers, bent down and kissed her. 'Don't bother reading it. It's just the standard release form for our Shenzhen factories. I'll sign on the plane and deliver it in person.

'I'll just have a quick look.'

'No need, it's boilerplate.'

He put a pen in her hand and moved it to where a plastic tab marked where she should sign. She scribbled her name, and asked Adam if he sure that this was the best time to vanish overseas.

'I know this is coming at the worst possible time, Tess, but I need you to look after Grandpa.'

'What if he gets worse while you're gone?'

Adam waved this away like a fly. 'He'll be fine. He's just had a little fall, it happens to heaps of guys his age. He's had a couple of weeks to lie down, watch some TV, pinch a nurse's arse. He just needed a rest and he'll be right as rain. You know he will.'

'Adam, he gets discharged from the hospital in a couple of days,' she protested, but her husband was already on his feet, kissing her cheek, headed for the door.

'I'll only be gone for a few days, and he'll be fine. He's a tough old bastard. He's been through worse before.'

———

Hunger. Even when the pain eclipsed almost all else, there was hunger. When Arkady's stomach shut down and the ache for food slipped away, it was replaced by another, for water, for a cool towel for his fever, for warmth, for kindness. When he surfaced from his delirium he could take stock for moments at a time and knew, again, that his life was over. The wound in his chest had gone bad and his blood was turning to poison. He could feel it when he was conscious, and even more so when he was not. As the fever surged and raged within him, memories of nights with Jan came to him, the way he smiled, the feeling of his fingernails caressing Arkady's back, and he was surprised, amazed, to find that he was excited.

Over breakfast one hungover Sunday morning before the war, a friend had wondered aloud why he always felt absurdly amorous when teetering on the brink of alcohol poisoning, and Arkady had joked that the body knew it was on the way out, and had summoned up the wherewithal for one last Darwinian stab at passing on his genes. Now, a few years later, dying in a bunk in a strange land, he remembered that. *Sorry, Darwin*, he thought, *that was never on the cards anyway.*

'Sorry,' he whispered in the dark, and laughed, and a voice from the darkness yelled at him to shut up.

How absurd, how very like you, you wreck, you lech, was what Jan would say if he had been there to cluck his tongue and shake his head in mocking disapproval. But of course he would never see Jan again, let alone touch him. Jan was long dead, at the bottom of a mass grave or ashes on the wind. What he wouldn't do to feel the man's hands on him one more time.

Not to worry, Arkady would be dead as well, soon enough. It was too dark to see the wound in his chest, but he could feel the burning in his blood and the itch creeping in where the stitches pierced his skin, eclipsing even the lice that crawled over him unchallenged. He was too weak to try to catch and kill them, too weak to do anything but wait.

Darkness, sleep, then a voice, Dr Mengele at the foot of his bed, reading a thermometer. 'This man has two weeks to live,' he said. 'If he has not died by then, or recovered, dispose of him.' Arkady tried to rise to argue, but he was already gone. Mengele's dismissal of him rankled, burrowed in deep. He was insulted. Until the Nazi's appraisal, he'd been quite happy to die; now he vibrated between life and death, torn away from peaceful oblivion by pique.

After the rage it was thirst. Who could have imagined such thirst? He dreamed of deserts, of waterfalls, of barren fields cracked by the sun, of taps. He startled out of sleep, and remembered that, at the end of the barracks where he lay, somewhere between five feet and a million miles away, there was a tap with cold running water.

He rolled out of his bunk and landed heavily, winding himself. He lay there for a while gasping, and then started crawling. One metre, two, three. He welcomed death, but not until he proved Mengele wrong by reaching some water. The tap was awfully far away though. He decided to rest, just for a minute, and closed his eyes. For a moment he was in Prague again, and then there were hands on him, rolling him over, tugging at his boots, scrabbling at his coat and for a second he thought Jan had come for him, but then he was out again.

For a long time Arkady drifted in the black, neither hot nor cold, not a bad place to be, and a much better place than the one he felt himself being pulled back to.

It was touch that brought him back, a man's fingers tracing his chest. For a warm, wonderful moment he thought of Jan, but no, Jan was dead, long dead. The hands on his chest weren't a lover's, they were too light. A doctor's hands, gentle and impersonal as a mosquito as they felt about his ribs and palpated his chest. Still, they called him back – it had been so long since he'd been touched by another human being, except in anger, that he hadn't realised how deep that hunger ran in him, deeper than the hunger of wasting muscle and bone, more profound than the thirst that had driven him across the barracks. He hadn't known just how much he missed kindness.

'Good morning,' a familiar voice said, and Arkady opened his eyes to find himself staring into Dieter's. 'How do you feel?'

Arkady tried to speak, but his voice was a cracked, pathetic thing. The doctor offered him a glass of water, helped him to drink it. He tried again. 'You should have let me die.'

The doctor smiled. 'Is that any way to say thank you?'

'*Pashol na hui,*' Arkady said.

Dr Pfeiffer smiled. 'My Russian is rusty, but you are welcome. I'm just sorry it took so long to find you. When you didn't report for work in the morning I went searching for you at the

Sonderkommando barracks. I have no idea how you ended up in the labs. I am sorry. Those responsible will be punished.'

Arkady tried to sit up, failed. 'Do you have anything to eat? Morphine?'

Dr Pfeiffer brought bread and vodka. Arkady went for the bottle first, then tentatively started on the bread. Dieter watched with a wry smile on his face.

'Better?' he asked, when Arkady stopped to breathe.

'As good as can be expected.'

'You were dead, you know,' Dr Pfeiffer said, lightly, his tone conversational. 'For fully two minutes. Of course, in this age death is a relative thing, but still, no pulse and no air for two minutes! It was something of a miracle for me to bring you back to life.'

'I forgot you were so modest,' said Arkady with a grunt. 'I don't believe in miracles.'

The Nazi grinned at him. 'No? This would be the time for it. They say there are no atheists at the end of a gun.'

'Perhaps, but I can tell you there are no gods in the middle of a war.'

'The war will not last forever. And then where will God be?'

'Wherever you Germans put him. You have science to justify anything, no? Your philosophers have killed him once. Surely you can drag him back to life like you did me?'

'The world needs men like you more than God, I think.'

'Is that why I'm here?'

The doctor looked appraisingly at Arkady. 'You are here because I need you. You're the best pathologist I've ever worked with, and without you my research will founder. Help me and you will survive this war. You have my word as a German.'

Arkady summoned up all the easy scorn he could in a moment, which was plenty: 'Great.'

'My word as a doctor, then.'

'Very good. Hardly worthless at all.'

'As a pragmatist then.' His tone, which had been wry until now was suddenly sober, and he leaned forward to lock his eyes on Arkady's. 'Right now you are the only thing keeping the children alive. Without you they will find no one to offer them anaesthetic, no one to tend to them after surgery, no one who cares about their survival.'

Arkady's eyes dropped from Dieter's and rested on his food, which seemed suddenly unappetising. The German continued, his voice soft and serious. 'I know you care about them. I know what you've been doing for them, with the toys.' The Russian started at this, but didn't look up. 'And, Arkady, I know you've been stealing medicine and food from me to give to them. I don't mind, not at all. I will even help you, if you help me. Let's continue our work here, and I will give you all you need to help the children; food, medicine, proper tools to make their toys, if that's what you want, and they will live. I can promise you that without your intervention, they won't survive the war. Not because I will kill them, but because you will, by neglecting their care.'

Arkady raised his eyes now, which were furious. 'What kind of offer is that?' he growled. 'What kind of monster are you?'

'Not a monster, a scientist, and one who needs a good assistant.'

'You are a parody of a scientist. You're Frankenstein, maybe. A shit fucking doctor, in any case.'

'Let me tell you a story, Arkady. All this talk of God and the Devil has reminded me of it. It is one of my favourites, from Hindu mythology. Siva the destroyer and Parvati the creator have a treasure, the greatest treasure they want to give to their favourite child. They call Skanda, the warrior, and Ganesh, the remover of obstacles, and tell them the prize goes to the first who can circle the world. Skanda immediately jumps onto his peacock and starts to race around the world. Ganesh, a little more thoughtful, a little less agile, simply walks a circle around his parents, who, as gods, *are* the world. Skanda, upon returning from his quest, is furious to find Ganesh has outsmarted him, until Parvati calms him down and reveals that he has been the treasure all along, just like Ganesh, just like all her children.'

'What is the point of that story?'

'The point is —' Dieter leaned across the table to freshen Arkady's drink '— sometimes you fight better when you don't fight at all. Pick your battles, my friend.'

SEVEN

Adam was woken by the call to prayer. The wailing gibberish sliced through the thick air, through the din of the air conditioner, piercing his stupor. He was hungover, worse than he'd been in years, worse than in living memory. For a moment he didn't know where he was and then he groaned when he remembered, thinking of the task ahead of him. *Jakarta. Fucking Jakarta.* While Shubangi had set up everything he needed to transfer the production of the Sarah dolls to Indonesia, he needed to inspect the factory in person, and sign off on it. He'd already printed off the necessary forms, and acquired Tess's signature, but now he had to deliver them in person. He was kind of glad, actually; what he was doing was sensitive, and he didn't trust anyone else to handle it with the requisite delicacy; nor, for that matter, could anyone know why he was doing it.

He'd arrived at the hotel after a gruelling twelve hours in transit. On his flight, he'd sat next to a plump middle-aged woman with a screeching western Sydney accent and the most frightening case of dandruff he had ever seen speckling the cloth of her halter-neck. They both dozed off during the flight and when he woke up he was slumped in her direction. He brushed a few stray flakes that had fluttered onto his lap, feeling ill. He did not like dirt, and he was not looking forward to Jakarta.

When he'd finally arrived, his taxi had crept through the choked streets, past the canals thick with rubbish and bordered by shacks built illegally over the rivers on stilts, just visible through the lamplight they cast on the water.

In years past, Adam had spent a half-dozen holidays in Bali, and thought of Indonesia as something seen from the window of a taxi, green and full of crumbling concrete statues of dragons and gods wrapped in cheerful black-and-white sarongs. Indonesia, as far as he knew, was a nation of smiling, helpful men in battered thongs who wanted to call him a taxi, bring him a beer, give him a massage. Jakarta was different. Here, the faceless, indifferent hordes in long pants and hijabs freaked him out. He had no idea what to make of this sprawling city; it felt as though he'd been lied to.

His first stop had been the bank where he'd arranged to have the money he would need in the next few days washed and converted into rupiah. It had taken a full hour and a half sweating through the traffic to reach his destination. He'd arrived at the bank shortly before close and had to argue his way past the security guards who spoke little English, only to confront a clerk who spoke none. It baffled Adam that anyone could run a bank without at least a basic grasp of English, but no matter how loudly and slowly he spoke, the bank man just stared blankly and blinked stupidly, little black dots of acne crowding his beady eyes further into fleshy cheeks, until he then unleashed a torrent of angry, impatient Indonesian. Adam, not used to being yelled at, was momentarily taken aback, but then raised his voice too. The clerk sighed, checked his watch, sighed again, and picked up a phone on his desk.

A manager was summoned from elsewhere in the building, a skinny, dark man who spoke with the singsong half-American accent of an international school, and fumbled with unfamiliar words in his struggle to keep up as Adam and the clerk barked at each other. It took half the night, and dozens of phone calls to Shubangi back in Melbourne, but Adam finally cleared the money and had it ready to go in the morning. Normally, this kind of thing was handled by Tess, so he'd no idea how stressful it was trying to secure something as simple as a bank transaction. His next appointment would be much easier.

From Australia, Adam had ordered an end to production at the Chinese factory that produced their flagship dolls, and across the world in Shenzhen, the factory floor was already being dismantled and reconfigured for some other enterprise. The millions of dollars he'd invested there had been redirected to Jakarta, where the cash would fund the production of the dolls in a cheaper Indonesian facility, minus fifty thousand dollars, which he would reroute back to Australia, and the account Tariq had given him. Time was running out. He did not believe the man would carry through on his threat if he was late with the money, but there was no point in pushing his luck

Adam had gone over the exchange with Tariq time and again, and each time it dredged up new feelings of hate and fear and guilt that his indiscretions had led him to this point, where some grubby stranger could barge into his office and demand his hard-earned. He brooded on it now, his mood growing darker as he waited for the bank to transfer the money into Tariq's account, and when they handed him the receipt he studied it glumly.

Adam had been exhausted and grumpy when he'd finally arrived at his hotel, so to cheer himself up he upgraded to the penthouse suite, just a few metres from the infinity pool, and the swim-up bar, that overlooked the city. Slumped on a submerged barstool, cool from the waist down and a pleasant warm breeze tickling his chest hair, Adam watched the chaos on the streets far below. With nightfall, the smog seemed to have gone to ground, and fifteen floors below, the swirling traffic, screeching horns and yells of hawkers underneath tarpaulins blended into a hazy rumble that barely reached him. The skyline, made ragged by rolling blackouts, empty lots, crumbling tenements that were half ruins, was a rough expanse of darkness, punctuated by a few glowing skyscrapers. At the top of many of them, the lights of their own rooftop pools shone out, and in one or two he could see women sluicing mermaid-like through the water. He briefly wished that a lonely businesswoman would wander up to the pool whom he could chat to and perhaps seduce, but then nixed that thought. He was, after his brush with disaster over Clara, determined to be a chaste and true husband. While it was good to be the kind of quick-thinking alpha male who could seduce strange women when the opportunity arose, it was entirely different, and much better, to be the kind of man who could but didn't. He was, he felt, searching inside himself, the latter.

He ordered another frozen margarita and let his bladder go, feeling the warm release of his urine into the pool. He had seen no reason to get up from his stool, and stayed there late into the night, ordering drinks and enjoying his own company, making plans for the morning, and all the mornings beyond that.

But now, at dawn, it was a different story. The rooftop room he'd insisted on meant that he was in the firing line of every loudspeaker tied to every mosque that broadcast the call to prayer. Sweating and grumpy, he pulled the pillow over his head to drown out the noise, and finally gave up on sleep. The wailing prayers gave way to a long religious sermon, where endless staccato sentences in Indonesian crashed against his hangover, followed by pregnant pauses for reflection. Adam cursed every prophet he could think of and looked at his watch. It was five in the morning and the sun, struggling to make itself known through the smog, was already unbearably hot.

He crawled naked from bed and, grabbing a towel to wrap

himself in, staggered to the pool. Nobody was around, so he let the towel drop and plunged in, diving deep and staying under as long as he could, swimming the length of the pool underwater with a few mighty breaststrokes.

After his swim, he called room service to bring him a bloody mary and sipped it, glaring from a lounge chair by the pool, out over the city and its repressive heat haze. His sweat fell off him in fat droplets, and every couple of minutes he had to wipe a thick film of grease off his face with a hand towel, which, seconds after he dropped it on the ground, would be replaced with a new one, freshly folded and refrigerated.

He couldn't help but take the weather personally; the heat that smothered him to a degree that felt like waterboarding, while remaining dry enough to make his lungs and throat rasp, seemed out to get him and him alone. The toxic, obfuscating smog that hugged the city looked, from up here, like a physical manifestation of a deep hostility that he could feel directed at him and everything he stood for.

Far below, as the day heated up, the seething mass of cars lost focus through the smog, blurring out to a dangerous game of Tetris. *Fucking idiots*, he thought. Finishing the bloody mary, he decided another was in order and, settling into the poolside bar, selected a piña colada off the menu.

A line of ants was marching from the kitchen, across the length of the rooftop bar, to a bank of waxy pot plants clustered around the spa. Using a thumb, he closed the end of the straw to trap the drink inside, and using his makeshift pipette, dropped a blob of sugary cocktail onto the brick by the pool.

Almost immediately a dragonfly peeled off from the buzzing miasma that hovered just above the water and landed next to it. Adam leaned in closer as it fed until his nose was centimetres away. It would plunge its tiny face into the sea of sugar and booze, stopping only to shake its wings once in a while, like it was rolling up its sleeves at the end of the workday.

'Easy, mate,' Adam told the bug. 'You'll do yourself an injury.' He was bored now, and heaved up to get another drink. While he waited for the painfully slow barman to deliver, he pinched his belly between thumb and forefinger, and was dismayed to find a layer of flab had grown under his skin since he'd last taken notice of himself. He would, he resolved, hit the gym first thing tomorrow.

Back in his seat, he leaned over to toast the bug and found it dying. Pickled by the alcohol, it lay on its back, little legs twitching helplessly while the army of ants swarmed around it excitedly. Attracted by the sugar, they'd lapped it up, and then turned their attention to the helpless dragonfly. For a moment they tugged to and fro, each eager ant trying to grab a piece of the insect, a limb, a wing, until, at some invisible signal, the ants surrounded the bug and lifted the body, as one, off the ground. Together they heaved the insect off, mandibles sunk in sugary flesh, little legs trotting, taking him home to the nest.

Adam, watching and sipping his drink, felt inexplicably sad to see the little guy go – his mood was sour now, his drink too sweet. Moving again to the side of the building, he cleared his throat and spat a blog of saccharine glob onto the street below, and was relieved to see that the gridlock had untangled itself, the game of Tetris won, and traffic was running freely. He asked a waiter to call him a driver, then dived into the pool and stayed underwater as long as he could.

After she parked outside the hospital, Tess sat for several minutes before going in. She waited first for the song on the radio to finish, then for her email to load on her phone, checked her makeup in the rear-vision mirror, and only climbed out of the vehicle when she was 100 per cent out of ways to delay the inevitable. The day before, the hospital had called and told her that Arkady had responded to treatment better than they could have hoped and was ready to go home. Since then she felt an inexplicable wave of dread that crested as she entered the building.

She didn't know what 'responding to treatment' meant, but she certainly wasn't full of hope. Vascular dementia wasn't so much a disease as the end of the adventure. It was the mind failing an obsolete body, a wearing out of old parts that couldn't be replaced. Arkady, elegant workhorse that he was, was breaking down.

Three weeks earlier, after she'd trailed the ambulance in her car, she'd more or less given up on Arkady. When she'd left him with the nurses, before they'd sedated him to run scans, he'd been violently confused. He'd tried to batter the nurses as they met him by the entrance and helped him into a wheelchair.

Struggling to stand, he'd yelled at the staff in German and

Russian, guttural and angry to her ears, but it was when he switched to English that her ribs clamped around her heart in dismay. Arkady's English was, if not perfect, perfectly formed, the vowels rounded and consonants crisp as his shirt collars. But as he bellowed profanity at the nurses, his speech was slurred, the emphasis dropping in and out.

'Fuck you,' he drawled at the muscle-bound nurse who held him firmly in his chair while another swabbed his bicep and jabbed him with a tranquilliser. 'Fuck-fuck-fuck – yoouuuu.' As the sedative had kicked in and Arkady relaxed back into his chair, the silence had done nothing for her anxiety.

In the time since the doctor delivered the diagnosis of dementia she'd been at a loss for how to react. How sick did that make him? Would he get sicker? Would his mind or his body give out first? And which was worse? She'd gone home that night and looked inside herself, taken inventory of her inner resources, and hadn't been at all sure that she had enough compassion in her to continue to love the old man if he went, leaving only a shell behind.

The disarray with which her own family had scattered meant that she had not been close to her own grandparents, and had not been around to see them decline. She was afraid of what would happen next, and wondered if Arkady was too. Would he understand that he was dying? That his consciousness would start to fade, and dim, until it went dark? Would he be scared of it? Would he even be able to understand?

They'd put Arkady on medication to thin his blood and steady his heart, and the doctors were monitoring his condition

closely. She'd gone in to visit him so many times in the days
after the diagnosis, returning less frequently as work demanded
more of her. While she'd seen little change in his condition, Adam visited just before his trip and reported back that
although Arkady was embarrassed, there was nothing wrong
with him beyond a stagnating boredom, and he'd started wag-
ing a charm offensive against the staff of the hospital to secure
his release.

'The last thing Grandpa would want is for us to faff about
and let his company stagnate while he's sick,' Adam had told
her. She noted Adam's use of 'his company', rather than 'our
company', or even 'my company', which she knew from long
experience meant that he was trying to distance himself from
something that was going awry within the firm. In the same
way, little Kade was 'her son' whenever he was in trouble at
school and needed bailing out, but 'our son' whenever he did
something worthy of praise, or in those moments when they
stood together watching the boy careen around the yard, and
they would look at each other with mutual gratitude. No matter;
whatever the problem was, she would let Adam handle it. She
was busy being terrified that she would lose Arkady, right up
until she opened the door to his hospital suite and saw him
again.

The old man was sitting looking out the window, and as
she opened the door he stood and smiled at her. He looked
wonderful, better than she did after weeks of anxious nights.
Although it was barely ten in the morning, he was dressed in
a three-piece suit, his shoes shined, his watch glinting on his

wrist where it peeped out of his shirt-cuff. He leaned lightly on a cane, which was new, but it matched his style so completely she tried to picture him without it and found already she could not. He grinned when he saw her, teeth huge and white in his craggy, handsome face. He was one of those men built like an American desert: majestic to begin with, but to whom the weathering of years had only been kind to.

'Hello, Tess,' he said, his voice clear. 'I feel I must apologise for my behaviour of late. I was not myself.'

She grinned, wild with relief. Her fears had been for nothing. 'It's nothing, Arkady, really, it's nothing to worry about. You just had a bit of a fall or a nightmare or something, and it happens all the time, and . . .' Arkady held up a hand, and Tess stopped rambling.

'Please, Tess. I'm fully aware of my condition. I was a doctor once, when I was a boy, and now I am not a baby. Please don't treat me like one, just because I have let myself grow old somehow. It is serious, but I have medicine, and things will be fine, I promise you.'

'Well . . . You look good,' she declared, and Arkady smiled down at his suit.

'I sent a courier to the house to pick up some of my things. I hope you don't mind, but I charged it to the company account. Normally I would have called first, but I found myself without my wallet. If a man doesn't have his dignity, what does he have, after all?'

Tess smiled. 'Of course.'

Arkady started moving towards the door, slower than

before, and with a slight clip in his gait when his right hip locked and he leaned into the cane. It was subtle, almost unnoticeable, like a gear sticking on a bicycle, and if she hadn't been watching for it she doubted she would have noticed anything had changed. He reached the door and turned back to smile at her.

'Now, if I can ask one more favour of you, would you take me to lunch? The doctors here are wonderful and I commend them on their professionalism and their kindness, but the kitchen staff are a different story.' He nodded grimly at a tray on which a grey sandwich and a foil cup of fruit salad lay untouched. 'I have not eaten so well since Auschwitz.'

Her attention rarely left Arkady through lunch, following his eyes as he read the menu, his hands as they gripped knife and fork – tight and efficient, wrists locked hard in the European fashion. She examined the set of his jaw as he chewed, trying to compare the man that sat before her with her mental picture of him before the stroke. She thought maybe he was moving a little more slowly, taking a little longer to eat. When Arkady read the menu she thought that something was wrong, that his eyes dragged a little, spent too much time moving from one side of the page to the other. Without looking up, Arkady spoke.

'While I am touched by your concern, I do not require this level of scrutiny. I assure you that if I'm going to keel over dead, then I will give you some kind of warning.'

She blushed, chastened. Even weakened, a little feeble, he still made her feel like a child when he told her off. 'Sorry.'

'Do not be sorry. Your worry is good. Your worry makes me happy. I am Russian, after all. Without some kind of angst we feel lonely.'

He flagged down a passing waiter and asked for the wine list.

'Are you sure you should be drinking, Arkady? You just got out of hospital. And I don't know if it will affect your medications.'

He waved this away. 'I have dementia. My brain is dying, Tess. A little wine will not hurt me now. Do you want me to die unhappy, as well as insane?'

'Don't tease me. It's not a joke.'

'Everything is a joke, Lubovka. If you had seen the things I have, you would know this.' His smile was sad, but not unkind. 'And besides, the whole idea that alcohol is bad for medicine is shit and lies. In the war, they were losing soldiers to the brothels, and a soldier goes to visit the women, he comes out with gonorrhoea, he gets sick and he cannot fight. They find that antibiotics will fix the soldier, but only so long as he stays out of the brothels. The second he gets drunk, he goes to the brothel, he gets reinfected. So, they tell the soldier that the antibiotics will not work if he drinks. So, he doesn't drink, he doesn't go to the brothel, he is cured.'

'Really?'

'Yes. It, like most of history, is a lie, but a good lie. And one which doctors keep up here, because Australians are animals, and if you do not take away their treat, they would never ever stop drinking.'

'Animals? Isn't that a little harsh?'

'Children, then. If you do not tell them a fairy tale, to scare them, they will not do anything you tell them.'

'True.'

'You can thank the war for that. For a great many things, actually: penicillin, amphetamine, the automobile. All the good things in life we owe to the great wars. As difficult as it is to admit, the things the Nazis explored pushed the world forward. The Americans gave amnesty to their physicists and got their nuclear technology. The rockets that made the Blitz possible also sent man to the moon.'

Arkady's tone was mild, but his eyes were steel. They drilled into Tess as she looked up from the menu, shocked.

'How can you say that, after what happened to you? Aren't you angry?' As the words left her mouth she felt the insignificance of the word 'anger', its smallness next to the atrocity she was asking about.

'Of course, forever, eternally.' Arkady shrugged, a small smile playing across his lips. 'But anger is unproductive. It is useful for a minute, if you need to flee, if you need to fight, but in the camps, neither of those things were an option, and in the aftermath, even less so. Those of us who survived had to learn to temper our hatred, or it would destroy us. We are not machines designed to be run red hot. We must rest, we must heal. If we cannot let go of fear and hatred, we will always be in the camps.'

'That doesn't sound like an easy thing to do. How long did it take you to feel okay? After the war, I mean.'

Arkady took a moment to answer. Without taking his eyes off Tess, he put down his knife and fork on the plate in perfect parallel, signalling he was done with food. 'What do you mean?'

'When did you stop feeling the weight of . . . what happened?'

'I feel it every day. It never went away. It never will. Not for me or anyone.'

'Oh.' Tess had no idea what to say next. The space between them was a vacuum, a perfect void she had no idea how to enter. 'I'm sorry.'

'I am too,' said Arkady, softly. 'More sorry than anyone could know.' He paused again, then the silence snapped, was extinguished by Arkady's booming voice, jolly, rounded, avuncular again. 'But what can we do now but try to live? We survived; the bad guys did not. And you know, I met my wife through the camps, built a life. If it wasn't for the war, I would not be here, I would not have Adam, or Kade, or you.'

'Silver lining?'

'My wife used to joke that Hitler was our matchmaker, that we would never have met without him. She got into a lot of trouble with her people for saying that – it is, of course, a terrible thing to say that anything good came out of the war, but there was that at least. Of course, he killed her in the end. Her poor liver.'

'So how are you supposed to forgive them?'

'They can't be forgiven.' Arkady put down the wine list and steepled his hands, thought deeply, put his words in order, moving the thoughts from one language to another. 'If one looks at the rise of the Nazi state, though, one can begin to understand. The German people believed that they were the strongest, the smartest, the most cultured, the most noble in the world, really believed it with all their hearts.' Here, the old man tapped his chest, and the memory of the scar over his heart came back to Tess. She pushed it away and reached for her drink. 'But at the same time, they'd just been defeated in a war with an enemy they saw as inferior; not just beaten, but humiliated and impoverished, undeniable evidence that the German State was imperfect. So they had to hold two conflicting ideas in their heads, which is not something a human being can do, and when that happens the ideas begin to mutate, to become perverted, and you start to look for an explanation, a villain. And if you don't have the strength to look outside your borders, you look for the enemy within. Historically, you take the portion of your society that you don't understand, the portion that is visibly different and demonstrably parochial and direct your blame and hatred there. Historically, also, sadly, this means Jews. In Germany, in Spain, and England, all the way back to Egypt.

'So, say you are young, say you are bright enough, but you are poor and frustrated and frightened by life. You grow up being told every day that you are poor because a Jew decided it should be so, that the Jews are after you, the Jews will take your job, the Jews will take your women. You believe it, of course, because you hear it enough times that it becomes fact, and facts become actions, become consequences. So you have a society built strong again, but its engine is hate, and like any engine it does what it is supposed to, which is run, day and night. To a machine, a Jew does not look different from a Gypsy, or a communist, or a homosexual, or a Russian. The machine runs on hate, and there is always something new to hate.

'Can you forgive it? No, probably not, but if you don't try and understand it, you risk it happening again.'

Tess was a little unnerved. 'Do you think it could? Happen again? Not today, surely?'

'Every great evil in the world was done because someone thought they had the answer. Let's civilise Africa, or colonise India, or close our borders to protect us from the evil outside them, or purge our cities of the evil people inside them. Then things will be better. Big ideas bring the world closer to its end. It would never occur to an evil man that he is evil, which is, of course, what makes him evil. Of course, that's what made what happened in the camps all the worse. Normal men, scientists and the bureaucrats who thought they were building a better world by what they did.'

'Surely the scientists knew better. They have no excuse.'

'Science is a religion, like any other. Examine your texts long enough and you'll find a rule that justifies exactly want you want to do, even demands it. What I did learn in the camps, from those scientists, is that a human being is no different from a rat. It will run through a maze if you reward it. It will run fast for cheese, but faster if the punishment is pain.

Avoiding death, horrible death, is a very nice reward. Even nicer than cheese.' He opened the wine list. 'But not as nice as wine.'

———

The building where the belongings confiscated from each trainload of prisoners were sorted and processed had been nicknamed Canada, after the country, which was rumoured by the starving prisoners to be a place of untold wealth and luxury. A work detail of female prisoners went through the pockets and found the treasures hidden by the civilians arriving at Auschwitz: jewellery, gold and diamonds, watches, cash from a dozen countries, Bibles, the compact Chumashes taken on journeys, love letters, records, sweets and bottles of wine. All the priceless sentimental objects smuggled into the camp by people who couldn't live without them, all now belonging to no one, all piled up to be truffled through by the Nazis.

All valuables were supposed to be sent to Berlin to fund the war effort, but much of it was pilfered by the SS overseers, and some of it went to Dr Pfeiffer. Dieter had recruited a soldier who had become addicted to morphine after being injured on the Eastern Front, and now traded valuable liquor and handfuls of gold for vials of the stuff.

Dieter instructed his man in Canada to look out for certain things he needed, either for his research, or for his comfort, and every few weeks he surprised Arkady with a gift. Now, instead of his striped uniform, he wore an immaculate three-piece suit, with only a tiny bloodstain on the lapel betraying its provenance. Tucked inside the suit pocket was a silver fountain pen, and on his wrist ticked a Swiss watch, a miraculous little thing that wound itself and kept ticking despite being dragged through time, travel, rain, snow, gas. At night, when memories of his torture in the Luftwaffe labs came back to him, Arkady held the watch up to his ear so that the reassuring tick tick tick drowned out his thoughts until his breathing settled and he could sleep again.

Even if he hadn't been a doctor, Dieter would have seen that his friend had changed since he'd been the subject of the experiments. He moved more slowly, as though his hulking body were a puppet dangling on loose strings; his delicacy with his tools was lost. Several times when preparing a blood sample his fingers slipped, cracking the glass and ruining the slide. Once, he cut his hand badly on a broken slide and sat staring as the blood welled up, dumb, as if he didn't know what was happening. Dieter surmised that the pressure experiments had caused some lasting brain damage in the Russian. There was trauma too; if Dieter didn't sedate him at night, he would thrash and cry out in his sleep. When awake he was fearful and would start at loud noises. Each time some evidence of the damage he'd done to Arkady presented itself, Dieter was overcome with regret and sorrow, and did what he could to make the man's life more comfortable.

Arkady never went back to the barracks above the crematorium. Instead, at the end of the workday, he would curl up on a cot in a corner of Dieter's office, where often he would eat his dinner with the doctor. Dieter managed to secure extra food from Canada, staples and treats that the dead had smuggled in with them from their hometowns: bread and pickles, and canned vegetables and fish and cured meat, bars of chocolate and bottles of wine. The two men ate anything perishable for dinner, but Dieter hid the food that would keep deep in the back of his closet where they wouldn't be found by any spot checks by the SS. When Arkady asked him what the point was of stashing food away when more than they could eat was coming through the door, Dieter smiled, held up his hand in the Boy Scout salute and said, in English, 'Always be prepared.'

A fortune in gold and cash was stored in ammunition boxes under a loose floorboard in Dieter's quarters, waiting for the end of the war, which was coming closer all the time. The American planes were overhead more frequently now, and while the bombs hadn't started yet, they would fall any day, he could feel it.

It had been a mistake to come here. The doctors he worked with were not men of science. If they had ever been, that was long over now, along with all pretence of procedure, standards and recordkeeping. The scientific methods lay discarded along with the mounting pyramids of bodies that were taken away by the Sonderkommando every morning. They were less doctors than spoiled children, brutalising their toys, tearing the limbs off one, sewing them onto another, discarding them without a thought when they broke.

They drank a lot, the two of them. They would finish work shortly after lunch and settle down to drink, talking or listening to records on the gramophone.

One night, halfway through dinner and a bottle of Canadian cognac, Dieter asked Arkady about the dolls, apropos of nothing, just steering up to the subject out of a comfortable silence.

Arkady was chewing, so he had time to think, swallow before asking, 'What about them?'

'It seems a strange thing for a doctor to do with his spare time.'

'So does murdering children.'

'Good point,' Dieter smiled. 'But I am still curious. Where does an educated young degenerate like yourself learn doll-making?'

Arkady hesitated, finished his mouthful and pushed his plate away. He wasn't very hungry, hadn't been very hungry since his ordeal in the laboratory. Before the experiments he would have killed, literally, for the food that was in front of him every evening now, but he continued to waste away. His thoughts, too, were not as clear as they once were, his emotions not so easily controlled. He still liked cognac, though, so reached for his glass and told Dieter the story of his father.

'My people came from Sergiev Posad, a little town about fifty miles outside of Moscow. My grandfather was a toymaker, as his had been, and his before that. We made *matryoshka*, you know, those little nesting dolls that fit inside each other. It was a procedure: cut the wood, it had to be the right wood, dry it for five years, no more, no less, then lathe it, lathe it, lathe it, eight times, then paint it. But they were beautiful, world class; the Tsar's children would collect them.

'But then, the revolution, and the Soviets nationalised the *matryoshka*. They became a point of national pride, you know, so handcrafting them was forbidden as inefficient, and all the *matryoshka* craftsmen were rounded up and moved to Moscow to work in factories that made these shitty, generic dolls. Of course, a craftsman is not a robot, and a man who could spend a week painting a doll is useless on a construction line, so Father could not find good work, and so he was poor, and disappointed to find himself in Moscow.

'In his spare time he used to make me toys, not nesting dolls, he no longer had the proper tools or the will to do that, but little things: stuffed bears, these floppy wooden puppets.' Here, Arkady put his arms out to mime a marionette. 'Simple things he could carve, simple things he could teach me. We were halfway through a rocking horse when he died.'

'That's a sad story,' said Dieter. 'But least he could make you happy with what he could do.'

'Yes. Although I suspect those toys made him happier than they made me. A man needs to be busy, especially when he's sad. But it was time we spent together, so the memories are good.'

Arkady's eyes were glassy now, a little drunk. Dieter poured him another. Dr Pfeiffer was a practical kind of drunk; no matter how tight he got, he always kept his head about him, a fact that had served him well through life, and especially well since the war had begun and the world fallen apart around him. 'So how does a toymaker from Moscow end up a doctor in Auschwitz?' he asked, gently as he could.

'Bad luck, of course, straight after good luck, which is the worst luck,' Arkady said, and, after a moment's hesitation he found himself telling the story he'd never thought he would tell anyone. About leaving Russia to study medicine in Poland, in part because he was drawn to paediatrics, a branch of medicine that had grown derelict in the Soviet Union, and partly because he wanted to put as much space between his family and the life he would live as possible. The story tumbled out of him, about falling in love with medicine, with Jan, a handsome young aristocrat he shared classes with, the walk through Krakow cemetery when Jan had kissed him, the anticipation and the terror of that, and the relief when he realised that the kiss wasn't, after all, a trap, just a kiss.

Then there was a whole new world that opened up as the two of them moved to a new life in Czechoslovakia. Prague was an epiphany, and there were long wild nights of beer and absinthe and smoky clubs where American musicians introduced him to jazz. And more than all of that, love, and the blindness that came with love, which meant he and Jan paid no attention as the world soured around them.

While he spoke about Jan, Arkady kept his eyes on the table, not ashamed, not exactly, but careful. He looked up when he was done to gauge Dieter's reaction, and found the German's eyes boring into him.

'That is disgusting,' he said, levelly.

'That I loved Jan?'

'That you love jazz. I follow the research of a doctor in Denmark working on a cure for your homosexual condition,

Arkady, but I'm afraid our best doctors cannot help with your taste in music.'

Arkady laughed a little, surprised by the German's levity.

'And Jan?' asked Dieter. 'Where is he?'

'I try not to think about him. He was a Jew, as well as being . . . like me.'

There was a long moment of silence. Even outside the office, the constant soundtrack of woe; screaming and gunshots seemed to recede, and the only sound was the tiny beat of Arkady's watch. Dieter took Arkady's hand and squeezed it, and then looked up to find Arkady's eyes welling up.

'I am so sorry, Arkady,' he said. 'It shouldn't have happened. None of this should. This is not your war. This is not our war. We are men of science. Neither of us should be here.'

'I will not be much longer,' Arkady said, bitterly.

'What makes you say that?'

'It's a war; there are sides, despite what you say. Both of us can't survive. I'm not your equal; I'm your servant. You know what happens to me in the end.'

Dieter frowned at the Russian's challenge, then stood up, and went to his hiding place under the floorboards to retrieve something wrapped in cloth. He placed it on the table and unwrapped it, and Arkady let out an involuntary groan when he saw what it was.

'When this is all over, we will make it right, Arkady. We will fix this world that other men have broken. But before that we have to survive, which means we have to get back to work.' Dieter picked up the little Sarah doll from its wrapping on the table and handed it to Arkady, who took it and held it like he might a baby. 'I need your help, Arkady. I need you.' He put a hand on the other man's shoulder, felt him shudder.

After that night, Dieter started to show more kindness towards the children. At first he started administering anaesthetic before amputating a limb, which he would have seen as an unthinkable waste a few months ago, then he started cancelling the operations when he knew that the outcome would have no scientific merit, and lying to Mengele about the result. And then spiriting medicine from the supply cupboard for those already ill. He did all this in secret from the other doctors, but in full view of Arkady, which made the Russian think perhaps it was all for his benefit. Regardless, it lessened the suffering of the children. In return for this, Arkady redoubled the effort he put into his lab work, concentrating hard even through the fog that was over him these days. They were, after all, a good team.

EIGHT

After making a couple of calls to push back the meeting he'd felt too shabby to attend on time, Adam dressed and went downstairs to where his driver was already waiting, leaning against the car smoking. As they crept through the streets of Jakarta, he downed a couple of bottles of vodka he'd snatched from the minibar. His hangover was starting to recede, and as the cleansing alcohol buzz settled over him so did some of the optimism from the night before.

There was a long wait at the entrance to the factory yard while a security guard checked the car out, running a bomb detector over the boot and scoping under the vehicle with a mirror at the end of a long pole. The driver rolled down his window and had a brief exchange with the guard, who stuck his head in to look at Adam. Adam summoned the politest smile he could muster and turned it to the guard who stared impassively at him from behind mirrored aviators. Finally, the guard nodded, said a word, and the boom went up.

A roller door opened to let the car drive straight onto the factory floor, where a manager, waiting to greet Adam, rushed forward to open the car door before his driver could. As the door opened, the chaos of the shop washed over him, the sound of thousands of articles of Javanese kitsch being lathed from wood and handpainted by the hundreds of workers crammed onto the factory floor. For a while the Mitty & Sarah Company had imported some shadow puppets made in this factory, largely so that Adam could convince Tess he had been sincere in his appreciation of her ideas, but they hadn't sold well and he'd discontinued the line. He remembered, though, that the box boasted that every doll was handmade, and handmade they were, by the rows and rows of nimble-fingered women who assembled them.

His ears flinched at the roar of the production floor, his skin flushed from the heat, and his nose prickled at the sawdust and the chemical varnish they used to treat the wood. Adam knew that scent; he'd smelled it in the Polish toy factories he had visited as a child. By the time the varnish had proven and the dolls had been shipped across the ocean, the scent would have faded until it provided the faintest nostalgic whiff. For now, though, the combined fumes of thousands of litres of the stuff collected in the airless factory, which was locked tight to discourage inspectors and photographers from NGOs from sticking their beaks in. Not far from where the car was parked, an old woman was dipping lathed puppet torsos into a rippling vat of the varnish. Her hands and arms to the elbow had taken on the sheen of very old, very expensive wood.

Adam shook the manager's hand, which, against his own soft, sweaty palm, was as rough and dry as a long-forgotten orange at the bottom of a fruit bowl. Calluses scraped against Adam's fingers as he retrieved his digits from the man's over-eager handshake. Those hands betrayed his origins on the factory floor, and a childhood spent labouring before that, as did his dark skin and ropy forearms. These things, which initially Adam found noble, and in a way reminded him of his own family story, started to seem grotesque as the visit wore on, and Adam decided he did not like the man. As the manager babbled about what a pleasure it was to see him and how excited he was that Adam was considering using his facility, and how far ahead of their quotas for the year they were, Adam saw the Indonesian for what he was: a jumped-up, slimy little bureaucrat who in the effort to rise above his fellow factory workers had sold them out. He was wearing a batik tunic that strained at his stomach where middle age was sending muscle to seed. The tunic still had creases in it, like it had just been removed from its packet. Adam suspected he kept the traditional dress in his office for when he needed to look both authoritative and exotic. The thought filled him with anger, not that the manager thought he would fall for such bald-faced manipulation, but that this slimy little toad-man would sell out his ancestry to make a quick buck.

Adam, after a walk across the factory floor, decided he'd had enough, and asked to be taken up to the showroom, which was housed in an annexe that hung suspended over the factory floor, with three sides of mirrored windows. It provided a panoramic view of the floor, and from the outside it presented as a dark, mirrored box. The overseer explained that it would draw the eye of anyone working on the floor if they looked up from their work, that the possibility someone might be watching them kept them from slacking off. That kind of low-level paranoia was a valuable motivator, from a management perspective. Adam nodded appreciatively, and spent a second savouring the clean frigid air, watching the work below. None of the noise of production penetrated the thick glass; the only sound was a Chopin nocturne being piped into the office through speakers, and the nervous scraping of the overseer's sandals on the carpet.

Adam paused for a moment to let the view sink in, and turned to watch the rows upon rows of women in hijabs bent over their workstations in silent concentration. Even from up here he could see the exhaustion on their faces, the mounting grime of the production process caking their cheeks.

Adam thought back to the gleaming Chinese factory that for the past decade had assembled and boxed all the Mitty & Sarah products for import into Australia. There, thousands of workers stood on automated construction lines, dressed in identical sterile overalls, gloves and surgical masks, all resolutely focused on performing one tiny task, tightening a screw, or polishing the plastic wrapping of a box as it whizzed past them on the conveyor belt. It had been beautiful to watch, as awe-inspiring in its own way as walking into one of the huge, empty churches he visited when he travelled through Europe as a child. The only sound from that factory floor was the mighty whirring of the extractor fans that sucked up the fumes and dust from the industrial process, and jettisoned it into the soupy Shenzhen air.

This was different. It was chaotic, and dirty, and loud, the floor febrile with women dashing about to fetch parts, the air loud with barking overseers. That said, it was cheap, far cheaper, to have the toys carved and painted by hand here in a warehouse in Jakarta than in the industrial powerhouses of China. There was even a certain kind of beauty to it. If you watched the chaos long enough, you noticed the patterns start to emerge, the cacophony and mess sliding into shape and the job getting done. Here, like the traffic on the streets, life found a way.

The overseer spoke, shaking Adam out of his reverie. 'As you can see, we've had no problem expanding production to meet your requirements. We've had to hire new workers, almost double our staff, but we've implemented a day- and a night-shift to make sure we meet your production targets.' He continued, droning on about schedules and quotas and efficiency and customer satisfaction, and Adam tuned out, hypnotised by the scurrying women below, only snapping out of it when an assistant brought Adam a prototype for the new Sarah doll, which he took and held in his hands.

Shubangi had sent the designs for the dolls a few days

earlier, and Adam, watching over her shoulder as she mailed off a PDF of schematics and Pantone codes and wood-grain measurements, had been unsure that her idea would work, but here, right here in his hands, was proof that it had. The doll was exactly the same as the ones from the old factory, and the factory before that in Gippsland, and the dolls from his childhood. The wood was different, but better, logged on the sly from Sumatra, and the dress Sarah wore was a little cheaper, a little more crackly when he rubbed it with a thumb and forefinger, but otherwise it was exactly the same. Bringing it to his face he smelled the warm, nostalgic scent of varnish.

It had worked. The audacity of this switch, all through a few well-placed emails, astonished him with its – his – brilliance. The same quality product, just made by cheaper people. They would still be shipped to their Melbourne warehouse, already in their retail boxes with the traditional copy stating they were handmade and designed in Australia, as well as the truncated history of the company, starting with Adam's handwritten spiel: 'Let me tell you a story about my grandfather.'

On the way back to his hotel from the factory he stared at the hawkers that wandered through the traffic selling batteries, phone chargers, magazines, deep-fried snacks. He admired their entrepreneurial spirit but pitied them for not wanting to be more than walking roadside stalls. To Adam the world was a place more full of wonder and opportunity than these people could imagine, and he had lost himself in thought about the astonishing potential that it offered a man like him when a beggar rapped on his window and startled him out of his happy thoughts. He was about to roll down the window and tell her to fuck off when he saw that she was carrying a baby under her arm, the child asleep, or maybe sick, its head flopping about alarmingly as she tapped on the window and made a pleading gesture with her free hand. Adam realised that the windows of the car were mirrored, and that the woman couldn't see inside, and he relaxed. She was just taking her chances that there was someone of means inside the car who could help her.

He pressed his nose to the window for a better look at her and realised that her hands were stained a dark brown from the wrists to the elbow, and for a moment he was sure she was the woman from the factory who had been dipping the dolls in varnish. He was startled, but only for a second, because what were the chances? She was just one of millions of beggars on the streets of Jakarta; there was bound to be a resemblance.

Momentarily disconcerted by the encounter, he pulled out his paperwork to take his mind off it. He ran the sums again and realised that with the money they would save shifting production to Indonesia he would turn a slight profit, even after all that money that would be siphoned off for Tariq, and the oppressive fog which had hung over him since his encounter with the man started to lift. Anyone could be successful, Adam reasoned, but to be given a black eye and come out on top made you a hero. And becoming a hero in the tradition of his grandfather was all he'd ever wanted.

———

They finished lunch: soup, salad, steak and a bottle of pinot noir, of which Arkady drank most. Afterwards, Tess, mellow after a glass and a half, helped Arkady into the passenger seat, then climbed behind the wheel and started for home. To fill the silence she told him how his room had been put back just the way it was, but with a couple of mobility bars stationed here and there should he need assistance getting up, and that a home nurse would come by daily to check on his wellbeing and anything he might need help with. When she stopped at the first set of lights and looked across, she saw Arkady's look of polite boredom.

'Tess,' Arkady said touching the back of her hand lightly as she put the car into drive. 'Take me to the office. I want to go over the books. Let's run the numbers, like we used to.'

'Oh, we don't need to do that, everything is going fine. Adam has brought in outside accountants to manage things for a while, and . . .'

'Oh good God!' Arkady raised his eyebrows in mock alarm. 'Hurry, then, there is no time to lose.'

Tess laughed. 'It's fine, Arkady. Take the day off.'

'Please, indulge an old man his vanity.'

She glanced at him again, smiled yes, and Arkady switched on the radio, punching through the stations until he found a tinkling classical station. He settled and closed his eyes, and soon he was snoring. Outside the window the houses got larger and larger then dropped away suddenly, as residential zoning gave way to light industry, grim shopfronts with handpainted signs for takeaway shops, panelbeaters, timber yards, brothels that she flashed by on the highway. Why were there always so many brothels out in factory zones? Tess wondered. Was it just because the rent was cheap? Were tradies as virile and insatiable as pornography suggested? Or did people from all over the city drive out here so they could get their kicks without being spotted? It was a disquieting thought, particularly with all the late nights Adam put in at the office. Her mouth twisted around the idea, and she only noticed the off-ramp she needed seconds before she would have passed it, and swerved to get on, cutting off a semitrailer behind her which slammed on screaming air-brakes, followed by a loud, angry blast from the horn. The driver flipped her off, slowing to yell obscenities at her, which were silenced by the two panes of glass and rushing wind between their vehicles, but she made the turn.

Shaken, she slowed to a crawl as she drove on, and glanced across to find Arkady staring at her wild-eyed.

'Sorry.' She frowned, then laughed in relief. 'What an arsehole.'

Arkady blinked and looked around. 'Where are we?'

'Nearly at the factory, Arkady. We just hit some traffic.'

'Oh.' Arkady exhaled heavily. 'Good.'

They drove the car straight onto the warehouse floor and parked in the spot reserved for visiting VIPs, sheltered from the beeping hustle of forklifts and picker-packers by a dividing wall, and close to the stairs that would take them up to the showroom. Adam had had them installed so that potential retail partners scoping out their products would be treated to a quick, sweeping glance of the industry underpinning the business, the rows and rows of pallets stacked to the roof that stretched further than the eye could see in the gloom of the warehouse, then a moment later arrive in the cool future-chic of the offices.

On his way up the stairs Arkady – he was definitely moving more slowly, Tess was sure of it – paused to catch his breath, looked out at the warehouse and nodded approvingly at what he saw, then trooped up to the top. They made their way to her office, where she left him to fix a couple of coffees. When she got back, he was seated, his head buried in paperwork, pen in hand, a small smile on his face. She stood in the door with the steaming mugs of coffee, her heart fit to burst. The old man was fine, just fine. It would all be okay. She placed the coffee next to him and he smiled, then went back to his books, muttering under his breath in German.

Often, in the past, when they were working in companionable silence, she would catch him muttering in German, absent-mindedly, the way another man might hum a pop song. One day she'd asked him about it, and he'd looked up at her in surprise, the white visible all the way around the blue of his eyes.

'What do you mean?'

'When you talk to yourself. You do it in German.'

'Do I? Well . . .' Arkady seemed taken aback. 'Force of habit, I suppose. I studied medicine at the German university in Prague. I guess doing homework takes me back there.'

'I don't understand why you didn't leave it there. Such an ugly language!'

'You think so? I think it is quite lovely, at times. There are words for things that only the Germans ever thought to put a name to.

'Like schadenfreude?'

'Yes,' smiled Arkady, putting down his pen and folding his long, elegant fingers in front of his face to hide a smile. 'But also, for example, *kummerspeck*, literally 'grief bacon', the weight you put on when you are unhappy.'

'I know the word,' Tess said.

'I believe you.' A hint of a teasing tone crept into Arkady's voice and he ducked to avoid the pencil Tess lobbed at him. She scowled at him, pretended at outrage, but she liked these odd, playful asides they sometimes had. Even when Arkady's tone could be brusque, talking to him was the only time she felt like a grown-up. '*Scheisskopf*,' she hissed at him, and he waved it away.

'An inelegant word. You can do better. Try harder. What is your favourite word? Mine is *saudade*. Portuguese. The desire for something that does not and probably cannot exist.'

'*Won*,' she challenged. 'Reluctance to let go of a beautiful illusion. In Korean.'

'*Luftmensch*. Yiddish for a dreamer, a visionary. "Air person". Like your husband, Adam.'

'*Sastranitsa* is a better word for my husband. Russian for "you shit too much".'

'But not my favourite Russian word. That's *chelovek-karova*, "man-cow". This means the fat, stupid prisoner you befriend and take with you when you escape from a gulag, for the express purpose of butchering him for meat as you cross the Siberian wasteland. I love this word. The fact that it exists tells you everything you need to know about the Russian soul.'

'Okay. That's – not a nice thing to do.'

'The Germans have their own versions. *Torschlusspanik*, or "gate-closing fear". Once upon a time, when barbarians would raid, the wealthy would close the gate to the city walls, leaving the peasants outside to be slaughtered. The angst that this might happen to you was *torschlusspanik*, but these days it means something like – the fear of diminishing opportunities as one ages.'

'Oh,' said Tess, 'believe me, I know that one.'

And Arkady, seeing he had steered her into melancholy, lightened his tone. 'But my very favourite word is Dutch. *Knuffelbeest*.'

'Which means?'

'Teddy bear. But literally "cuddle beast".'

'Oh, that is good. It reminds me of the Australian word "puggle".'

'What is this puggle?'

'It's a baby echidna.' She googled it, found a picture, showed Arkady, who laughed at the photo of the absurd little creature.

'You are right,' he said. 'That is a beautiful word.' He paused for a moment, then laid his hand on her shoulder and squeezed. 'You will make it a toy, this *puggle*. A plush toy. It will make a million dollars.'

She'd laughed then, but in the end she thought about it, and she'd looked into it and found another toy company had already had this idea, and had trademarked the word. At the time she'd been struck by two facts: that it was possible for a company to lay claim on the name for the young of an entire species (was nothing safe from lawyers?), and that Arkady's instinct for business seemed infallible.

Now, back in the office with Arkady, as if nothing had changed, Tess felt content for the first time in weeks. She didn't notice Arkady open and leaf through the file she'd left neglected on the desk, with the collected evidence of money laundered from the company. He cleared his throat and she started, moved to snatch the folder off him. He laid his hand down over it, gently resisting her efforts to take it.

'Oh, don't read that, Arkady. It's . . .'

'You mentioned this, before I got sick. That someone is stealing from you?'

'From the company,' she said, already regretting it. 'Someone has been stealing from the company. For years, someone had been siphoning money away from our accounts.'

Arkady looked at her levelly, his face perfectly blank. 'How much money?'

'I'm not sure. Hundreds of thousands, at least. I keep looking further back, and the further I go, the more is missing. Then you got sick, and I stopped, and . . . I shouldn't have told you, I'm sorry.'

Arkady stared at her. For a long time he said nothing, and then finally he said, softly, 'It is me.'

'What do you mean? I'm not sure you understand.'

'Someone is taking money from the company. It is me. I am . . . What is the English? Cooking the books.'

He asked her to bring him the evidence of laundering that she'd found, and then demonstrated, matter-of-factly, how he'd done it. Every so often, as the company's money snaked its way around the globe, a little of it disappeared. A few thousand from a factory floor in India; a secret cache of euros that vanished in a Portuguese port. And that money, secreted across the globe, was where his real empire was. Arkady rummaged through the old filing cabinets nobody but him had touched in years and brought out documents: bank account numbers, details of safe deposit boxes, stock portfolios.

For all that the world cared, the company was a fairly profitable little family business that had done well for itself thanks to decades of perseverance, but the public face belied the real purpose of the company, which was simply to launder cash from canny investments. For the first time, she began to realise that the day-to-day business of the Mitty & Sarah Company was only the facade of a huge, nebulous fortune that swirled and secreted itself all around them. On any given day, they had maybe ten million dollars in toys gathering dust in the warehouse, but, elsewhere, in stock exchanges and banks accounts across the world, the company's real worth was ticking over, appreciating, drawing money to itself. As soon as Arkady had accrued a few hundred thousand over the years he spirited it away from the toy concern as quickly as he could, into bonds, trusts, shares, Arabian oil and American war bonds, Australian coal and Chinese manufacturing. The revenue from the web of cash dwarfed, many times over, the money that the toys brought in.

'But why?' Tess asked. 'Why have you done this? And kept it secret?'

In his youth, Arkady explained to Tess, he had made money from his dolls, but not enough to keep himself safe. To do that he would need to spin his modest fortune into enough money for several lifetimes. 'Any fool can make a fortune if he works at it. Keeping it is another story. When we were growing up in old Russia, my mother kept urging my father to bury his money in the backyard. My father laughed at her, until the Soviets took all his. Then he was no longer laughing. That's a lesson I have never forgotten.

'If I bury money in my own backyard, maybe it will be safe, maybe not. Maybe someday somebody will come to look for it. So I have buried my money in everyone's backyard, Tess. You should do the same. Take some money and hide it away, away from the business, even away from me. You never know what will happen in your future. Life will always surprise you. Ambition, luck, people: things are never ever what you think they will be.'

Arkady closed the file, pushed it over to her. 'A person is defined by the secrets they keep, Tess. I am trusting you to keep mine. I know I can trust you, yes?'

Tess was bewildered, nodded, shook her head, tried to think it through, a million questions clambering for real estate in her mind, none of which would be asked, because her son had just been dropped off by his babysitter, and was barrelling down the hallway to her office. Little Kade popped his head around the corner and squealed with delight to see his great-grand-father. He ran to tackle Arkady, who staggered and laughed and ruffled his hair. Then Kade took Arkady by the hand and led him, half dragged him, to the showroom, chatting happily about school, and a goal he'd almost kicked, just barely missed, and a new kid at school with a funny accent, and so on, while big Arkady laughed and made approving noises and Tess plodded after them.

In the showroom, each individual product was carefully placed and precision-lit with overhead lamps so that buyers could wander through the neat rows of toys and play with them at will, while the media manager would scurry behind, replacing the toys in their designated spots, moving the limbs back, posing them precisely as they were: action figures in mid kung-fu kick; dolls with teapots raised, pouring their imaginary tea for imaginary friends. In the centre of the room, under a spotlight just subtly brighter than any other in the room, sat a pair of the original Mitty and Sarah dolls, holding hands, rosy mouths smiling, wood lustrous and shiny.

Kade was nearly seven years old, but young for his age, and still as close to either tears or joy at any given moment as he'd been when he was two. Earlier in the year he'd gone away on school camp and taken his teddy bear, and had then been sent home inconsolable after some of the other boys teased him about it and threw it in the river.

Slow and sweet-natured as he was, he was easy prey for

bullies, and their experiments in after-school care had been disastrous. So they were happy for him to while away his time in the showroom unsupervised. Now and again, if Adam wanted to impress the potential of a new toy on their retailers, he would make sure he brought them by just as Kade was discovering it, zooming about the room or giggling with pleasure as he rolled around the floor with it.

The showroom was locked, and Kade vibrated with impatience for entry, hopping from one foot to another. Tess punched in the code to the room (one of Adam's ideas – a key would have done just fine, certainly there was nothing in there that cost more than the security system, but he liked the impression it made on guests) and the door swung open.

Kade stood on the threshold for a second, his hands on his hips and his eyes raking over the familiar rows of toys, searching for changes that only he, who'd half grown up in this room, could see. He reminded Tess of the young surfers who haunted the beaches near her childhood holiday home, who spent hours watching the waves, listening to the secret language of tides and currents and rips, the promises therein. Then he spotted what he was looking for, a new line of water guns that they'd just purchased. He made a beeline for them and started to play, imitating the rattle of gunfire with voice, making Rambo-rolls under the tables.

Tess stood next to Arkady and together they watched Kade hurl himself around the room. After a moment the old man spoke without taking his eyes off the boy.

'Isn't he wonderful?'

Tess's heart swelled: pleasure and pride. 'I know. And just look at him go. I know that maybe this spoils him, but, God, doesn't it make you feel young watching him?'

Arkady turned and smiled at her, then leaned over and said, in a low conspiratorial voice, 'Can I tell you a secret?'

'Sure.' Tess shrugged. 'What's one more, right?'

'I tell his parents that I take him with me on these trips because he helps me choose what to buy, but that's not quite true.'

'What do you mean?'

'The truth is, the boy is kind of an idiot. A nice idiot, but still an idiot.'

Tess started, turned to Arkady. 'What?'

'But idiots have their uses!' Arkady said merrily, tapping the side of his nose. 'They don't ask questions, at the borders, in the hotels, at the offices, when you turn up with the child. "Here is my grandson, his name is Adam, good Jewish boy, isn't he cute? I couldn't bear to leave him behind."' He turned and his eyes were sharp and cruel and elsewhere. 'They don't suspect a thing, and even if they did, are they going to bring it up in front of a child? No, of course not. Why would I go to Europe? Why would I ever come back after the things we did?'

Tess, not sure what he was talking about, still felt something cold wrap itself around her heart. They stared at each other – Arkady conspiratorial, Tess confused. 'I'm not sure I understand what . . .' she began, and at that moment little Kade rushed up to them brandishing his toy rifle.

'Bang!' he yelled, pointing it at Tess. 'Bang! Bang! Bang!'

He was swivelling it around to point it at the old man when Arkady's cane cracked the boy across the face.

One moment the old man was smiling and leaning sleepily on his walking stick, the next the stick arced up and caught little Kade across the cheek. The sound of wood on flesh and bone echoed through the stockroom, followed by a few seconds of shocked silence.

Nobody had ever hit Kade before, and the boy was at a loss, as the force of the blow knocked him arse-backwards. He sat, stunned, staring up at his great-grandfather who stood over him, the cane still raised, his eyes wild. His arm came down again and Tess, spurred out of shock, reached out and caught the walking stick, wrenching it away from Arkady.

'What the fuck!' she demanded, grabbing the old man by the shoulder and turning him to find his eyes foggy now, his jaw slack and quivering. The cane dropped with a clatter. '*Es tut mir leid,*' he whispered. '*Verzeihung.*' Then he was gone, out the door, running towards the stairs on broken old hips, and it was only then that little Kade came out of shock and started screaming for his father.

———

There was a sense now, on both sides, that time was running out. The ovens ran day and night, the smoke from the chimneys dirtied everything, even the clouds, which hung low and greasy and spat back rain too soiled to wash away the film of dust and bone and human fat that had settled on the buildings. The fields of bodies, the walking dead all in rows, shivered on their way to factories where nothing was being built. Soon, even the grey skies were blacked out by swarming aeroplanes.

The Allied bombers, unchallenged now by the Luftwaffe, were overhead almost all the time, flying over the camp on their way to the Eastern Front. Every day they had less distance to travel, as the Red Army swarmed across Poland on its way to Berlin.

The SS who ran the camp reacted to the threat in different ways. Some of them redoubled their efforts, improvised, dumped thousands of people in mass graves dug in the surrounding fields, pouring gasoline over them to set them alight. Others retreated into drink. Some of the guards were so drunk they could barely walk, just slowly stalked their patrol route, pistols drawn, heavy-lidded eyes barely open for trouble.

Dieter was woken up in the middle of the night to treat a solider who had been shot through the shoulder when his bunkmate, too drunk to stand and turn out the light in their barracks, had tried to shoot out the bulbs. If his aim had been just a little worse the bullet would have found his friend's head, but instead it sank into the fleshy part of his arm and passed through. He came in cursing and slurring, his bunkmates laughing as though it was the funniest thing they'd ever seen as they walked him into the surgery, arms around him like they were stumbling home from a cafe.

As Dieter cleaned and sutured the wound, he looked up at Arkady, who stood across the surgical table, and muttered, 'You know, give these idiots enough time and they'll kill themselves long before your people get here,' which drew a rare a smile out of the Russian.

Dieter was worried about his friend. In the months after his torture, he'd changed. He spoke when he was spoken to, but rarely engaged in conversation. He did his work quietly, but didn't offer new theories or opinions on their research. At night he ate very little but drank steadily. He got thin. Some nights he listened to one of the jazz records that Dieter had secured for him at great cost, but usually after dinner he would curl on his cot in the corner and work on one of his toys.

In his time off, Arkady travelled between the crematoriums and traded money and jewellery from Dieter's stash for items collected from the trainloads of prisoners: bolts of cloth, buttons from coats, tufts of hair.

Using what he could find, he improvised. A teddy bear made from an evening dress and stuffed with odd socks and buttons for eyes kept a little Hungarian boy company while his sister was having a gangrenous arm amputated. A set of chess pieces carved from bone, the black side coloured with char, went to a bookish pair of twins who'd expressed a love of the game.

It amazed Dieter that Arkady could still extract a little imagination from the children, as effortlessly as a tooth or a litre of blood. He broke up an antique hardwood chair, which had somehow washed up in Canada, and used the splinters to make a *dreidel* for a little boy who hadn't spoken since his mother had been executed in the selection line in front of him. The boy took it without a word, but sat spinning the toy for hours on end, passing the time.

Most nights he worked on the doll he called Sarah, the one he was making in the likeness of the little girl who was being moved back and forth from Mengele's zoo to be infected with various bacteria, then with experimental treatments. It was rough, but grew more sophisticated every night. Arkady would sit with it in his lap, scalpel in one hand, for hours, for the most part not carving, just running his hands across the doll's features, then, finally, raising the blade to lathe off a tiny sliver of wood. When he had the doll's features just as he wanted them, he fashioned working articulated limbs for her, joining them to the body with surgical sutures. He stained the wood a dusky pink with a disinfectant solution and used a marker pen to give the doll eyes, lips, a nose. When a recently healthy young woman turned up on his autopsy table, he salvaged the cloth from her pyjamas to sew a small dress, and harvested her hair – long, flowing and black – which he painstakingly stitched onto the doll's head.

Dieter watched his friend and his strange hobby with a rising sense of dismay. He knew that something had gone very wrong with Arkady. It was more than emotional trauma could account for. Something was broken inside him.

He no longer questioned what he was doing. When Dieter gave him an order, he followed it without arguing, even the day he went into the labs and found the tools for surgery laid out for him, the twins on the table. They were restrained with leather straps but conscious, their mouths gagged to muffle screaming, but their eyes wide and wild as they followed his hand as it moved to pick up a scalpel.

The guidelines were already drawn over the backs of the

children, thin directives in black ink that showed where each incision would be made, where the stitches would be threaded. He'd learned how to follow these marks practising on cadavers during his studies in Prague, but right now his mind was in a place years before medical school, in the workshop with his father, as the toymaker drew patient lines on a plank of wood before cutting along them with a jigsaw. He'd loved that job as a child, the way each piece would be carefully cut out and then joined together, so a couple of lifeless slabs of wood could be portioned, lathed and, with ingenious tongue-in-groove assembly, be brought to life.

Dieter watched Arkady sew the identical twins together near the spine without complaint. Sections of skin were flayed and raised, then sewed together with the corresponding flesh on the other twin so that they sat back to back and wrist to wrist. Arkady threaded the delicate veins in the wrist through the body of other twin as instructed, then closed the operation, snapped off the sutures and left the room to clean up without a word.

Mengele had wanted to see if a conjoined twin could be created by surgically attaching two identical twins. The experiment failed. Later, Arkady vivisected the twins, harvested their organs and boiled the flesh off their bones, then prepared the skeletons for Mengele's collection. When, a couple of days later, little Sarah, the model for his doll, died on the same table, he finally put the doll away, in a suitcase under his bed.

NINE

Seconds after Adam had checked his luggage, he realised his phone was inside his suitcase. He'd put it in there the night before so he wouldn't forget it when he left the hotel at dawn, then had blanked on it completely. He stared forlornly as a conveyor belt whisked it away, to some place deep in the bowels of the airport, and the lady at the check-in counter assured him it would be impossible to retrieve before he landed in Melbourne. Faced with a long flight without his phone to entertain him, he bought a *Sports Illustrated* at a newsstand and settled in for his transit to Bali.

In Bali, his connecting flight was delayed by five hours, a wait he could neither believe nor stand the thought of, and so he caught a taxi from Denpasar down to Kuta beach and found a bar. He downed a vodka and soda quickly, then another, and was just starting on a third when two young men in thongs and Australian-flag singlets shuffled in from the beach, jostling each other, and sat next to him at the bar.

'Buy us a beer!' one said to his mate.

'Nahcunt. S'your fucking round.'

'Yeah, but nah, I got the last one. Don't be such a fucking Jew.'

'Excuse me.' Adam found himself addressing them before he'd thought it through. 'Sorry to bother you, but what the fuck did you just say?'

After they bounced him out of the bar Adam was dismayed to find that not only was he shaken, he was literally shaking. He'd walked into the fight filled with righteous fire, pushed one of the bogans and swung at the other, and then suddenly found himself bent over in agony. A bouncer had appeared from nowhere to twist his hand behind his back at an angle that threatened to wrench it out of the wrist joint completely. He'd found himself leaning into the pain, his body obeying the screaming tendons rather than his brain, and allowed himself be dragged out of the pub, onto the road, and dumped gasping in the gutter, where he'd scrambled away in the manner, he realised looking back on it, of a coward.

He checked his watch, and, seeing he still had hours to wait, wandered down the street and came across a massage parlour, with teenaged touts in short shorts lounging out the front. He stood in front of them, smiling at them, a little tipsy, prevaricating.

He had a thing for Asian women. Something about them drove him crazy, most likely that they were out of his reach. He had a way with a certain kind of woman: those who had grown up with enough money that they appreciated its importance, but poor enough that their parents often fought about it. If her father was angry, distracted and disappointed by the world, and the fading beauty of his ageing wife, all the better. When he was growing up, almost every girl he knew had some iteration of this childhood, and it created certain faultlines in their character, existential tremors that, through a combination of flattery and passive aggression, he had learned to exploit. He had an instinctive ability to spot in a crowd, a group, a party, the woman whose past meant her standards for decent treatment from men would be way too low to put up any decent defence against him.

The Asian girls, however, were closed to him. They were from a different culture, implacable in the way they met his stares, somehow challenging without acknowledging that they'd seen him watching them. He did not know where the cracks in their bravado lay, where the scars in their egos were; they would never be his. For this reason, perhaps, he found himself gravitating towards them when letting his fantasies out for a walk.

He paid for an hour at reception and was shown through to a dimly lit studio and left to undress and lie down on the table. He slid his shirt and jeans off, then removed his watch, the much battered self-winding Rolex his grandfather had smuggled from Europe and gifted to him when he took over the reins of the company, and took a shower, sluicing the sweat and anger off his body. Then he heaved himself up onto the massage table, lay down on his stomach, willed himself to relax. He soon grew impatient with the soothing music being piped into the room, though, and was even less impressed when a beautiful Balinese girl entered and gave him a competent, professional massage.

If he was being honest with himself, he would have admitted that he didn't actually like massages – what he liked was the hand relief that came at the end – so he found that when he grew excited moments into the massage and the masseuse just ignored the elephant in the room as the hour went on, he became increasingly annoyed and uncomfortable.

This cruelty was exacerbated by the way she found every worn-out joint and tension knot in his body like she was reciting a litany of ways his youth had deserted him.

Parts of him he'd thought evergreen screamed in protest, and there was an especially angry cry from his recently manhandled arm. When he turned over and the masseuse started working his upper torso, he realised that the hard-won pectorals that rippled under his singlet when doing bench presses and chest flies in the gym turned out to be, on closer inspection, just fatty steaks that slid unsettlingly under his skin. At the touch of her disinterested, utilitarian fingers, his erection wilted, along with his mood.

He walked out of the parlour and flagged down a taxi to

take him back to Denpasar and an aeroplane that would return him to his family, and it was only as he was lining up to board that he realised he'd left his grandfather's watch in the shower. It was still there, thank God, waiting for him after a mad dash back through peak-hour traffic. When he got back to the airport, his plane was delayed, miraculously, and he clambered on, finally enjoying a little bit of luck, settled into his seat and went to sleep, his luggage, still holding his phone, safely tucked away in the cargo hold beneath him.

———

Adam's phone rang out, and then again, and then again. Tess left a voicemail. 'Where are you? You have to come home, you have to come home right now.' An hour passed, and another, and still no answer. She left another message. 'Arkady is sick, and I don't know what to do,' she snapped, half into the phone, half at herself.

She tried her own family: none of them answered. She left messages. She swore, cursed the fuckers rotten and blue, out loud at first, then silently, when she realised that she was disturbing Arkady. After his fit in the showroom she had taken him home, put him to bed. She did not know what else to do.

Every so often her hand reached for the phone to call an ambulance, but stopped. Her gut told her that if he went into the hospital he would not come out.

Instead, she sat by his bedside and spent a long time watching over him, scared and helpless. Angry as well, suddenly angrier than she could ever remember being; searing, incapacitating fury that rose up and clouded over her and made her tear her breath from the air in ragged strips. She could actually see red, which she'd always thought was a figure of speech, but no, a red mist drew down over her vision from the top of her eyes like a television losing reception, and she realised, firstly, that she had no idea where her husband was, where even in the world he was, or what he was doing, although she was sure that whatever it was would be foolish; and secondly, that she hated him, really hated him, with all she had. This was not what she had signed up for.

Tess had known not long after her wedding that anyone who claimed marriage was about compromise was an idiot. It was about endurance. Tess had known before most of her contemporaries that marriage was, for most people, the art of wilful blindness.

Much, probably most, of what Adam did drove her crazy. The way he ate like a homeless kitten, mouth open, molars gnashing and jaw clicking. That he drove the company, and, by extension, her life, like a stolen car, careering wildly in all directions, leaving a string of broken promises, initiatives and employees for her to clean up. The fact that he was profoundly, existentially selfish, to the extent where she wasn't quite sure he understood that other people were people, with lives and worries of their own, and not inanimate playthings to be worn out and discarded.

For all these years, whenever she thought she'd reached the limit of tolerating Adam's boorishness and ineptitude, he would blindside her with uncharacteristic sweetness: a gift, or reservations at her favourite restaurant for her and a friend, or, rarest of all, an apology, and an acknowledgement that she'd been right in some fight he'd picked over their clashing management styles.

The longer she sat now, though, the clearer things seemed to become for her. She'd gone into marriage with her expectations carefully managed. She had known it wouldn't be easy; she could not have imagined it would be so hard. Or that the best part wouldn't be her husband at all, but her unexpected bond with her grandfather-in-law. He was the first person she'd ever known who cared more about her than himself, a facet of humanity that, until she'd experienced it, she'd never even known she needed.

She kissed Arkady on the forehead, felt the cracks in her lips graze the rice-paper folds of his skin, and turned the lamp off to go downstairs. The lights in Adam's home office were automatic and switched on as she walked in. There must be, she surmised, some clue here that would help locate him; a hotel booking, a business card. It was imperative that Adam was here for Arkady, but she could find no trace of him. His emails were locked, his social media accounts strangely neglected. Normally he could not go more than a couple of hours without checking in on Facebook or Instagram. With mounting gloom, she fossicked through his desk drawers, his shoulder bag and, finally, his leather jacket, which was draped over the back of his chair.

She checked the side pockets, smoothing out crumpled receipts hoping they would shed some light on where Adam had disappeared to, but nothing: fast-food receipts and petrol station dockets. Adam's clothes were anathema for laundry, his pockets always full of forgotten things; no matter how carefully she checked, there was always a clandestine tissue that covered everything in fine white schmutz. She reached into the inside pocket of Adam's jacket and retrieved a crumpled-up ball of paper, which she folded open and smoothed out on the desk to reveal a photo. Here was Adam, with a schoolgirl.

'Oh.'

Tess could remember the happiest moment in her marriage, in her life, could pinpoint exactly where it was and when. The night they'd brought little Kade home from hospital, she and Adam had placed the baby down in his cot and stood, frozen, side by side and watched him sleep. The gloom was cut by a single beam of light shining in from down the hall and there was no way to tell how much time had passed, and no need to.

Without a word they'd stood over him for hours on end, murmuring to each other about the features inherited from this long-lost relative or the other, marvelling at his tiny fists, the almost invisible rise and fall of his chest. That night, that dreamy half-real stretch of time, was the first in her life she understood what it meant to be alive. There had been many more nights like it, even after the exhaustion, stress and despair of actually raising a child had kicked in, but that was still the one perfect moment she'd had, and was, really, more than she had ever expected from her life. That was the memory that remained perfect and untouched, no matter how many times she took it out to polish it and make sure it still shone.

Tonight, watching her grandfather-in-law fade was a neat bookend to that. Where she'd felt her son's potential growing and stirring while she watched, she could see Arkady slipping away, and the feeling it shook out of her was helplessness.

Once when she was little, before her parents' divorce, her family had spent Christmas at their beach house near Sorrento. It had been a strange, gothic summer, the days stifling and the nights freezing, the air thick and sullen. She remembered her parents as brooding, silent presences that became angry whispers through the thin walls after dark.

Their troubles with money were starting to pick at the edges of their marriage, and while she was too young to understand that, she knew enough to keep out of their way. Her big brother, on the other hand, was old enough to see what was coming, but still young enough to take it out on her, and she'd quickly learned to avoid him as well, and the Chinese burns and dead legs he dealt out whenever he caught her.

Most of the time she hid from him by playing quietly in the garden, where dry fountains and concrete statues were overgrown with ivy, and an ancient tennis court had given over to saltbush and weeds. She'd found a four-leaf clover in a patch growing through the sand and had been absorbed in a search for more, nose pressed to the lawn, and hadn't noticed her brother sneaking up on her until he jumped out, startling her.

'Pete!' she screamed, swiping at him while he laughed and danced back. 'Don't be a dickhead!' His laugh faded into a smile and he held up his hands, signalling a truce.

'Come,' he told her. 'I want to show you something.'

She followed reluctantly as he led her past the tennis courts, to the back of the garden where the property ended with a clump of vines and torn chicken wire. Pete pulled back some vines to reveal a hole cut through the fencing, nodded for her to go ahead, then led her through a forest of stunted gums that gave way to parched saltbush and finally to a path leading to the edge of a cliff, high up on the bluff of Sullivan Bay. There, past the hollows and dunes where the wind blew the sand up into drifted banks, the ground stopped abruptly at a limestone cliff. By inching carefully forward, she could stand and see where the water lapped against the rocks below. Her brother pointed down and urged her to look.

'At what? It's just water.'

'Can't you see it? Look closer.'

She glared suspiciously back at him, then inched a little further out, so that her toes crept over the cliff and held fast like a monkey's, then leaned out over the precipice. Looking straight down into the ocean she could see nothing but blue; but then, as she watched, the turquoise faded into a darker blue, then a blue-grey, then all at once a huge creature, a giant flat arrowhead trailing a dragon's tail, glided up to the surface, turned a lazy circle and dived again. She shrieked and jumped back.

'What was that?'

'Stingray!' Pete boasted knowingly. 'Giant stingray.'

'Wow!' She was thrilled, her mood spiking, her heart rattling her rib cage, the horror of the family holiday forgotten.

'What's it doing there?' She leaned back to try to spot it again. 'What does it want?'

'Oh,' her brother said in the tone of a schoolteacher, moving beside her so they both stood on the edge of the cliff, the skin of their arms brushing, 'they live deep at the bottom of the ocean, and only come in to the shallows to feed.'

'On what?'

'Oh, you know . . .' Pete said airily, 'fish, octopuses . . . little girls!' As he said the last words he grabbed her, suddenly, by each shoulder and shoved her hard out over the void, her neck whiplashing back painfully, his hands holding her half out over the water while he laughed. 'Don't fall in!' he implored her in a singsong voice. 'It's a long way down!' After a few seconds he pulled her back and tossed her to the safety of the ground, then wandered off screaming with laughter, wiping happy tears from his eyes.

She'd stayed crying in the scrub all afternoon. Her bladder had betrayed her while she was dangling out over the water, and she'd stripped her ruined underpants off and buried them in the sand dunes so her parents would never know she'd wet herself and turn their anger onto her. There was shame, but also the start of a lifelong habit of stoicism in the face of others' selfishness. She would be better, always better, than those who let her down. Quietly, without making a fuss about it, she would be stronger, work harder, be nicer than everyone else. She would wage a cold war against the world; icy calm in the face of her brother's, and others', cruelty. For hate's sake, she would become a better person than they could ever be.

And then, decades later, she'd met Arkady, whose heart was just like hers, and watching him fade now, she thought about that day at the bay, the stingray, the horrors that lurk under still water. Every time he opened his eyes, they swivelled around to find her. She could not fathom what his thoughts were, or even if he still had any. His blue eyes had never missed much but they were clouded now, and looking into them as they rolled around and focused on her, she wasn't sure there was anything left behind them at all.

She thought back to one of the first times they'd gone to lunch together, back in the early days when he was taking her through the laborious process of sourcing the parts for the Mitty and Sarah dolls from around the world.

'You know,' she'd told him, 'I used to play with a Sarah doll when I was a little girl. I used to wonder where she'd come from, but I never imagined it was so complicated.'

'Where did you think they came from?' he asked her, his eyes twinkling.

'I'm not sure. I guess I just assumed they'd always been around.'

Arkady laughed then. 'In a way, in a way. I'm not a young man, you know.'

Tess smiled, and asked, 'Why Mitty and Sarah? Where did you get those names?'

Arkady went suddenly quiet, his eyes stopped shining, he grew sombre. 'Well, Mitty is short for mitzvah, which is a Hebrew word that means a good deed for God.'

'And Sarah?'

'Well, Sarah.' Arkady took a long time to answer, chewed his food slowly, had a long swallow of wine. 'Sarah means princess. I knew a girl once, Sarah, and the doll was a little version of her. Little princess Sarah.'

Arkady's breathing, which had been ragged, was now so slow she had to keep lowering her ear to his mouth to assure herself that it hadn't finished altogether. She laid her head next to his lips so they almost touched and she just barely heard him whisper her name.

'I'm here, Arkady,' she said.

Arkady made a wet hacking sound, and his tongue slid out of his mouth as he grappled for the words. 'Adam?' His eyes opened and rolled slowly over to Tess, who didn't know what to say. Arkady saw that she was stricken and let out a sob, then whispered in horror, 'He knows.' A tear rolled down his face. 'He knows. He found out.'

'He found out what? Who found out?' Tess reached out to wipe his tears away and said the first thing that came to her mind that might put him at ease.

'Do you mean Adam? And the money? He doesn't know about the money, Arkady. Nobody does. I won't tell anyone your secret. Nobody knows a thing. It's okay.'

'Oh, thank God.' Arkady smiled, reassured. 'He must never know. We didn't know. It all made sense back then. We weren't to know.' He mumbled something in German, and looked at Tess again. The fog burned off then, and inside the collapsed mess of his face, his eyes burned fiercely. 'You must never tell him. Promise me.'

'I promise.'

'Look after him. He cannot do it by himself. He is not like us. You must protect him.'

Tess had smiled and nodded. 'It's okay, Arkady. Hush. Try to sleep.' The old man sighed and relaxed, and he slept.

Why was she not to tell Adam about the secret trust funds? Did Arkady not trust him to look after it? All that money, buried in all those backyards.

Tess watched Arkady's eyes flittering under their lids, as if he was watching something inside his mind that was a world and half a century away. She wondered what it could possibly be. Arkady had never talked much about his life, but Tess knew enough to know that wherever his mind had taken him, it probably wasn't good.

Downstairs in the study, Tess considered the photo, waiting to see what her reaction would be. She tried Adam's phone again. It rang out once more, landing on voicemail. Suddenly furious, she threw her mobile against the wall in a clumsy overhand lob that bounced it ineffectually back at her and caught her on the toe. She swore, then, snatching up a pillow, pressed it against her face and screamed with anger at her useless fucking husband, at her tender feelings for the old man upstairs that had caught her by surprise, for the self-pity that racked her with sobs. Clutching the pillow she sank to the floor and brought her knees into the fetal position, and cried until she was empty and the pillow was ruined with tears and snot.

Then she got up and walked to the computer, where she wrote Adam an email telling him that his grandfather was dying, and so was their marriage. It was over. She wrote in long and great detail of the mounting stress and woe he caused her and the fact that she thought he was a dud, and had never lived up, not even once, to the most fleeting of her lovers from before their wedding. She poured it all out, like she had to the pillow. When she was done, she read it all back, twice. Her finger hovered over *send* and then, with a click of the mouse, she deleted it.

She washed her face, had something to eat, and by and by was feeling better. A memory came to her, of a time when she and Adam had embarked on a bitter, screaming fight about the possibility that little Kade, their special child, who was developing far too slowly, might actually have some kind of developmental disorder. Adam had been unwilling to listen, she'd been unable to back down, and it was only after he had stormed out of the house that she became aware that Arkady had heard the whole thing, and found her crying alone in the kitchen.

'Oh God.' She was mortified. 'I'm sorry, we didn't know you were here. God, you must think we're idiots, fighting about nothing, after everything you've been through.'

Arkady boomed with laughter. 'Sadness is sadness. It's a strange part of the Australian character that you make suffering a competitive sport. There's a Catholic heart to this country and a Protestant head, which is why, after all these years, you have no idea who you are. It is a particularly Protestant foolishness to think that you can be more miserable than a Russian. Go and make up with your husband; have a good life. Promise you'll do this much for me. Suffering will wait.'

She smiled at the memory and went back upstairs. The room was dark and still, and even before she crossed the room and found his breath and pulse stilled, she understood that Arkady was gone. She closed her eyes, waited a long moment, opened them. Nothing in the room had changed. It seemed strange, that the world still spun on, indifferent.

She pulled back the sheets and slipped into bed beside Arkady's body, lay on her side next to him, pulled the quilt up over them both to make a cubby. Inside, the dark was perfect. She slipped her hand up under his shirt and traced the jagged lines of the surgical scar that bisected his chest, wondered again where, or who, it had come from, realised that now she would never know. The air grew stale, but she lay there with her arms around Arkady until the heat faded, and her fingers met cold skin wherever she moved them. Such a strange feeling, to feel cold skin on a human, but then, this was not Arkady, just the cold carcass of the man. Arkady himself was more than meat, had been something immortal and wonderful, and part of that was part of her now.

But still, she would lie with him for another moment. Whatever she had to do next, it could wait, would wait, as long as she needed it to.

———

One afternoon, the Sonderkommando rebelled. Using shovels and axes, they overpowered their SS captors and stuffed them live into the ovens, and, using gunpowder smuggled in by Jewish slaves from a munitions factory, they tried to blow up the crematoriums. Arkady looked up from his work, startled by the explosions, and left the medical building to investigate. From the entryway he could see smoke billowing from the direction of the gas chambers – more than the usual amount from the chimneys. He could hear machine guns, and the pop pop pop of rifle fire, the snap of grenades. For a moment he hesitated, wondering if he should join the fray. He knew where Dr Pfeiffer kept his pistol. This could be a chance to fight his way out, to take out the handful of Nazis that held them. He could help save the other prisoners. He could save the children.

As he dithered, a young prisoner appeared. He was grizzled and bloody, hit in the stomach, a round which Arkady could see at a glance had gone through and exited the man's back, just missing the spine. It would have been extraordinarily painful but he still held onto an automatic rifle. 'Where are they?' he screamed at Arkady. 'Where are the doctors?'

Arkady looked at the weapon, out across the courtyard, beyond the electric fences to the birch woods. He could run. It wasn't far; it wasn't insurmountable. Out the door and to the left, a sprint past where the firing squads worked, where not that long ago he'd been hung up and tortured, and on to the fence. A tiny stretch of dirt with rough-quarried gravel strewn through it to try to thwart the mud, but which only rendered the road a field of tiny knives that shredded the bare feet of the prisoners.

Two rows of barbed wire threaded through bowed concrete posts, tall and thin, stooped towards him like a broken man, hardly taller, in fact, than a man. Sometimes the electricity went out. If the explosions down the road at Birkenau had taken out the power, then he could slip through and escape.

Of course, that wouldn't be an escape. It would only be a deferral. The posts were not the problem; the problem was what lay beyond them – thousands of billeted soldiers, and beyond that an endless indifferent wasteland, an enemy of infinite might and cruelty. A world that despised what he was, that would never accept him, whichever way the war ended. He was safest here. His home was with Dieter.

He heard himself say, 'That way! They are over there! Go and kill every last one of the sons of bitches,' and he pointed towards the troop canteen. The prisoner looked in the direction Arkady indicated, then back at him. His eyes narrowed and he shoved past Arkady into the surgery. Dieter, who'd come in from the pathology lab to see what the noise was, saw the prisoner, then his gun, and realised that he was about to die.

He stared at the barrel of the rifle, surprised at how large and black the mouth seemed. He'd never been on this end of a gun before. A second passed as the prisoner's finger hovered over the trigger, enough time for Arkady to tackle the boy to the ground. The gun went off as they crashed, and a spray of bullets arced uselessly through the room. The prisoner landed heavily on top of his weapon, but Arkady hadn't realised how weak he'd grown, and even with his gut-wound the boy shrugged him off with an elbow. He reached for his gun again, bringing it up to shoot the Nazi doctor, but Dieter had found a weapon, one of the heavy chair legs that Arkady was slowly turning into toys, and he brought it down across his assailant's face.

It took a few blows to drop the boy, and when he was done, Dieter stood panting over the mess, spattered with blood. He dropped the club and it clattered to the floor.

'I'm sorry,' Dieter heard himself say to the boy. 'Forgive me.' He kneeled to check the boy's vitals. He would not be getting up again.

Arkady crouched down next to him, put a reassuring hand on his shoulder, told him that it was okay. 'He had been through hell, he was crazy, he would have killed you, and then me.'

'Well,' the German said. 'Thank you.'

'I'm not going to let them hurt you, Dieter.' He smiled at his friend and said the thing that he told himself every night while he sat on his bed and worked on his toys: 'This isn't our war. It is nearly over.'

Soon the gunfire stopped as the SS retook the ruined barracks. There was a long pause as they lay the captured Sonderkommandos down on their stomachs on the lawn outside the barracks and, one by one, shot them in the back of the head. The first shots echoed through the camp, but soon they were drowned out by the bustle as everyone, from Dieter's lab to the surviving crematoriums, got back to work.

TEN

The clouds that had threatened to break all through the funeral changed their mind at the last minute, dispersing and drifting off. The mourning party gathered by the graveside, now drenched in too-warm spring sunshine. To Adam, rain would have been preferable to the heat that beat down upon them, making people loosen ties and shed overcoats. He watched Tess's brother, Pete, slip out of his jacket, and was furious to see he was wearing a short-sleeved shirt underneath, sweat stains blooming from his armpits. Adam had never liked Pete, thought him a small-minded bohemian dimwit who confused scruffiness, latent alcoholism and a disagreeable temperament with artistic ability. The fact that the man couldn't find a shirt with cufflinks to wear while they buried Arkady was just too much.

The whole thing was below his grandfather's dignity and, scanning the crowd, for a moment his sombre mood coloured with anger at the pretenders who'd showed up. Then he nodded approvingly at a group of Orthodox Jews who stood in a clump near the grave, suffering stoically under their greatcoats and fur shapkas while their faces reddened and their sidelocks dripped with sweat. These Jews, friends of his grandmother's come to pay their final respects, were his grandfather's type of men, loyal, tough and pious, and he was touched that so many who knew his grandma from so long ago had come.

The rest of these people, on the other hand, they could go fuck themselves. The graveyard was packed with those who were clearly only paying lip-service to his grandfather. They were there not because of who he was or what he had achieved, but, rather, because of what he had done for them. Paunchy, pale businessmen stood jammed between headstones, surreptitiously checking their phones, while a procession of representatives from the slew of charities that Arkady had supported filed in, made sure they were seen, then disappeared.

Adam stood at the grave next to his wife, who was receiving mourners as they shuffled up, took her hand, murmured a few words and moved on. He glanced down at the coffin and felt a cold, sharp stab of grief tear through him; he looked away, swallowed hard. He would not cry, not here. 'Just look at all these fucking imposters,' he muttered.

Tess looked at him, appalled. 'Behave yourself, Adam,' she

hissed. 'You're not the only one who's upset.'

Her voice snagged on the last word, and she fished a tissue out of her sleeve to wipe her eyes. Adam was taken aback. As a rule, Tess didn't let her emotions get the better of her.

'What, Tess?' he asked. 'Am I supposed to be nice to these people, these . . .' he searched for the word, '*parasites*, who feed off my family my whole life, longer than my whole life, taking advantage of Grandpa's good nature, knowing that because of the things he went through, he would help anybody who said they needed help? Look around you: these people, too lazy to work, have come for one last feed and to see if they can squeeze anything out of the old man.' His voice was rising now, he could hear the hoarse edge as the anger crept in, but he didn't care. 'He would —'

Tess grabbed him by the arm, cutting him off, her nails digging in hard through the Italian wool of his suit. 'Adam! Get a grip; this isn't the time.'

'Why not? When is there going to be a better time? Grandpa would be rolling around in that box if he knew that half the people turning up to his funeral are . . .' here he pointed in turn at Pete and the closest woman, 'faggots and sluts and . . .'

Tess stopped him with a look and after a long, careful pause said, very quietly, 'And when did you ever have a problem with sluts, Adam?'

'Huh?'

'Never mind.' Tess was already walking off, drying her eyes; she had a funeral to work.

Adam stared after her. She was impossible to read, and he pondered the fact that, somehow, after so long, he was no closer to working her out. One moment he thought he knew her like his own reflection, but then she would turn, would say or do something to surprise him, and he would realise he barely knew his wife at all.

Adam felt that he was supposed to chase after her, offer her more sympathy, but the procession of mourners kept coming, and he stood, smiling grimly, as punter after punter gave him their condolences. As the sun crept higher, his smile grew more strained, his temper worse with each supplicant. None of these people knew what he was going through, none of them really cared. They were sad, not because they had lost Arkady, but because they had lost his money. He half recognised some of the faces in the endless stream from when he was a child. None of them, he realised, were friends. There was nobody here that Grandpa would call for coffee and a chat; just cogs in some great commercial machine that he had kept running with his own sweat and blood. This realisation filled Adam with sorrow, even more than the fact of the coffin at his feet. Making an excuse, he ducked away to compose himself.

He only returned as the crowd gathered at the graveside for the prayers. The coffin was lowered into the grave, in a space Arkady had bought decades ago next to his wife's. His-and-hers burial plots had been the first purchases he'd made for him and Rachel after their wedding bands and their house. When Rachel's friends had teased him about his Russian fatalism, he had held up his hand in a mocking Boy Scout salute and said,

'Always be prepared.'

A priest led the mourning prayer, and gave a eulogy that was heavy on praise for Arkady's achievements and light on religion. In the past, Arkady had made it clear that he wanted God as far away from his death as possible. Still, despite his strict instructions not to bring the Bible into it, the priest broke into his theological boilerplate, reciting the parables you heard at every funeral – Jerusalem and Jericho, the Levite, the Samaritan.

Adam stood sullen, brooding, his attention drifting from his annoyance at the priest fucking up his grandfather's very simple burial wishes to the realisation that the final years of Arkady's life must have been bitterly lonely. Why hadn't Adam spent more time with him? At the end of the prayers, the mourners lined up in rows on either side of the grave, and Arkady's relatives took their places.

In deference to Rachel, even though they were not to be buried in a Jewish cemetery, they would follow the tradition that all the family would help shovel earth onto the coffin, and as the most senior mourner, the job first went to Tess's father, Trevor. *This is bullshit*, thought Adam as Trevor Coughlin shuffled to the front. Poor Trevor, fat, bald, ineffectual Trev, who had never worked a day in his life, who had never provided for his family, who hadn't shouldered the burden of history the way that Arkady had, who didn't care half as much for the old man as Adam had – that he should be the first to throw the dirt was wrong, and his grandfather would never have allowed it had he been alive. Trev sunk the shovel in and flipped a smattering of dirt.

'Fucking pathetic,' Adam muttered under his breath, then found himself springing into action, moving towards the mound of dirt. One hand closed around the handle of the shovel, the other brushing the startled Trev away so he stumbled back and, for one awful moment, looked like he would topple over into the grave, but he righted himself just in time. Adam was already digging, a solid, satisfying shovelful of dirt, which he hefted up and onto the coffin. He watched it thump, full of force and weighty with feeling, on the oak, then went back in for another heaping of earth. Two, three, four shovelfuls, enjoying the feeling, the twinge in his muscles, the satisfaction of weight and movement, until the pile of dirt was gone and his shoulders ached and clicked with the heaving. He stopped, panting, and handed the shovel to the next in line, and then was striding off, oblivious to the people who shifted to get out of his way.

———

Tess caught up with Adam in the car park, where he was pacing and checking his watch. She walked up behind him.

'Adam, what's going on?'

Adam looked at her, looked at his SUV, pointed at the hearse, which was double-parked in the middle of the lot.

'The hearse is blocking me in.' He shrugged. 'Have to wait for them to leave.'

'No, I mean, where are you going? What are you doing? What's wrong with you?'

Adam turned to look at her, surprised. 'What do you mean?'

She stopped for a minute, frustrated, not even sure where to begin, landing, in the end, on: 'You just walked out of your grandfather's funeral!'

Adam started yelling. 'That is not my grandfather's funeral!' he hollered, pointing up the hill. 'My grandfather was a hero. He deserved a hero's funeral, not a fucking day in the park.'

Tess had grown up in a family that, deformed by wealth and artistic ambition, had used histrionics as currency. As the youngest daughter, she'd learned that she would never out-shriek or out-weep her elder siblings and parents, so she had learned to wrap her anger in calm, softly spoken couplets. She knew that the way to hurt someone bearing down on you with self-righteous anger was to sideswipe them with absolute, ice-cold calm.

'How would you know?' Tess asked, coolly. 'Did you even know him?'

Adam's jaw set hard and he took a heavy step towards his wife. 'How fucking dare you,' he growled.

'How fucking dare you!' Tess stepped forward and jabbed him in the chest. 'Where the fuck were you? Where have you been? You knew he was dying.'

'I was busy . . . I had – business.'

'You should have been there.'

'But . . .'

'You should have been there.' Her composure slipped, and she was crying now, the tears hot down her face. Mourners were starting to file out of the cemetery gate and stopped when they saw the fight in progress, not able to leave without going past the couple and the conflict. Tess didn't care, not at all, not any more. 'You should have been there. I was there. I was there when you should have been.'

She could see Adam gearing up to fight her, taking a deep breath to begin shouting, and she cut him off. Something had changed inside her, crystallised. She wasn't even angry any more, just resigned.

'But then you disappear off to Asia with God knows who, right when Arkady needs you the most, and you're not there when he dies because, presumably, you were right in the middle of someone, and that's not something I will forgive, ever, because that's not something he would forgive.'

Everything seemed very clear to Tess now. She was figuring out, as she stood in the car park and Adam's fumbling excuses flew by her unheard, that all the anger and disappointment she'd repressed through the years was still inside her, as well as a limitless well of something that, as it burned away whatever feelings she still held for Adam, she recognised as ambition, as the call of destiny. She held up one hand to silence her husband, and spoke, loud and clear enough for the mourners nearby to hear. 'I loved Arkady. He meant more to me than you ever did, but he loved you, and you let him down, and it's patently fucking clear that you'll never be half the man he was. This is done.'

More mourners were around her, a circle of black suits topped with concerned faces, and a babble of sympathetic noises. Tess pushed through them and then she was running, through the car park and onto the street, and ignoring the voices calling after her. She knew that she should feel ashamed but only felt scorched and broken and free.

She'd left her purse and her phone in Adam's car so she walked home, losing her heels after the first kilometre or so and walking barefoot on the nature strips where she could, hot-footing it across the burning footpath when she couldn't. She was happy to walk; it gave her time to think. By the time she made it home she'd carefully re-evaluated her life, turning over each item and making a snap judgement. The friends she'd just disgraced Adam in front of could go; she didn't need them. The respect of the business community, gone; good riddance, she'd never been able to stand them, and she was sure the feeling was mutual. There was nobody left to pretend to be happy for; Adam was on his own. Everything was burned to the ground, and that was fine and good. There was nothing to hang around for – she would take the money Arkady had stashed away, then take Kade and go far away, back to New York, raise her son as a good man a world away from his shitkicker father. The walk home was long and she used the hours to decide what to take, and how to explain to Kade, who'd thrown a tantrum before the funeral and stayed home with a sitter, that they were going on a holiday, just the two of them. The sun was going down by the time she returned, and she was ready.

She packed their suitcases, taking just bare essentials, and was wheeling them out the door when the landline started ringing, and she found out, to her amazement, that her husband had somehow managed to ruin everything, one last time.

———

In the end the Nazis destroyed the crematoriums themselves. The war was lost, and, like men sobering up, they were shying away from what they'd done when they were drunk on cruelty. Everywhere Arkady looked they were destroying evidence. They were burning files by the building-full, driving thousands of prisoners at a time on forced marches through the freezing night in a panicked effort to escape the looming Russian justice. Mengele had slipped out quietly, taking some of his research with him, but most of it abandoned, destroyed, a final insult to all the people he'd killed in his deranged experiments. Before long, the rest of the Nazis – soldiers, bureaucrats, doctors – followed, as their hellish machine collapsed and the parts scattered. Soon only a few stragglers remained to tie up loose ends.

From inside Dieter's office, above the howl of the blizzard, Arkady and his companion listened to the symphony of screaming, gunshots and heavy boots running helter-skelter.

'This doesn't mean the end for you, Dieter,' Arkady urged. 'You are a good man; you were acting on orders. The Russians will understand. I will speak to them. I will vouch for you.'

Dieter smiled, sad, but resigned. 'Thank you, Arkady. I know you mean well, but what we've done here is . . . It would be hard to explain.'

'Well, then you run! Take a car from the motor pool and drive west, drive until you reach Switzerland. Plead asylum. I'll come with you; we'll escape together.' Arkady went to Dieter's desk and, after a moment's search, located a map, spread it out, traced a road with a finger. 'Here, Dieter, come look.'

Dieter did not humour the notion of the map. Instead, he waited a long, long minute, then spoke carefully. 'Arkady. I ordered that you be arrested and taken to the labs. It's my fault you were tortured.'

Standing behind him, Dieter saw Arkady grip the table and his knuckles whiten, the muscles in his back tense, the angry red flush bloom up his neck. The carotid artery in the side of his neck, the one that fed the brain, bulged with the pressure.

'Why?' he said softly, after a pause. 'Why would you tell me that?'

'Because I want you to know that I am sorry. That I never wanted to hurt you.' He spoke softly as he walked up behind Arkady and laid a gentle hand on his shoulder. 'Because there is no other way.'

The needle slid into Arkady's neck and Dieter's thumb plunged the syringe. Arkady turned, one hand grasping his neck, eyes bulging and glassy. He charged at Dieter, catching him and bringing him to the floor, but the fight was over before it began. There'd been enough of the chemical in the injection to kill five men – Dieter wasn't taking any chances. He got Arkady in a headlock and held him while he bucked and convulsed, until he no longer frothed at the mouth, until long after his breathing had stopped. When he was sure the other man was dead, Dieter stood up, and started moving. He had a lot of work to do, and not much time.

First, he swapped the files he kept on Arkady Kulakov, both as a Sonderkommando and a test subject, with the ones he'd doctored with his own photo and dental records. He tore up the originals, put them in a wastepaper basket, splashed rubbing alcohol on them and then burned them to ash.

He lit another match to partially burn the doctored records, to make it look like he had tried to destroy the files and failed. As he singed the edges, it reminded him of watching Arkady make a treasure map out of paper and old coffee, for his children. A tear welled up in each eye but he wiped them away, pushed the rest down. No time for that, not now, not ever.

Next, he stripped to the waist and, taking the automatic tattoo gun in his right hand, he carved a shaky serial number into the forearm of his left. With a pair of clippers, he shaved his head in front of the mirror. There was the matter of his blood-group tattoo, black letters under his arm that were given to all SS, in case they needed a transfusion while unconscious. If the Allies found that tattoo, it was over for him, so he upturned a vial of caustic acid across it. He was unprepared for the pain, and his fingers slipped, spilling the rest of the vial across his ribs and back. Gasping, he found a neutralising agent and doused himself with it, then, gritting his teeth, examined the damage in the mirror. The skin down his arms and shoulder blade on the left side were scorched red, and already starting to peel. It would not heal pretty, but he needn't worry about his SS tattoo.

Then, taking a deep breath and a scalpel, he made a deep incision in his chest over his heart, to match the one he'd given Arkady. More rubbing alcohol on the wound, then a little ash from the trashcan rubbed into it. He didn't want infection, but he needed it to scar. Suturing the wound was harder than he'd anticipated; he got it done, although by the end his hands were shaking badly from the pain and his fingers could barely manage the buttons on the old striped prisoner's uniform he'd been saving for the occasion.

Finally, when he couldn't put it off any longer, he kneeled down next to Arkady and undressed him. He hesitated for a minute over whether to leave Arkady his Rolex, but decided he might need it for a bribe, and slipped it into a pocket. Rigor mortis was on its way, so he struggled to shuck him out of his trousers and shirt. 'Faster,' Dieter told himself. 'You must move faster.' Once his friend was naked, he used a scalpel to remove the skin with Arkady's serial number, then dressed Arkady's body in his own SS uniform.

The two men had been almost exactly the same size, once upon a time, but the Nazi uniform swallowed Arkady whole, his shrunken arms and legs just sticks under the wool and leather. Nothing to be done about that now.

He fetched a beaker of acid and carefully, one by one, dipped Arkady's fingers into it to remove the prints, wrinkling his nose at the smell. Once he was satisfied the other man couldn't be identified, he fired a single shot into Arkady's temple, and wrapped the dead man's fingers around its grip. He stood back, observed the scene, made sure he'd forgotten nothing, tried to look at it from a Red Army soldier's point of view. Here was just another Nazi, taking the easy way out. Now, apart from the Nazi doctors fleeing across Europe, there would be no witnesses. In the weeks leading up to this, Dieter had been careful to liquidate any adults in the camps who could identify him.

The children, those who were left, would never know who he had been, just another monster in a white coat.

Then, a little gasoline about the place, a match to light the lab up, and out into the snow, moving as quick as his wounds allowed to beat the Russian tanks he could hear rolling in. The Red Army, at the end of this war where all pretension of civility had been used up long ago, was marching into the camp, this place where humanity had reached its nadir. It was a collision that did not go well for the Germans who hadn't been smart enough to flee or kill themselves, as they were rounded up by the Russians and executed. There would be no Geneva for them.

The snow was thick enough that he could scurry from building to building in relative safety. Out in the blizzard, he heard a German screaming, and a deep Russian voice, full of humour. 'Don't waste a bullet on this one. Do him slow.' Dieter, who'd practised his Russian every night with Arkady, understood all too well. He froze, moved forward a little, froze again. Moving slowly, carefully, wrapped in itching prisoner's stripes and a greatcoat, he crawled through the night to reach the smoking ruins of Birkenau.

There he burrowed, like a roach, under the burning brick, and once he was deep enough he lay there through the night, shivering, listening to the hollering of Red Army squads who had discovered caches of food and alcohol and were distributing them among the prisoners. On the breeze, laughter and singing reached him as men and women were nourished with food and kindness for the first time in years.

The night was long, a babble of despair and joy, the sound of a humanity stretched like a rubber band to breaking point snapping back into shape. The soldiers didn't find him until the morning, when the sun rose. A Russian solider, huge, reeling from booze and the horrors he'd seen and committed through the night, heaved a lump of concrete off Dieter and uncovered him. Dieter opened his eyes and saw, silhouetted against the rising sun, the man's greatcoat, the rifle across his back, the shapka on his head.

'Hey!' he called to his comrades. 'Hey! There's a survivor here. He's alive! I think he might live!'

And Dieter, moving feebly, crawled up through the rubble and spoke in Russian. '*Da*,' he croaked. 'Yes, I will live.'

ELEVEN

After the funeral, and the wake, not being able to get onto Tess and not knowing what else to do, Adam had gone into the office to be alone as he'd given everyone the day off to mark his grandfather's passing. He slumped heavily into his office chair and after a moment's consideration fetched a bottle of vodka from the drinks cabinet he'd put in after he'd started watching *Mad Men* and wanted to introduce a touch of sophistication to his office. He sat in the dark, alone with his thoughts, drinking. Time passed, and when the bottle ran out, he fetched another. He had dozed off until the phone rang and he startled awake.

'Mitty & Sarah,' he croaked into the phone. 'How can I help you?'

'I want to talk to the owner.' The voice was an older woman, twangy and high with outrage, the broken bowstring of an inconvenienced Australian.

Adam, slow with drink, paused for a moment before answering. 'Why?'

'I want to complain.'

'Oh,' Adam grunted in relief. 'Good. Go on then.'

'For you people to say that you are an Australian company, when all you've been doing is lying to us for years and making your toys overseas and . . .'

Adam cut in, tired, with the scripted response he normally used. 'Some of our products are manufactured overseas, yes, but all of our toys are designed according to traditional methods since we were founded by my grandfather . . .' The word stuck in his throat, and suddenly his eyes were moist and his throat thick. He moved the phone away from his ear and stared blankly at it for a moment, the voice still yammering, furious and tinny. He looked down, brought it back to his ear and picked up the thread. '. . . So if you think I'm ever going to buy one more toy off you, you can think again, and what's more it's disgraceful, just disgraceful, that you represent yourself as a proud Australian company when you are probably just a bunch of Chinese and . . .' Adam slowly, quietly, put the phone down and let the lady talk into the void.

Now his mobile was ringing. It was Tess, and for a moment his heart surged with hope that she'd forgiven him. When he picked up the phone, though, her voice was calm, icily so. 'Adam, what the fuck have you done?'

'Nothing . . .' he protested, wondering how she'd possibly heard that conversation. Adam thought hard, then pivoted. 'I mean . . . What do you mean, what have I done? Specifically, I mean.'

'Do you have any idea what happened to your little party in Jakarta?'

'What?'

Tess's voice was cold with rage. 'You moved our business, our flagship fucking product, to some fucking sweatshop in fucking Indonesia, which has just exploded and taken out half a fucking orphanage.'

It was all over the news. The factory in Jakarta he'd hired to take over production of the Mitty and Sarah dolls had been pulling 24-hour shifts to meet demand, and a floor manager, stressed out and overtired, had mixed volatile chemicals in the wrong order. The explosion had taken out the production deck and all the workers with it. The fire had barbecued the entire workforce before spreading into neighbouring factories. Human rights investigators were crawling through the ruins which were already thick with news crews. Flicking through the TV channels, he found the same scene over and over, the same footage shot from half a dozen angles, of burned and mangled corpses piled together in a smouldering human grease trap. Here and there among the bodies was a miraculously pre-served Sarah doll, slightly charred, but smiling. Adam felt a little proud that, even after the explosion, the quality of the dolls was undiminished. He hit the pause function on the remote control, and the broadcast froze. The room seemed too quiet now, so he turned on the radio, the golden oldies station. Good tunes. They didn't make them like they used to. He flicked some switches, and piped the radio through the PA in the warehouse.

Taking the bottle of vodka, he wandered out to the warehouse and staggered up and down the aisles, swigging from the bottle and singing along with Crowded House. 'Hey now, hey now.' In the next room he could hear his mobile going off, and all the extensions in the office, but he just sang louder to drown them out. 'Hey now, hey now. Don't dream it's over.'

His life was over. The company, certainly, was over; everything his grandfather had built was now forfeit. Adam had not only fucked up the company, but he'd shamed his grandpa, just hours after he'd buried him. All around him, invisible in the air, laying down to rest inside the internet for all of eternity, were pictures of smiling Mitty and Sarah dolls piled up next to burned women and children. The bottle was empty now, and he threw it overarm, sent it sailing out into the darkness of the warehouse as far as he could, listening to the satisfying, clean shattering noise. *Hey now, hey now.*

He mounted the stairs to the Kindergarten one by one, stopping to steady himself on the rail. When he got to the top, he clambered over the guardrail, to where dusty crates of discontinued lines and one-off prototypes were stacked. The boxes weren't stored in any particular order, and Adam tripped more than once making his way to the edge of the platform. He crawled to the precipice, the factory floor fifteen metres below, then stood, contemplating the drop. It would be easy, the flopping forward, the sailing through the air, the crack of skull as he hit the concrete, the splat of brains. For a minute he luxuriated in the fantasy, in Tess hearing the news and falling to pieces, begging God for her husband back, sorry for hassling him over a few indiscretions and misjudgements.

He fell then, but backwards, into the Kindergarten, and lay on his back laughing. There was a centimetre of dust caked on the floor, and he waved his arms and legs to make the shape of an angel. He reached across to a nearby crate to pull himself up but the wood was old and brittle and he accidentally ripped the side clean off, then swore as an avalanche of toys spilled out, squeaking and rattling around him. A toy monkey marched towards his head, banging its cymbals together, and he sat up to grab it, ripping it apart with his hands and hurling the two halves out into the void.

'Shutup,' he slurred. He'd always hated that monkey. As a kid he'd sometimes wake up from a nightmare and see it staring at him from the top of his toy chest, with its beady little eyes, and he would have to drum up the courage to slip out of bed and turn it around. He realised that the crate he'd ripped open must be decades old, shipped from warehouse to warehouse as the company grew, and it was full of stock samples from the seventies and eighties, all of which were toys he'd grown up with.

Slowly, he picked through the crate, and echoes from childhood came back to him as his fingers wrapped around each of the toys. Old memories stirred in his muscles. Adam was distracted now, calm; suicidal intent forgotten as he started to play.

He recalled being given each toy by his grandfather during their summers together in Europe, a new scene springing to mind the second he touched one of them. He picked up and briefly played with a Rubik's cube, a *Ghostbusters* figurine, a *Ninja Turtle* doll, and he thought of the hundreds of hours he'd spent staging elaborate battles between Donatello and the Foot Soldiers.

He remembered the fantasy worlds he used to build for these toys to live in. He would fill all the hours at home – his dad too busy to play, and no friends his own age because of the summers spent treasure-hunting in Europe with Arkady – planning commando raids behind enemy lines, just him and his toy soldiers. In these games, he would imagine himself as his grandfather during the war, and make long complicated lists of what kind of provisions they would need to escape occupied Europe: how many loaves of bread and jars of sauerkraut, how many bullets for his weapons, how many knives for Nazi throats.

Getting on his hands and knees and burrowing further into the crate, he found a handful of fur and the second he touched it he knew what it was, a Cheburashka. His grandfather had given him one on a trip behind the Iron Curtain many years ago, and Adam had fallen deeply in love with it, dragging it everywhere with him until the fur had grown mangy, and it had been patched up time and again.

Cheburashka was a stuffed toy, a bear of sorts, with big round ears, and a soft belly. He'd known nothing about the strange creature, but he'd loved it to bits and made up an elaborate backstory for it. Years later he'd learned that it was a mainstay of the Soviet childhood, had come with songs and cartoons and friends and a mythology he completely missed. As an adult he'd looked into picking up the intellectual property in Australia and found that it had become something of a cult item in former Soviet countries, the original dolls fetching huge sums on eBay, and he'd regretted not keeping his. After making the mistake of taking it with him to a school camp he'd had the shit kicked out of him by some kids for carrying around a doll, and on returning home he'd thrown it, tearfully, in the bin.

Here now, though, was Cheburashka, back from the grave, hand of God in play. Adam held it, stroking the stiff, dusty fur of its ears. The feel of the fur brought a memory back to him, the day he'd been given the doll, him sitting rapt on an office floor, stroking the toy's big flopping ears, while in the background Arkady argued with some looming adult in German, growing more and more heated, until finally, the fight apparently won, he stopped yelling, and Adam looked up to see his grandfather closing an attaché case with a satisfying clunk. Before the lid was shut, Adam caught a glimpse of the stacks of bills that filled the case, all different sizes, all different colours, just like Monopoly money.

Every time they'd gone on a trip to Europe, Arkady had had one or two of those meetings, always in a European language, always somewhere dark and quiet, and never in the bright, fun toy stores Adam preferred to visit. One time he'd asked his grandfather about these special visits, and the old man had made him promise never to speak of them to anyone but him. He'd bought him the Cheburashka as a reward for keeping silent.

Getting up, Adam walked back, clambered over the guardrail, and returned to his office. He was well past debilitated now, in the eye of the drinking binge, having passed through all visible signs of intoxication and no longer showing symptoms, the perfect alcoholic clarity. He sat in the desk chair stroking the Cheburashka.

On the television, the image was still paused on a close-up of a little girl's mangled hand, the fingers burned and fused together around a Sarah doll, the doll with its hair burned off but otherwise miraculously untouched. In its own tiny hand, the Sarah doll was clutching the little 'An Aussie Company' green and gold flags he'd ordered them to be packaged with.

Adam looked at the screen, and then back at the Cheburashka, with its matted and clumped fur, then at the screen again, at the footage of the corpses. Deep in his brain, boozy synapses rumbled to life. He went to the drinks cabinet and rummaged around until he found a little Australian flag cocktail umbrella, which he threaded into the Cheburashka's little hand.

Holding it up to the light he saw that he'd had an idea, a little blurry, but one that would save the company and his marriage all at the same time, and muttered a silent prayer of thanks to his grandfather, who was still looking out for him from another world.

TWELVE

Then there was the fearful crawl across Europe, by foot and in the back of trucks, as he was passed from the Russians to the Americans, through Germany and France. A truck to Marseille across a bombed and broken country, a night boat through the Pyrenees, and finally the months in Lisbon, where he found a room below a tavern that was above the law, and beyond the conflict that had ruined the world.

Somehow, when all else was starvation and snow on stone, here the winter was warm. It was a place steeped in watery sunshine and sardines, salted cod, tart wine from stone jugs, more than he had imagined was left in Europe. Meat was available as well, despite the protestations of his landlady, who claimed fresh meat was as rare as kindness these days. At least, until he produced enough money and she brought him a great slab of marbled steak, fried in the German style with a glorious dab of wholegrain mustard on the side. His body thrilled as she placed it in front of him and the scent filled him up, until he cut into it and the blood welled up from the raw heart of the meal, the way it did on a surgical incision, and he was suddenly ill. He gave up on eating, concentrated on his wine instead, and slipped the steak to the whipped but optimistic housedog that lurked under the table.

In the cantina above his room he found that he could, for the first time in memory, relax, as long as his back was to the wall and his eye was on everyone entering the bar. He'd stopped panicking every time he saw an Allied uniform, or a face that could have been familiar, passing by on the street. He spent the days drinking until it got dark enough to walk the streets without fear, and he was amazed that the world still spun. Civilisation went on the way it always had, like it always would, as if it couldn't be snuffed out overnight. How surreal to walk on cobblestones and under archways that hadn't known artillery shells or fire-bombing, to see a teenage girl lean out of a second-floor window to flirt with her boyfriend, or to hear two Portuguese men arguing over the price of a fish in their weird slippery language. Elsewhere in Europe the slaughter hadn't yet stopped. Here it was as if it had never started.

It took a few months to procure the papers he needed to follow Mengele to Brazil, and then at the last minute they fell through, leaving him stranded on a transit visa in London, unsure how to proceed. He flailed about, wasting a small fortune on useless bribes and false hopes from unscrupulous fixers, until finally one gave him a choice: America, Canada, Australia. 'Canada,' he said, half jokingly, 'I hear that the life is good there.' No, not Canada, too close to America; he would never be able to relax living next to that country of avenging evangelists that was, as far as he could tell, populated entirely by sharply tailored soldiers with clean teeth who survived on prayer and chocolate and cigarettes.

He knew nothing about Australia, but Australia it would have to be. On the boat over he stayed in his cabin as much as he could, reading books in English, expanding his vocabulary, getting his story straight. He worked late into the night rehearsing the conversation he would have with immigration officials when he arrived, preparing responses for every conceivable conversational cul-de-sac and practising them until they were perfect. He experimented with flattening out his English to make it more Russian. By the time he docked in Melbourne his accent sounded, to the bored customs officer who processed him, generically European, like an Englishman who had spent too long abroad.

The customs officer took the papers Dieter had bought at great cost and flicked through them frowning.

'Name?'

'Arkady Kulakov.'

'Age?'

'Twenty-three.'

'Profession?

'Doctor. I am a doctor.'

'Not any more you're not.' The man marked the papers and handed them back to Dieter. 'Welcome to Australia.'

He felt keenly the weirdness of this place. The buildings looked like home; the cool blue cobblestones underfoot made his shoes ring with nostalgic notes. The sunlight here was different, though, starker somehow, and it hit the eyes at a different angle. The air too hot, too dry, it tore at his lungs while he fumbled to loosen his tie. Gentle waves pushed at the shore behind him, and ahead the streets stretched out, endless and foreign. Seagulls wheeled and cried overhead, banking gracefully, turning to keep one eye on the litter that piled up, the divine opportunists who inherited the beaches and rubbish dumps of the world.

Across the road from the docks, a fat man sweating under his hat clocked Dieter standing uncertainly on the brink of his new life, and waddled over to him.

'Are you lost?' the man asked him in German, which sent a jolt of pure fear through Dieter. He ignored the question, making a show of being baffled by the language. The stranger tried again, same question, but the German syllables softened into songful Yiddish. Again, Dieter looked confused, then responded:

'*Ruski?*'

'*Da, nemnoga, angliyskiy?*'

'Yes,' said Dieter, 'Just a little.'

The man had an offer for him, a room in a boarding house nearby, and a job in a factory adjoining it where war had made workers scarce. 'It's not glamorous, but I'd say it's a damn sight better than whatever you're used to.' His eyes flickered from Dieter's face to his jacket, which was worn and grimy despite a long campaign to keep it clean on the journey over. 'Life will be easier now, friend. A new set of troubles begins, but the worst is over.'

He offered Dieter a card for a bakery, a line-drawn sketch of a bagel, a name and an address.

'Thank you.'

The man smiled, showing a mouth full of teeth, rotten where gold caps had been yanked out. '*Nichivo*. We must look out for each other.'

The bagel man clapped a fraternal hand on Dieter's shoulder and moved on, approaching more stragglers from the boat who stood in uncertain clumps. Dieter studied the card for a moment, and, for lack of a better idea, approached a yellow cab that was idling by the road, the driver leaning against the bonnet, smoking a pipe.

The driver kept the pipe going as they climbed into the vehicle, so Dieter slid the window down, enjoying the breeze as the car wended down the beach road, making several turns before rolling up Chapel Street. Through the window Dieter stared at the Australians passing by, unnerved by the size of them, huge features, huge guts, ruddy and sweaty like they'd all just been disgorged from a sauna. From the back of this taxi, it seemed like the whole country was forever in a Bavarian beer garden, on the first day of summer, everyone drunk and jolly and sunburned by the afternoon.

He looked up and caught the driver watching him in the rear-view mirror, his wide blue eyes framed in the glass.

'You look like you've been in the wars,' he offered.

Dieter wasn't familiar with the expression, and agreed. 'Yes. I was in the wars.'

'No shit? That must've been rough.'

'Rough, yes. Terrible thing.'

'Gotta lotta mates who went over there, whole lot less who came back.'

'Yes.' Dieter's new proficiency in English was failing him. 'It went badly for us all.'

'Is it true what the papers are saying about Poland?'

'I do not want to talk about it.'

'Fair'nuff.' The driver shrugged. 'So you over here for family?'

'No, there is nobody. Just me.'

The driver took the hint, turned back to the road.

The cab dropped him off outside a block of flats next to a factory on Chapel Street. Across the road, labourers in shirts and suspenders were loading crates of jam into a truck. Dieter climbed out of the cab, retrieved his suitcase from the boot and carefully counted out the pennies to the cab driver.

It took him a few minutes to find the right place. A sea of pedestrians parted around him as he stood in the middle of the footpath. The scent of South Yarra assailed his nose: the funk of horses as they clipped by dragging carts filled with produce up and down the road, bread baking and bacon frying, and above it all the heady, yeasty fug of alcohol that permeated the whole strange city.

Dieter paid for three months' rent in advance and the land-lady showed him up to his room, handed him the keys, told him, 'If you need anything, Mr Kulakov, I'm just downstairs,' then left him alone. The room was cramped and stuffy with the shutters closed, but when he threw them open the cacophony and light of the street crashed into the room. Nobody could see into the room, but just to be safe, Dieter closed them again.

A striped horsehair blanket lay at the foot of the bed. He picked it up and held it to his nose. It smelled clean. He placed his luggage on the bed and opened the lock, and the over-stuffed suitcase sprung open, with all the things he'd saved from Auschwitz. A doll named Sarah, rough-carved from wood and dressed in rags, stared up at him. He picked it up, held it for a moment, then tossed it across the room, where it landed with an ugly wooden clatter. Dieter would not need it for a while.

He spilled the contents of the suitcase onto the floor, then, feeling around carefully at the bottom of it, he found the release for the false bottom, sprang it, and took stock. Most of the gold he'd set out with was gone, frittered away on too-expensive bribes at borders and checkpoints, or extortionate fees for the smugglers and forgers who'd sold him the doc-uments he needed to get here. Terrified of getting caught with too much of the fortune he'd earned from Auschwitz, he'd spent the months leading up to the liberation salting the money away with friends in industry and banks. Now it was hidden across Europe, in vaults and companies that had grown rich on slave labour. One day he would go back to reclaim the money he'd had to leave behind, but first he would start a new life, here where nobody would think to look for him. This new country was good at forgetting, knew how to keep a secret, and would help him build a careful chrysalis to protect him from the things he'd done.

There would be a year spent as a factory worker, carving little wooden toys alone in his room at night, like he'd watched Arkady do for all those months they'd spent together. When the toys were passable, he started to sell them. Sometimes, he would play up his European charms to tap into the pretension of a Melbourne that was slowly becoming, under the weight of waves and waves of post-war immigration, more cosmopolitan. Other times, he would tell Arkady's sad story of how he carved toys in the concentration camps to provoke sympathetic fingers to open wallets. The toys, he knew, weren't good product, but he was, and he knew what people wanted to hear. He wasn't selling toys; he was selling an idea of lost civilisation to homesick Europeans stuck at the end of the world.

Soon he would buy a shopfront, then a workshop, and then a factory. He would pay for each expansion of his business with some of the gold he'd stolen from Auschwitz, discreetly sold a little at a time over the years to avoid raising suspicion.

Each year he grew richer, and each year it grew harder to live with the mounting past. To keep it from crushing him, he would start drinking, and when that stopped working, he would start going to a synagogue near his first factory, an unobtrusive little building that was serene and solemn and gave no clue to the blinding heat and clattering trams outside. He would stand up the back of the service, swaying drunkenly a little. He liked the sermons, liked listening to the musical lilt of the Yiddish, which somehow helped his homesickness over his dead Europe, and made his guilt paw and tear at him, a pleasant, flagellant kind of ache, at the same time. Best of all he liked the prayers, the chants, the cantillations; the melody and the impenetrable Hebrew would wash over him and empty his mind for a while.

One day, leaving the temple, he bumped into Rachel, a young Polish Jew who walked with a limp because she'd been crippled in the camps, and who worked as a cantor for the synagogue. Soon they would fall in love and raise a family, and when she died young because of the things the Nazis had done to her all those years ago, nearly everything he lived for would go with her, everything except his work.

Three decades would pass and, with his Adam, his sweet, idiot grandson, along to complete his disguise as a kindly Russian expat, he would travel back to Europe and track down all his old comrades who had come out of hiding, now working as doctors or executives for companies producing computers and luxury cars. Retrieving the money he'd hidden with them, laundering it through his toy company, he would expand and cement his wealth, and carve an unassailable empire for himself. He would be famous as a toymaker, never having made more than a handful of toys. His real trade he would carry with him to the grave.

That would take time, though, and for now, on his first day in Australia, Dieter picked up a handful of gold teeth, which gleamed darkly in his palm, even in the gloom. It wasn't much, but if he found the right people to help, if he was careful, there was enough: more than enough to start again.

———

Tess wasn't sure exactly how Adam had managed, in the few days she wasn't watching over him, to engineer an international humanitarian disaster with her fingerprints all over it, but there you go. The factory that he'd moved production to had burned to the ground taking hundreds of child workers with it, but not, sadly, the documents held within a fireproof safe in the factory office, documents detailing the transfer of hundreds of thousand of dollars from Mitty & Sarah accounts to an Indonesian bank and into the sweatshop deathtrap, documents that, unaccountably to her, held her signature of approval.

These tied the company, and their request for additional workers and overtime which had stretched the capacity of the factory to breaking and caused the disaster, squarely to Adam and, as the CFO of the firm, to Tess.

She marvelled anew that, despite the myriad ways in which her husband had fucked up time and again during their marriage, he always managed to find ways to surprise her.

She had been hours, minutes, away from walking out completely to start a new life when ramifications began raining down; shit from a fan. In the hours and days after the fire, the media swarmed over the good name of the company and began to pick the meat from its bones. Whatever happened next, it seemed Mitty & Sarah was done for. The method by which they'd operated for decades, chasing ever-shrinking profit margins by buying cheaper and cheaper shit from the developing world, had imploded, almost literally. They could no longer make their money like that, which meant if she was going to survive, she had to find a way to rescue the company.

While the world watched, clucked its collective tongue, tweeted, waited for them to make their move, she realised that she was, in a practical sense, shackled to the company, and by default to Adam. He'd fucked up so badly that to simply leave would ruin her; even if she somehow escaped the criminal liability that the Jakarta documents might expose her to, what other company would hire her if she walked from the ruins of this one? No, she would have to fix it, for her own sake, and for her son's, and because of her deathbed promise to Arkady. She'd realised too late that he'd considered her the only person in his life he could really trust and he'd groomed her for power because he wanted her to have it. Her husband had come very close to destroying everything Arkady had built, so now she was taking back what was his, and making it hers.

Arkady, who she now realised had cared for her more than anyone ever would, had asked her to keep his secret, which, she was sure, meant the money he'd secreted away in his safe havens over the years. She still had no idea how much there was, or where it was hidden; every time she followed the leads in the files Arkady had left behind, she found more, small fortunes spirited away from the Mitty & Sarah coffers, as well as occasional, inexplicably huge injections from private bank accounts in Europe. She still didn't know what to make of it all. If she was going to keep her word to him, she would need to play the long game. Slowly, one day at a time, with the patience and diligence Arkady had taught her, she would find the money, move it from where Arkady had buried it to her own secret accounts. Once she'd found it all, she would bury it, as Arkady had instructed, a million miles away from the home she would continue to share with Adam, for now.

When she was ready, she would cut Adam loose. Until then, he would stay with her, a *chelovek-karova*, a man-cow she had taken with her to help her escape, the two of them scurrying away together across the ice, fast friends until the time came to butcher him.

The Mitty & Sarah Company as it had existed for half a century would close, the staff retrained, as the corporate entity shifted to become a charity. From now on, the company would be the Kulakov Foundation. They would no longer sell toys, not exactly. Instead, they would sell an idea.

Only one product would be sold, and that would be manufactured in small, community-run workshops in the parts of Jakarta devastated by poverty, before being imported to Australia where it would be packaged and shipped out across the world. Lubovka Bear was a plush toy, styled in the likeness of the late Arkady Kulakov, that came dressed in a three-piece suit, with a certificate detailing how the money spent on the bear would benefit the developing world; a pamphlet with statistics about malaria nets, the digging of wells; a picture of a smiling child.

It was actually Adam's idea, in a final irony, the idea that would save the company after he'd destroyed it. Not long after the disaster, Adam had turned up at their house, reeking of vodka, ranting maniacally and clutching a manky stuffed bear and an Australian flag. The charity, the bear, the symbol.

Tess had engineered the pivot. Although she'd been overcome with loathing for him when he'd pitched it to her, she couldn't help but admire it. Their profits had been falling for years and they weren't going to come back. The only sales they made were from people who had grown up with the toys and wanted their children to experience some of the magic they remembered through rose-tinted nostalgia.

Listening to Adam rave about charity, waving the derelict toy in her face, Tess had realised that children didn't use their imaginations any more, but every adult liked to imagine that they were a good person. Everyone wanted to make a difference, and by buying a Lubovka Bear, they could. Across the world, wars would continue to destroy countries, new ones would rise from the rubble, and in sweatshops and on farms and on streets everywhere the poor would struggle against time and disease and indifference to survive, and from their combined efforts, the money would slowly trickle up to Tess and her customers, who wanted nothing more than to feel good about themselves.

With the help of a crack squad of public relations people, they sold the story. They started with a few hand-picked journalists, who digested the story a piece at a time at a series of expensive dinners paid for by the Kulakov Foundation.

By the time the news cycle came to an end, it was clear to the public that Adam Kulakov and his company were both victims of a great tragedy and heroes who would help make amends. Along the way, the buck had been passed, and in the public eye the former Mitty & Sarah Company were dupes, the victims of unscrupulous labour practices by Third World profiteers. This subtext, the same across all the papers that carried the story, helped soothe the rumbles against the Kulakov Foundation, told the world this new incarnation of their company would fight for better labour conditions in Jakarta. Australia already knew all about Indonesia, after all, a country of people smugglers and colonial oppression and child slavery. Unfair, undemocratic, sinister.

In the month since the disaster, Tess had set about quietly dismantling the company and putting it back together. The bears themselves would make, at best, a modest profit, but after liquidating the old company they would have more than enough to sustain the vast administrative fees required to run a not-for-profit, and still a little left over to throw to the third world, and for Adam to keep himself busy.

Adam was bashful, chastened, on his best behaviour, but she knew that his contrition would only last until the excitement of his new adventure wore off. Some cockroaches refused to die, no matter how hard they were stamped on, but they all went scurrying when you turned the lights on, at least for a while. He would need to be kept busy while she made her moves, and the Kulakov Foundation was a perfect role for Adam.

With each day, the world shrunk, and as it did every hour

brought endless horrors, captured on phone cameras, uploaded instantly for all to see. Every time an Australian turned on the television they were hit with the deluge of war, famine disease, terrorism. So much suffering; all the lost children, starving, flies on their faces, drowning facedown on a foreign beach. Too much, too ugly to look at, but the Lubovka Bear was a nice, clean way to help, and behind it stood Adam Kulakov, handsome, charming, affable – the face of good old-fashioned Australian kindness.

Earlier in the day, she'd written his speech for him, helped him rehearse it, kissed him on the cheek and wished him luck. As Kade played on the floor not far from her desk, and she planted the seeds for her new life from the computer at the Kulakov Foundation office, Tess kept an eye on the television. Adam would soon be speaking at a press conference to outline his vision for the Lubovka Bear, asking for donations from business leaders, and from the wider public.

It was, she had to admit, the one thing he was really good at, standing in front of a room full of people and selling a very simple idea. Nobody could take a lie and believe it with such pure sincerity as her husband. He could spend the rest of his life at fundraisers and awards nights and public-speaking events, rolling out his charm, which he would always have in his limited, blowhard way, and basking in the attention, a happy child in a playpen. Even after she was gone, he would, like she'd promised Arkady, be looked after, even if he would never know the extent of what he had missed.

There would be time for that, of course, but later, and for

now, as on the monitor Adam took to the stage, she got up, stretched, then sat on the floor to play with her son. There would be time for that too.

———

Although he'd been rehearsing the speech for days, he still felt nervous. He checked his reflection for the hundredth time, and practised a wink in the mirror, then realised that he had a smear of lipstick on his cheek, where Tess had kissed him good luck earlier, her lips cool on his skin. He wiped it off, smudged his foundation, and swore, picked up the compact to fix it.

'Here.' Shubangi, once head of product, now head of philanthropy, stood in the door, and moved to his side. She took the sponge off him and reached up to swipe it down his face. 'Like this, you have to blend it in.'

'Thanks.'

'Are you nervous?'

He shook his head. 'Not at all.'

'Good. You'll be fine. You've got this.' She finished blending the foundation over his cheek and dabbed at it to finish it. 'There, beautiful.'

He would be fine; he knew it. In the first few days after the accident, as the press had worked out who was responsible for the Jakarta inferno, he'd existed in a twilight state of misery and panic, but he'd soon started to enjoy his notoriety. After a lifetime of dreaming about being famous, there he was, his name splashed all over the front page of the papers, of the internet. As the press accrued, he stopped panicking as he read his name in damning news articles, started to enjoy the rush and plummet of his stomach as the adrenaline soaked up through his fingers with the newsprint.

Now, standing backstage, Adam paced nervously back and forth, then stopped, forced himself to take a deep breath, take stock. He realised that he had changed, was better. He'd been hard done by and had risen to meet the challenge, and along the way the feeling of flabby inferiority, of not being good enough for the line he'd been born into, had burned off. He felt lean, strong; he was, he decided, finally a man. He would nail this, and then he would go out and celebrate. Perhaps, he thought, if he could get away from Tess, he would call Clara, see what she was up to.

Stepping out from behind the curtain onto the stage he waved away the smattering of applause. Taking his place behind the podium, he unfolded his speech. 'Let me start by saying that this isn't about making money. This is not about taking money. This is about giving. It's about giving back.

'Please. Do not applaud me. Lubovka Bear, well, it was my idea, but it is just an idea. Like all big ideas, it takes work to make it a reality. I meet a lot of people with big ideas, ideas that will change the world for the better, but we must all work together to make it happen.

'What happened in Jakarta was a tragedy, tragic, on so many levels. Our thoughts should be with the families of the dozens of women and children who lost their lives, and also with the thousands of people who have lost their livelihood. These people are the victims of those who would take advantage of their fellow men for profit, who stop at nothing to cut corners. As the CEO of the Mitty & Sarah Company, I'm ashamed to say that I, too, fell victim to these foreign profiteers, and invested in these factories of death. This is why the Kulakov Foundation was born, and this is what we will fight.

'We must not let those who would take advantage of our generous nature, our way of life, the opportunities we offer, to stop us from doing the right thing for those who have suffered in this tragedy, both in Australia, and our friends overseas. You do not run from the past, you use it to make the future brighter, which is something the greatest man I've ever known taught me.'

When the applause died down he leaned forward and spoke into the mic. 'Let me tell you a story about my grandfather.'

ACKNOWLEDGEMENTS

In no particular order:

This project was supported by the Prague UNESCO City of Literature in consultation with the Melbourne UNESCO City of Literature Office. Special thanks to Kateřina Bajo, David Ryding and Justyna Jochym. *Děkuji*, thank you and *spoko*.

Michelle Garnaut sent me to India a million years ago where much of this book was born. Her generosity through the M Literary Residency program made it all possible. Thank you.

Additional support was provided by the Copyright Agency Creative Industries Fund, whose continued investment in Australian literature is vital and invaluable.

Everyone from Sangam House, especially Arshia Sattar, Rahul Soni, Pascal Sieger and Mangala.

Victoria Khroundina for teaching me the finer points of the Russian language. Olga Peshkova for the rest. Antonia Baum for similar reasons.

Werner Pieper, whose recollections and insights into the Third Reich were invaluable.

Chris and Jill Lunn and Marieke Hardy for lending me peaceful places to work.

Early readers: Hanna Silver, Paul Garland, Catherine McInnis, Adam Wajnberg, Elizabeth Flux, David Vaughan, Shane Pieper, Miriam Gregory, Leticia Gregory, and McCoo, even if to get her to read the manuscript, I had to cross out '*The Toymaker* by Liam Pieper' and replace it with '*The Conflicted Professional Woman* by Shonda Rhimes'.

My agent Grace Heifetz, tireless defender of author's rights who championed this novel.

Louise Ryan who not only championed this novel but sold copies, and so earns bonus points.

All the Penguins, including but not limited to: Melanie Ostell, Rebecca Bauert, Johannes Jakob, Tracey Jarrett, Alex Ross, Anyez Lindop and all the sales reps.

Special thanks as well to all the booksellers out there fighting the good fight. I love each and every one of you more than everyone, especially you, holding this book right now. Thank you.

Zelda Catzgerald, who I have neglected terribly these past years.

Nikki Lusk, copy editor extraordinaire and troll mate.

My editor, Cate Blake, who, I will admit, had some small part to play in creating this book. There isn't enough space in these pages to thank her profusely enough for all she has taught, and continues to teach, me about writing. Besides, she will be so sick of repairing this thing line by line that she will probably be too tired to ever read this. Nonetheless, thank you.

ACKNOWLEDGEMENTS

Most of all, this book owes a debt to all the survivors of the Holocaust who lived to tell their stories, who ensured that we never forget, whose legacy will remain to remind humanity what we are capable of when we become proud of our indifference, then cruelty. In particular I must thank those who shared their memories with me, especially Raissa and Vladmir Glouzman whose generosity sent me to Berlin for the first time where the idea for this novel took shape, and Mietek Silver, whose wisdom I've tried to do justice to in these pages.

Thank you.